Hearts Restored

Serenity Crossing: The Hartwell's Book #2

TARA BAISDEN

STERLING RIDGE PRESS LLC

Cover designed by Sterling Ridge Press LLC

Published by: Sterling Ridge Press, LLC www.sterlingridgepress.com

ISBN: 978-1-966093-50-3

Dedication

For every woman who was ever told she was too much — and became more anyway. This one's for you. Pull up a rocking chair. Stay awhile. Serenity Crossing has been waiting.

"Unless the Lord builds the house, the builders labor in vain." — Psalm 127:1

***

They say, Write what you know. So I wrote about strong coffee, small towns, big families with loud opinions, and two people who were absolutely certain they didn't need anyone — right up until they did. To my readers: you are the reason I get to do one of the things I love most in this world. Every message, every review, every time you tell a friend about one of my books — that is a gift I will never stop being thankful for. This story belongs to you now. Take good care of Sarah and Ethan for me.

"They will rebuild the ancient ruins and restore the places long devastated; they will renew the ruined cities that have been devastated for generations." — Isaiah 61:4

Always Love,
Tara

Contents

Chapter 1

Ethan Cole pulled open the front door of Hartwell Construction and stepped out of the August heat. The lobby smelled like strong coffee and the faint sweetness of cedar, with framed photographs of completed projects lining the walls. A woman behind the front counter looked up from her computer screen with a warm smile before he'd made it two steps inside.

"Good morning," she said, pleasant and unhurried, in the way people in Serenity Crossing had of making even strangers feel like expected company. "What can I do for you?"

"Morning." He shifted the leather portfolio under his arm and returned the smile. "Ethan Cole. I have a nine o'clock with Sarah Hartwell."

"Of course, Mr. Cole. Let me ring her for you." The woman picked up the desk phone, pressed a button, and waited. "Sarah, your nine o'clock is here." A pause. She nodded once and set the phone back in its cradle. "She's ready for you. Head down that hallway and take your first left. Her office is the last door on the right."

"I appreciate it."

He followed her directions past the front counter and into a narrow hallway that ran the length of the building. The walls were lined with more project photographs, before-and-after shots of renovations and restored facades that told a story of careful, deliberate work. He, being an architect, noticed these things. The framing was consistent, the lighting in each image professional, and every project featured the kind of clean craftsmanship that spoke louder than any slogan mounted on a wall. There were no motivational posters. No glossy mission statements. Just the work, presented without commentary, and Ethan found that more convincing than anything else could have been.

He took the left turn and saw the open door at the end of the short hallway. A nameplate beside it read S. Hartwell, Owner.

Twelve years. He hadn't seen Sarah Hartwell since the afternoon they'd both walked across the gymnasium stage in their caps and gowns at Serenity Crossing High, collected their diplomas, and gone in opposite directions. He remembered the girl she'd been at eighteen. Lead cheerleader. Sharp, competitive, fiercely smart, and completely uninterested in giving him an inch of ground on anything, from class rankings to student council elections. She had been the one person in that entire school who refused to be impressed by him, and he'd spent four years finding that both infuriating and oddly fascinating without ever having the vocabulary to sort out why.

Sarah Hartwell stood behind her desk with a coffee mug in one hand and a warmth in her expression that stopped him for half a second. Nothing about the woman in front of him matched the version he'd been carrying in his memory. She was taller than he remembered. Her dark hair was pulled back in a low knot, a few loose strands framing her face, and her hazel eyes were steady and direct as they met his. She wore a fitted flannel shirt with the sleeves rolled to her elbows and jeans that looked like they'd seen a job site before breakfast. Her hands were wrapped around that coffee mug with the casual grip of someone who'd been up since dawn and had already accomplished more before nine o'clock than most people managed by noon.

But it was her smile that caught him. Not calculated, not cautious. Just real. Like she was genuinely pleased to see a face from a long time ago, and she wasn't going to pretend otherwise.

"Ethan Cole," she said, and there was a note of surprised recognition in her voice. "Well. It's been a hot minute since I've seen you."

"It has," he agreed. He crossed the room and accepted the hand she extended, her grip firm and warm. "Sarah. It's good to see you."

"You too." She released his hand and gestured toward the chair across from her desk. "Sit, please. Can I get you some coffee? I should warn you...we brew it strong around here, so if you prefer the weak stuff found at the local gas station...well, you're just not strong enough for the way we like it."

He laughed. "I'll take my chances."

She poured him a cup from a small carafe on the edge of her worktable and handed it over before settling back into her chair with the kind of easy authority that made the office feel like an extension of who she was rather than just a room she occupied. There was a small dish of individually wrapped caramels on the corner of her desk. A framed photograph of what looked like a large family gathered on a wide porch, and a hard hat hanging from a hook on the wall beside the door. The space was organized but lived in. Warm without trying to be.

Ethan took a sip of the coffee. She hadn't been exaggerating. It was strong enough to strip paint, and he liked it.

"So," Sarah said, leaning back slightly in her chair and regarding him with friendly curiosity. "Ethan Cole, back in Serenity Crossing.

I heard you'd moved back home and taken over your father's firm. How's the transition going?"

"Slow," he said, and it was honest. "My dad built something special with Cole & Associates Architecture, and stepping into his shoes has been... an education. He ran that firm like he ran everything. With a lot of care and no wasted motion. I'm still learning the rhythms of it and, to be honest, still learning how to fit back into small-town life."

"Your dad was the real thing," Sarah said, and the shift in her tone was subtle but genuine, a softness entering her voice that told him she meant every word. "I was so sorry to hear about his passing, Ethan. Phillip Cole was one of the most respected men in this town, and that's not just talk. He was a good man, and he left his mark."

The words settled into a place in Ethan's chest that still ached. Eight months since the phone call from his mother that had redrawn every line in his life. Eight months, and the grief still had the power to tighten his throat when someone said his father's name.

"Thank you," he said. "That means a lot. He thought the world of this town and the people here."

Sarah held his gaze for a moment, steady and kind, and then let the silence pass naturally without rushing to fill it. He appreciated that more than she probably knew.

"So," she said after a beat, and her expression shifted back to something warmer, lighter. "Twelve years. Last time I saw you, you were giving your speech to our graduating class that I'm pretty sure was designed specifically to irritate me."

"Ahh... my salutatorian speech," he said as the corner of his mouth tugged upward. "You beat me by two-tenths of a point for valedictorian, if I remember right."

"You remember correctly." Her eyes brightened with what he could only describe as the ghost of their old competition, stripped of its edge and warmed by time. "I'm glad to know that still stings a little."

"Only on days that end in Y."

She laughed at that, low and genuine, and the sound of it did something to the room that he wasn't prepared for. It made the space feel smaller and warmer at the same time, like the walls had shifted inward by an inch. He became suddenly aware that he was noticing her in a way that had nothing to do with high school memories and everything to do with the woman sitting across from him right now.

He set that awareness aside carefully, the way he set aside a blueprint he wasn't ready to examine yet, and brought himself back to the reason he was sitting in this chair.

"I should explain why I'm here," he said.

She folded her hands on the desk, and the playfulness in her expression made room for the same professional attentiveness he'd seen in the photographs lining her hallway. She was listening now, fully and without distraction, and he recognized in that shift the kind of discipline that came from years of being the person in the room who made the decisions.

"It's the Granville Theater," he said.

Something moved through her face at the name, quick and genuine. Not surprise, exactly, but recognition. The kind of look a person gets when you mention a place they haven't thought about in a while but never quite forgot.

"The Granville," she repeated quietly.

"Memories from there? Thoughts?"

"I grew up going to that theater," Sarah said. "Every kid in Serenity Crossing did. Saturday matinees, school plays, the church Christmas play. I haven't been inside that building since it closed, and that's been what, about fifteen years now? But I remember it. I remember the velvet seats, the buttered popcorn, and the chandelier in the lobby that looked like it belonged in a castle." She paused, and her expression shifted to something more careful, more professional. "What about it?"

Ethan leaned forward slightly, and he could feel the weight of everything he was about to say pressing against the inside of his ribs, the way it always did when he talked about this project.

"My father dreamed of restoring the Granville," he said. "It was his legacy project. The theater has been in my family for three generations. My grandparents met there. My parents fell in love in that building. My dad spent the last year of his life quietly putting the pieces in place to bring it back to life. He was in talks with the city of Serenity Crossing, and they agreed to back the project. He secured a historic preservation grant. He even drew up preliminary sketches for the restoration. I found them in his desk after he passed." He paused, letting that land. "He never got the chance to make his dream come true. So I'm going to do it for him."

Sarah was quiet for a moment, and the quality of her attention told him she understood exactly what he was telling her. This was not a sales pitch. This was a son honoring his father's last unfinished work.

"That's a big undertaking. What kind of shape is the building in?"

"The bones are solid. The brick exterior is sound, the roofline is straight, and there's no structural failure in the foundation. But fifteen years of sitting empty has taken its toll. Inside, I've got water damage from a minor roof leak backstage, sagging acoustic panels, plaster deterioration, outdated electrical throughout, and plumbing that predates most of the building codes we'd need to meet now. The original features are still there: the terrazzo flooring in the lobby, the pressed-tin ceiling, and the proscenium arch with the murals. But they need careful restoration, not replacement. The whole project has to honor the building's history while bringing it up to modern code, and that's a tightrope I would rather not walk with anyone who doesn't understand preservation work."

He could see her mind working behind those steady hazel eyes, cataloging every detail, running preliminary assessments the way builders do when you describe a project and they're already mentally walking through the space.

"What's the city's involvement at this point?" she asked.

"I met with the mayor last week. The city is still fully behind the project. My father's agreement with them is intact, and the mayor's looking at this as an economic investment for Serenity Crossing. A restored Granville brings tourism revenue after it reopens. It puts this town back on the map as a cultural destination in the Smokies, and that's something the city council wants."

"And the preservation grant?"

"Secured. My father had that locked down before he passed. There are compliance requirements tied to it, timeline expectations, documentation, and oversight protocols that we'll need to follow to the letter. But the funding is real, and it's in place."

Sarah nodded slowly, absorbing all of it. "Who's handling the architectural side?"

"I am. My mother is still managing the day-to-day operations at Cole & Associates, and there are two other architects on staff who can handle the firm's active projects. But the Granville is my sole priority. I'm not dividing my attention on this. Every design decision, every material selection, and every detail of this restoration is going to come through my hands, because that's what my father would have done and that's what this building deserves."

She studied him for a long moment, and he had the distinct impression that Sarah Hartwell was not a woman who made professional decisions based on sentiment. She was weighing everything he'd said, measuring the scope against the resources, the emotion against the logistics, and arriving at her own conclusions in her own time.

"Why us? Why Hartwell Construction?" she asked.

"Because my father chose you." The words came out simply, without decoration, and he meant them exactly as they sounded. "Hartwell Construction was at the top of his list for contractors on this project. Your reputation for quality craftsmanship and your experience with renovation work made you his first choice, and I trust his judgment. I've also done my own research since coming back, and everything I've seen confirms what he already knew. You build things right, and you get the job done, Sarah. That matters to me more than anything else on a project like this."

Something shifted in her expression at that, so brief he might have imagined it if he hadn't been looking directly at her. A flicker of something warm beneath the professional composure, there and gone before she let it settle.

"I appreciate that," she said. "And I appreciate you coming in here and laying all of this out honestly instead of leading with a sales pitch." She sat forward in her chair and folded her arms on the desk. "I'm going to be straight with you, Cole. I'm interested. Everything you've described is undoubtedly the kind of project I'd want my name on. But I don't commit to anything I haven't seen with my own eyes, especially a building that's been sitting vacant for years. Before I can give you any kind of answer, I need to walk that building top to bottom and corner to corner. I need to see the structural reality for myself, not just hear about the architectural vision."

"I'd expect nothing less."

"Are you free this afternoon?" She was already reaching for the planner on her desk, flipping to today's page. "Say around two o'clock?"

"Two o'clock works."

"Good." She closed the planner and looked up at him.

"I'll bring the grant documentation with me," he said, standing and gathering his portfolio. "And my father's sketches, if you'd like to see them."

"I would," Sarah said, and she stood as well, extending her hand once more. "Very much."

He took her hand, and her grip was just as firm and sure as it had been ten minutes ago

"Two o'clock, then," she said.

"Two o'clock."

She walked him as far as her office door and offered one last smile that carried the easy warmth of a woman who was exactly where she was supposed to be and knew it. "It was good to see you, Ethan. Really."

"You too, Sarah."

He made his way back down the hallway, through the lobby, past the receptionist who wished him a good day, and out the front door into the full weight of the Tennessee summer. The heat wrapped around him as he crossed the gravel lot to his truck, and he climbed into the cab, set the portfolio on the passenger seat, and sat there for a moment with both hands resting on the steering wheel.

He hadn't expected that. Any of it.

He'd walked into Hartwell Construction with a clear agenda: a project to pitch, a contractor to hire, and a building to save. He had prepared for a business meeting. He had not prepared for Sarah Hartwell.

Not for the woman she'd become. Not for the confidence or the warmth that coexisted with her directness like they'd never been at odds in the past. Not for the way she listened, fully and without pretense, or the way she said his father's name with the kind of respect that told him she understood what this project really meant to him. Not for the laugh that had made her office feel like a different room.

She was not the girl he remembered from twelve years ago. Not even close.

Chapter 2

Sarah Hartwell pulled her black F-150 to the curb on Beech Street and cut the engine, her eyes already moving across the facade of the Granville Theater. The brick was darkened by decades of weather and neglect, and the old painted sign across the second story read GRANVILLE THEATER in lettering so faded it looked more like a memory than an advertisement. The marquee still jutted over the sidewalk with a kind of stubborn dignity, its red trim chipped to a rusty rose, several of the changeable letters missing behind dusty glass. One corner of the underside sagged slightly, and rust freckled the metal supports. Aside from those minor details, the bones of the structure looked decent from the front, at least.

Ethan was already standing on the sidewalk beside a navy-blue truck, a leather portfolio tucked under one arm and a to-go cup in his free hand. He'd beaten her here. She wasn't surprised. The man she'd sat across from in her office this morning had struck her as someone who showed up early to everything and probably considered on time to be five minutes late.

She grabbed her clipboard and the small flashlight she kept in the center console, dropped her phone into her back pocket, and stepped down from the cab. The August heat was thick, the kind that pressed against your skin like a warm cloth and made the air shimmer above the blacktop.

"Nice wheels. I have to say, I never pictured you as a truck girl." Ethan said as she came around the front of the truck.

Sarah looked at him with an expression she reserved for men who were about to learn something. "Well, what else would you expect? I own a construction company." She patted the hood once as she passed it. "She hauls lumber, tows trailers, and has never once let me down. More than I can say for most things."

He laughed at that, a short, genuine sound. "Fair enough."

"You been waiting long?"

"About ten minutes. I wanted to walk the exterior again before you got here to see if I noticed anything I hadn't before."

She tucked the flashlight into her back pocket beside her phone and turned to face the building fully. "All right. Let's start out here."

They stood side by side on the sidewalk and looked at the Granville. Sarah let her gaze travel from the roofline to the foundation, reading the building the way she'd read every structure she'd ever worked on.

"Roofline's straight," she said, pointing with the end of her pen. "That's the first thing I look for in a building this age. If the roof has shifted, everything underneath is suspect. This one hasn't moved." She stepped closer to the brick and ran her fingers along a section of mortar near the entrance. "Brick's in solid shape. You've got some repointing that needs to happen along the lower courses where mois-ture's been sitting, and this section here near the foundation has some efflorescence, which tells me water's migrating through, but that's manageable. The stone accents around the upper windows are still seated well. Whoever built this building used quality materials and knew what they were doing."

"My grandfather hired a crew out of Knoxville," Ethan said. "Brought in masons who'd worked on theaters across the state. He wanted it to last."

"Well, he did good." Sarah stepped back to take in the full facade again. "The marquee needs structural assessment up close, but from down here, the frame looks sound even with the sag on that corner. That's likely a connection point that's corroded, not a load issue. Fixable." She made a note on her clipboard. "The front doors and the poster cases need restoration, not replacement. That wavy glass in the door panels is original, and you don't throw that away."

"Agreed," Ethan said. She glanced at him and caught something in his expression that went beyond professional agreement. He was looking at those doors the way a person looks at the front porch of the house they grew up in.

"You ready to go inside?" she asked.

He pulled a set of keys from his pocket and stepped forward to unlock the heavy wooden doors. The brass handles were tarnished nearly black, but the mechanisms turned smoothly, and the doors swung inward with a low groan that echoed into the dark space beyond.

The first thing Sarah registered was the smell. Dust and old wood and the faint, trapped sweetness of decades of popcorn oil soaked into plaster and fabric. It was the smell of a building that had been sealed up and left to breathe its own air for fifteen years, and it told her things before her eyes adjusted to the dim interior. No mold. No rot. No standing water. The building was dry, and dry was everything.

The lobby opened up wider than she'd remembered, and as her eyes adjusted, the details began to emerge. A high, pressed-tin ceiling painted in what had once been cream and gold, the pattern still visible beneath the grime. A chandelier hanging from a center medallion, its crystals dulled with dust but intact, every arm still in place. And beneath her feet, terrazzo flooring with a mosaic border in muted blues and burgundy, cracked in hairline fractures in a few places but structurally sound.

"Oh," she said quietly, almost to herself, and then she was moving.

She crossed the lobby with her flashlight out, sweeping the beam across the ceiling, the walls, and the floor, cataloging everything. She paused at the ticket booth, a beautiful octagonal glass structure with its peeling paint revealing layers of history underneath, forest green beneath faded ivory. She could see where the wood framing needed attention, but the glass panels were intact and the proportions were perfect.

"This lobby," she said, turning slowly to take in the full space. "Ethan, this is remarkable. The tin ceiling alone is worth preserving. You see these medallion details?" She pointed her flashlight upward, illuminating the pressed pattern around the chandelier mount. "That's handcrafted tin work. You don't find this anymore. A restoration crew can clean and repaint this to look exactly the way it did when this building opened, and it'll be stunning."

"My grandmother used to say the lobby was designed to make you feel like you were stepping into somewhere special before the show even started."

"She was right. Whoever designed this understood that the experience begins the second you walk through those doors." Sarah moved toward the concession stand along the left wall, running her hand across the marble countertop. Cool, veined, and filmed with years of neglect, but solid. The old popcorn machine still sat behind the counter with its chrome trim clouded but complete, and the hand-lettered menu boards overhead were still legible. Popcorn 75¢. Coke 50¢.

She smiled at those prices. "The concession area needs to be modernized for today's health and safety codes, but the bones are here. That marble counter stays. The layout is actually efficient for the space. With updated equipment and some reworking of the service flow, this area can function beautifully without losing any of its character."

She made notes as she moved, her handwriting quick and sure. Ethan walked beside her, and she noticed that he was watching her work with an attention she wasn't entirely sure how to read. It wasn't the scrutiny of a client checking up on a contractor. It was something quieter and more focused, as though he were recalibrating something in real time and not quite finished with the math.

She pushed through the wide double doors into the auditorium, and the space opened up around them like a held breath finally released.

The ceiling soared, supported by curved beams hidden behind decorative plasterwork. Ornate molding framed the proscenium arch at the far end, and above the arch and along the upper walls, faded murals of mountain landscapes and stylized clouds stretched in muted colors that were still visible beneath years of accumulated grime. The auditorium floor sloped gently toward the stage. Rows of original theater seats filled the space, their red velvet upholstery worn to a dusty rose, some cushions sagging, but the iron frames bolted solidly to the floor. A center aisle and two side aisles divided the rows, their burgundy carpet patterned in gold scrollwork, threadbare along the walking paths but holding.

Sarah stood at the top of the center aisle and let the room settle around her. She'd been inside hundreds of buildings in her career and had assessed structures in every stage of decay and neglect. She'd learned a long time ago that the first few seconds inside a space told you almost everything you needed to know. This room told her plenty. It told her the building had been loved once and loved well. It told her the neglect was cosmetic, not catastrophic. And it told her that the people who'd built this theater had invested in it with the expectation that it would still be standing a hundred years later.

"I used to sweep this aisle," Ethan said from beside her. "When I was ten, maybe eleven. My dad would bring me here on Saturday mornings, and I'd sweep the aisles while he walked the building with a notepad, checking on things, making lists of what needed attention. He was always making lists." He paused, and she could see his jaw work once before he continued. "I thought it was boring at the time. Sweeping the same rows every week, picking popcorn out of the seat tracks. But looking back, those were some of the best mornings of my life. Just me and my dad in this big, quiet room."

"The auditorium's in better shape than I expected," she said after a moment, running her hand along the cast-iron armrests as she went. "The seats need to be reupholstered or replaced, but the frames are solid. The plasterwork on the ceiling has some deterioration along the south wall. Those murals." She tipped her head back and studied them. "Those are going to need a specialist. You don't paint over that, and you don't try to restore it yourself. But they're saveable."

"I've got a preliminary list of preservation specialists my father was in contact with," Ethan said. "Including a muralist based in Knoxville who's done work on three National Register properties."

"Good. Hold on to that. We'll need them." She crouched down and pulled back a section of carpet, examining the floor beneath. "The subfloor here is solid. No give, no soft spots, no sign of water migration from underneath. That's a win." She stood and turned her attention to the walls, shining her flashlight along the baseboards and up toward the acoustic panels that hung from the ceiling. "Those panels need to come down. They're from the seventies, they're sagging, and they're covering up original plaster details that are worth saving. Once they're removed, we'll be able to see the full condition of the ceiling and do any plaster repair that's needed."

They made their way down to the stage that spanned nearly the entire width of the auditorium, deeper than she'd expected, built to accommodate more than just a movie screen. Heavy velvet curtains hung from a metal track, their fabric faded from what had once been a rich crimson to something closer to a washed-out clay. The fabric was brittle along the fold lines. Sarah touched the edge of one curtain carefully and felt it crumble slightly between her fingers.

"These curtains are done," she said plainly. "They'll need to be replaced entirely." She walked further onto the stage, and the boards creaked beneath her boots, some of them flexing more than she liked. "The stage floor is going to need significant work. You've got boards that are warped, some that are soft, and I can see nail holes and scuffs that go down deep enough to compromise the surface layer. Depending on how far the damage goes, we might be looking at a partial or full replacement of the decking, but we'd keep the same species of wood and the same plank width to preserve the look."

She moved to the edge of the stage and looked out over the auditorium from the performer's perspective, and for a moment, she understood something about this building that went beyond joists and load calculations. Standing on this stage, looking out at those rows of worn velvet seats sloping up toward the back wall, she could imagine what this room had felt like when it was full. The sound of it. The energy of a crowd settling in, the rustle and murmur, the lights dimming.

"My grandparents fell in love on this stage," Ethan said. He'd stepped up beside her, and he was looking out at those empty seats with an expression she hadn't seen on him before. Not grief, exactly.

Something closer to reverence. "They were both in a school play. My grandmother always said she knew the moment she saw my grandfather walk out from behind that curtain in a costume two sizes too big that she was going to marry him." A faint smile crossed his face. "She told that story every Thanksgiving."

Sarah looked at him and saw something she hadn't expected to see in Ethan Cole. Tenderness. Not the polished confidence she remembered from high school, and not the professional composure he now wore like a well-fitted jacket. Just a man standing on a stage where his family's story began, holding the weight of that story as carefully as he could.

They moved backstage together, into the narrow corridors that ran behind the stage. Two dressing rooms with long mirrors rimmed in round bulbs, most of them shattered or missing. A costume storage closet lined with empty racks. A small green room with mismatched chairs and a folding table. And along one wall of the backstage corridor, the evidence of the roof leak Ethan had mentioned in her office. Water stains spread across the plaster in a soft, irregular bloom, and the surface bubbled slightly where the moisture had settled.

Sarah pressed her palm flat against the wall beside the stain and held it there for a moment, feeling for give in the lath and plaster beneath. "The good news is the framing behind this wall is still solid, I would guess. The water damage here is surface level. The leak needs to be addressed from the roof side first, and then we strip the damaged plaster, check the lath, and re-plaster. The mildew smell back here tells me there's been standing moisture at some point, so we'll want to test for anything behind the walls before we close them up again, but I don't think we're looking at a major remediation issue."

"That's consistent with what I found in my walkthrough," Ethan said. "The leak appears to be localized to this section. I had a roofer come out last week to do a preliminary assessment, and he identified the entry point. It's a flashing failure along the backstage roofline junction, not a whole roof issue."

She made another note on her clipboard. "Roofing should be the first phase of work for this restoration. You seal the envelope before you touch the interior."

He nodded, and she caught the slight lift at the corner of his mouth, as though he appreciated that she'd said exactly what he would have said. She noticed that about him, how he listened without the impulse to talk over her or redirect the conversation. In her experience, men in his position, architects in particular, tended to treat the walkthrough as their show. Ethan was letting her lead, and the ease with which he did it told her it wasn't performance. He simply respected her expertise.

It was different from the Ethan Cole she remembered. The boy she'd competed against for four years of high school had been brilliant and fully aware of it, with a competitive streak that matched her own and an arrogance that had driven her up the wall. This version was quieter. More settled. He still carried himself with confidence, that hadn't changed, but the sharp edges had been smoothed by something. Time, maybe. Loss. The kind of life that teaches you how much you don't know.

They climbed the narrow staircase to the balcony, and Sarah tested each step with her weight before committing to it, a habit so ingrained she didn't think about it anymore. The stairs held firm. At the top, the balcony curved across the back of the auditorium, its railing made of carved wooden panels and brass trim, tarnished but still elegant. She leaned against the railing carefully, testing its give.

"This railing needs reinforcement," she said, stepping back. "It's got lateral movement that tells me the connections at the base have loosened over time. Not unsafe for us standing here today, but nowhere close to code for public occupancy. The balcony seating structure itself looks solid, the support columns are sound, and the floor up here feels good underfoot. But I'd want to get underneath this level and inspect the joists and connections before I sign off on the structural integrity. That's a priority item."

"Understood."

She looked down at the auditorium from the balcony perspective, and from up here, the full scope of the room was visible in a way it hadn't been from the floor. The sweep of the seats, the arc of the proscenium, and the murals stretching along the upper walls. It was a lot of building. A lot of history. A lot of work.

"Let's look at the bathrooms," she said, and they made their way back down and through the lobby to the restroom facilities. As she'd expected, the plumbing was the weakest element in the building. Outdated fixtures, corroded pipes visible beneath the sinks, and toilets that predated current water-efficiency standards by at least three decades. The tile work on the walls was original and beautiful, a pale green ceramic with a decorative border, but several tiles were cracked and the grout had deteriorated badly.

"Full plumbing overhaul," Sarah said, straightening up from her inspection of the pipe connections under the sink. "No getting around it. Everything in here needs to be brought up to current code, and we'll need to expand the facilities to meet ADA accessibility requirements and occupancy standards. The good news is the tile can be preserved where it's intact, and we can source matching tiles for the sections that need replacement. But the plumbing infrastructure itself is a gut job. New supply lines, new waste lines, new fixtures, new everything."

"What about the electrical?" Ethan asked as they walked back into the lobby.

"That's the other major system I want to address." She pointed her flashlight at the base of a wall-mounted light fixture near the auditorium entrance, one of the tulip-shaped frosted glass shades she'd noticed throughout the building. "Your electrical throughout this entire building needs to be brought up to the current code. That means a full rewiring. Panel upgrade, new circuits, code-compliant outlets, emergency lighting, exit signage, and a modern fire alarm and suppression system. On a building this size with this occupancy classification, the electrical scope is significant. But it's straightforward work. My crew and the subcontractors I use have done it on buildings this age before, and we know how to run new wiring without tearing out the walls. You fish it through; you don't demolish to get to it."

They'd completed the full circuit of the building by then, and Sarah led them back into the lobby, where the light from the front windows fell in dusty columns across the terrazzo floor. She set her clipboard on the marble concession counter and turned to face Ethan.

"All right. Let's talk about the grant documentation."

He opened the leather portfolio and spread the paperwork across the counter. Sarah leaned in and read through the documents, her eyes moving steadily through the grant terms, the funding amount, the compliance requirements, the timeline expectations, and the documentation protocols. It was thorough work. Phillip Cole had been meticulous, and the grant itself was well-structured, with clearly defined milestones and a funding amount that made the project realistic.

"Your father did his homework," she said when she'd finished reading. "This grant is solid. The funding covers the majority of what I'd estimate for a restoration of this scope, based on what I've seen today." She tapped the page with her pen. "But I want to be upfront with you. On a project like this, especially with a building this age and this many unknowns still behind the walls, there's always a possibility that costs run higher than the grant amount. You open up a wall and find something nobody predicted, or a material source falls through and you're paying a premium for an alternative. It happens."

"It does," Ethan agreed without hesitation. "I've seen it enough in my own work to know that budgets on preservation projects are educated guesses until you're inside the structure. I'm prepared for overruns. The grant is the foundation, but it's not the ceiling."

"Good. That's what I needed to hear." She appreciated that he hadn't flinched at it. Some clients heard the words "additional costs," and their whole demeanor changed. Ethan just nodded like a man who knew that the unexpected was part of the process.

She set the grant documents back on the counter and looked at him directly. "I want to ask you something, and I'd like a straight answer."

"Go ahead."

"What's your level of commitment to this project? Not the professional answer. Not the one you'd give the mayor or the grant committee. The real one."

He held her gaze, and she could see him deciding how much to say.

"This building is the last thing my father was working toward before he died," he said. "I'm doing this to finish what he started, to honor his dream, and to give my mother the peace of seeing his legacy completed." He paused and set both hands on the marble counter. "But that's not the entire truth. The whole truth is that I left Serenity Crossing twelve years ago, and I barely looked back. I built a career in Nashville, and I was good at it. I let that success become the reason I didn't come home more often. My work consumed me. I missed holidays. I missed Sunday dinners. I missed my father's last year of life because I was too busy being important somewhere else." His voice was steady, but there was a rawness underneath it that cost him something to let her hear. "I didn't get to tell him I was proud of him. I didn't get to sit in this building with him one more time and listen to his plans. I didn't get to say the things you think you'll always have time to say until the phone rings one morning and all that time is gone."

Sarah didn't move. She barely breathed.

"So, my level of commitment?" Ethan said. "This project is personal now; it's my attempt to make up for my past failures as a son. For every holiday and weekend that I should have come home. I should have spent time with my parents instead of chasing something I thought mattered more. I'm not walking away from this building, Sarah. I don't care what it costs, how long it takes, or what we find behind those walls. This is the most important thing I'll ever do in my life. It's my 'I love you, Dad'... something I didn't say often enough."

Sarah looked away, picked up her clipboard, and held it against her chest. She'd asked for a straight answer, and she'd gotten one. More than one. She'd gotten a window into a man she was still learning to reconcile with the boy she'd known, and what she saw through it surprised her in a way she hadn't been prepared for.

"Say no more," she said, turning back toward him. "Here's what I need to do. I'm going to go back to my office, run the numbers on everything I've seen today, and put together a formal proposal. Scope of work, phasing plan, preliminary cost estimates, timeline. I also know a designer who specializes in historic restorations, and I'll be pulling her in on this project." She paused, then corrected herself with a faint, honest smile. "If I take this project. Which I haven't officially said yet."

"Noted," Ethan said, and there was warmth in the word that matched the slight amusement in his eyes.

"I want you to understand something about the timeline. A project of this scope, this building, this level of preservation work? This isn't a quick renovation. We're looking at several months and a lot of detailed work, most likely extending well into next year. The phasing alone is going to require careful sequencing, and the grant compliance milestones will add to that. If you're expecting to have this theater open by early spring, I need to reset that expectation right now."

"I'm not expecting fast," he said. "I'm expecting right."

"Then we'll get along just fine." She made one final note on her clipboard. "I can have a formal proposal ready by Wednesday morning. Does ten o'clock work at your office?"

"Ten o'clock. I'll be there."

They walked toward the front doors together, and Sarah paused at the threshold where the dim, cool interior gave way to the bright wall of Tennessee heat outside. She looked back once at the lobby behind them. The chandelier. The pressed-tin ceiling. The terrazzo floor with its mosaic border tracing a pattern laid down by hands that had been gone for generations.

This building deserved what it was about to get. And she wanted to be the one to give it.

"Wednesday, then," she said, stepping through the doors and into the sun.

Chapter 3

The Daily Grind was humming with its usual Wednesday morning coffee crowd. Maggie Cole set her coffee cup down, leaned forward across the small table she and Ethan had claimed by the window, and she proceeded to tell him about the Anderson porch situation like a woman delivering a field report.

"Karen Anderson called the office yesterday afternoon and asked if Mark could add a screened section to the back of the porch instead of leaving it open. She said the mosquitoes near the creek are, quote, ungodly, end quote." Maggie Cole said. "Mark told her it would change the roofline pitch and add three weeks to the timeline, and she said she didn't care because she hadn't been able to sit outside past six o'clock all summer without being eaten alive."

"What did Mark propose for the roofline?"

"He's thinking of some type of shed extension off the existing gable. He said it's the cleanest option structurally, and he can keep the sight lines consistent with the original design."

"That's the right call. Tell him to draw it up and I'll review it before he sends it to Karen. She'll want to see renderings, not just plans. She's visual from what he's told me about her."

Maggie nodded and took a sip of her coffee. Ethan watched her the way he'd been watching her for the past month since he'd moved back home, with a care he tried to keep invisible. She looked good this morning. Her silver-streaked brown hair was pinned back neatly. She wore a pressed blouse and slacks that told him she'd already decided this was an office day, not a stay-home day. That distinction mattered. In the weeks since he'd moved back to Serenity Crossing, he'd learned to read her mornings the way a farmer reads the sky. The days she got dressed for the office and came downstairs with her purse and her planner were the good days. The days she stayed in her robe past seven in the morning and drifted through the house in silence were the ones that cost him sleep.

The Daily Grind was filling up around them, with the steady rhythm of a town that ran on coffee and conversation before the business day began. The front door opened and closed in a near-constant rotation, letting in brief waves of August heat that mixed with the smell of fresh-roasted beans and warm and sweet breakfast items from the bakery case. Voices layered over each other in the comfortable noise of people starting their day with coffee and conversation. A couple of men in work shirts were discussing a fence line near the register. A woman with a toddler on her hip was ordering something complicated with extra foam. A man in a suit that looked like it had been purchased before the current decade was reading the Serenity Crossing Chronicle at a table by the window.

Ethan liked this place. He'd been surprised by how quickly he'd taken to the morning routine of it, the way he and his mother would drive into town together, park behind the office, and walk the block and a half to The Daily Grind before starting their day. In Nashville, his mornings had been solitary and efficient. A run at five-thirty, coffee from the machine in his kitchen, at his desk by seven. There'd been no lingering. No company. No reason to sit in a room full of people and listen to the sound of a town waking up.

He hadn't known he needed this until he had it.

"Your father used to order the same thing every morning," Maggie said, looking down at the table. "Large black coffee and a blueberry muffin. For eight years I came here with that man after this place opened, and he never once tried anything different. I used to tease him about it." She smiled, and the smile was real but thin, like fabric stretched over a frame that wasn't quite the right size anymore. "He'd say, 'Maggie, when a man finds what he loves, he sticks with it.' And then he'd look at me like he wasn't talking about the muffin."

Ethan felt the words land in his chest the way they always did when she talked about his father, a quiet ache that sat right beside the gratitude of hearing her say his name with warmth instead of just pain. Eight months since the phone call that had changed everything, and the grief still moved through their lives like weather. Some days were clear, some days overcast, some days a storm that neither of them saw coming.

"He was a creature of habit," Ethan said. "I don't remember him ever ordering anything different at a restaurant, either. He'd look at the whole menu and then order the same steak he'd had the last twelve times."

"Medium rare, baked potato, no sour cream," Maggie said, and she laughed. A small laugh, brief and genuine, and Ethan held onto the sound of it like a man holding a candle in a drafty room.

The front door opened again, and Sarah Hartwell walked in.

Ethan saw her before she saw him, and for a few seconds that felt oddly suspended, he watched her move through the room with the same purposeful ease he'd noticed at the Granville on Monday. She was dressed for a workday: fitted jeans, a clean button-down with the sleeves already rolled to her forearms, and boots that had seen real use. Her hair was pulled back in a low ponytail, and she carried herself the way she always seemed to, with a certainty that didn't need to announce itself. She stepped up to the counter, greeted the woman behind the register by name, and ordered without consulting the menu.

His mother was still talking about something, the Anderson project timeline, he thought, and he was still listening. Mostly. He was also aware that he'd been thinking about Sarah Hartwell more than was strictly professional over the past two days, replaying moments from the walkthrough that had nothing to do with plumbing or electrical panels. The way she'd crouched to check the subfloor with the same focus a surgeon brings to an operating room. The way she'd stood on that stage and looked out at the empty seats and understood, without him having to explain it, what that room had meant to the people who'd filled it. The way she'd asked him for the real answer about his commitment and then held completely still while he gave it to her.

Sarah's order came up. She picked up her cup, turned to scan the room, and her eyes found his.

He lifted his hand in a wave that felt natural enough, though the timing of his awareness suggested he'd been waiting for exactly this moment. She smiled, bright and easy, and waved back, then started making her way through the tables toward them.

"Sarah Hartwell," Maggie said, following his gaze. "Oh, good. I haven't talked to her in weeks."

Sarah reached their table and set her coffee on the edge.

"Good morning, Mrs. Cole... Ethan."

"Sarah, sit down for a minute," Maggie said, pulling out the empty chair beside her. "You look like a woman on a mission this morning."

"Always," Sarah said with a grin as she slid into the chair. "How are you doing?"

"I'm doing all right, sweetheart. Keeping busy at the office. Trying to keep this one in line." She tipped her head toward Ethan, and the gesture carried the particular brand of maternal affection that was equal parts pride and gentle teasing. "How are your parents? I saw your mother at church on Sunday, but we didn't get a chance to visit."

"They're good. Daddy's busy at the mill, as always. Mama's already planning her fall garden and pretending she's not also planning Jim's wedding from behind the scenes."

Maggie's face lit up at that. "Jim's getting married? Wait... I think I heard something about that... Grace Bennett... right?"

"Grace, yes. They got engaged a few weeks ago. The wedding's set for November."

"Oh, that's wonderful. Grace is a lovely young woman. Gosh, I remember when she and Jim both were just wee little things. Your mother must be over the moon."

"She's trying to play it cool, but she's already been to the quilt shop three times this past week buying more fabric for their wedding quilt, so I'd say the cool act has some cracks in it."

Maggie laughed, and it was the second real laugh Ethan had heard from her this morning, which made it a noteworthy day. He sat back in his chair with his coffee and let the conversation move between the two women, content to be on the edge of it. There was something about watching Sarah with his mother that he was enjoying. The ease of it. The way Sarah leaned slightly forward when Maggie spoke. The way she asked follow-up questions that weren't filler but genuine interest.

How's the garden doing this year? Did you enjoy Pastor Warren's sermon last Sunday?

And Maggie responded to it all. She opened up in a way that Ethan enjoyed witnessing, offering details and small stories.

"Ethan tells me you two walked the Granville on Monday," Maggie said, and her voice shifted just slightly, the way a room shifts when someone opens a window. Still warm. But with something moving through it.

"We did," Sarah said, and she glanced at Ethan briefly before turning her attention back to Maggie. "It's a beautiful building, Mrs. Cole. The craftsmanship in that theater is something I don't see very often, and I've been inside numerous old buildings."

"Phil loved that place," Maggie said. "He spent so much time researching... making plans for the restoration. I'd walk into his office at home, and he'd have six tabs open on the computer, reading about restoration techniques and preservation methods, and I don't even know what all. I'd say, 'Phil, it's ten o'clock at night,' and he'd look up like he had no idea what time it was." She paused, and her fingers tightened slightly around her cup. "He had plans for that theater. Big plans."

"He did," Ethan said quietly. "And they were good plans."

"The building needs work," Sarah said. "But the bones are solid. The original features, the terrazzo floors, the pressed-tin ceiling, and the proscenium arch—all of that is worth saving."

Something moved through Maggie's expression at those words. A flicker of something fragile and guarded. "The chandelier in the lobby," she said. "Phil's mother picked it out herself from a catalog and had it shipped all the way from a company in Virginia."

"It's still in great shape," Sarah said. "Every crystal intact. It just needs to be cleaned and rewired, and it'll look exactly the way it did."

Maggie nodded slowly, and Ethan watched her take that in the way she took in most things these days, carefully, one piece at a time, holding each one up to the light to see if it was safe to keep.

"I'm glad you took the time to walk through it with Ethan. Phil had a high respect for you and your work, Sarah... I just want you to know that," Maggie said.

"That means a lot to me, Mrs. Cole," Sarah said. "Truly."

The table was quiet for a beat, and then Sarah glanced at her watch and straightened in her chair. "I apologize, but I need to run. I've got crews at two different sites this morning, and I need to check in with both of them before our ten o'clock appointment, Ethan." She looked at him with a grin. "I'm looking forward to discussing the project in more detail."

"I'll be there," he said.

"Good." She stood and pushed the chair back into place, then touched Maggie's shoulder lightly as she passed. "It was so good to see you, Mrs. Cole. If you need anything, don't hesitate to call."

Maggie smiled at that, a warm, full smile that reached her eyes. "It was good to see you too, dear. Why don't you come by the house sometime, Sarah? I'll show you what I've done with the hydrangeas this year."

"I'd like that."

Sarah picked up her coffee and headed for the door, weaving through the morning crowd. Ethan watched her go, tracking her through the front windows as she stepped onto the sidewalk.

"She's a good one," Maggie said.

Ethan took a sip of his coffee. "Yeah," he said. "She is."

He was still watching as Sarah reached her truck, opened the door, and paused for just a moment with one hand on the frame. She looked back toward Main Street like she was running through her mental checklist before the day swallowed her whole. Then she climbed in, and her black F-150 pulled away from the curb and disappeared around the corner.

Maggie picked up her cup and looked at him over the rim with an expression he recognized from thirty years of being her son. It was the look she gave when she'd noticed something and was deciding whether to say it out loud.

She decided not to. She just took a sip of her coffee and smiled.

Chapter 4

Sarah pulled her truck into one of the angled spaces in front of Cole & Associates Architecture. She sat for a moment with the engine idling, the proposal binder on the passenger seat beside her, and the contract in a separate folder clipped on top of it. She'd put in a few extra hours of work late last night, adding the final touches on both. The proposal was clean. The numbers were fair. The timeline was honest. Enough margin was built in to account for the kinds of surprises that old buildings liked to keep hidden behind their walls.

She wanted this job. She'd known that since she'd walked out of the Granville on Monday. She wanted it the way she wanted every project that tested the full reach of her skills, but this one had something extra. History. Craft. A building that deserved to be brought back to life by hands that understood what they were holding.

She cut the engine, gathered the binder and the folder, and stepped out into the heat.

Cole & Associates occupied a converted two-story Victorian set back from the sidewalk on a quiet side street just off the town square.

It was the kind of building Sarah noticed, the way most people notice a well-tailored suit on the right person. The proportions were excellent. Original clapboard siding painted a warm slate gray, white trim, a deep front porch with turned spindle railings, and tall double-hung windows that let in light without sacrificing the structure's historic character.

Maggie Cole met her at the front door before Sarah had made it up the porch steps.

"There she is," Maggie said, and pulled Sarah into a hug. "Right on time. Come on in."

"Thank you, Mrs. Cole." Sarah shifted the binder under her arm and followed Maggie through the front door into a reception area that had clearly once been the home's parlor. Hardwood floors, a fireplace that had been preserved as a design feature rather than sealed off, and a front desk where a woman Sarah didn't recognize was answering the phone. The walls held framed architectural renderings and project photographs, and the entire space had a quality that Sarah appreciated.

"Ethan's in his office," Maggie said as they walked down a wide hallway toward the back of the building. More framed projects lined the walls. Sarah recognized a few of them, local buildings she'd driven past her entire life. A church addition on the south side of town. A farmhouse renovation out past the lake.

"Mrs. Cole, I'd love it if you'd sit in on the meeting," Sarah said as they reached the closed door at the end of the hall. "This project was your husband's dream, and I think it's important you hear my full proposal and ask any questions you might have."

Maggie paused with her hand on the doorknob and looked at Sarah with an expression that softened her face. "I'd like that very much," she said.

She opened the door, and Ethan looked up from behind a large oak desk. His office was clean and organized, with a long drafting table under the window and rolled plans standing upright in a wooden holder against the far wall. A set of bookshelves took up the full length of one side, loaded with reference volumes and binders and a few framed photographs she couldn't see clearly from the doorway. He'd taken off the jacket he'd been wearing at The Daily Grind this morning, and his button-down was open at the collar, sleeves rolled neatly to the forearm.

He stood when they walked in.

"Morning again," he said with a smile

"Morning," Sarah said, and set the binder and folder on the edge of his desk.

He gestured toward the two leather chairs arranged across from his desk. "Please sit down. Both of you."

Maggie settled into the chair closest to the window, and Sarah took the one beside her, pulling it slightly forward so she was angled toward both of them. She opened the binder to the first tabbed section and laid it flat on the desk between them.

"All right," she said. "Let me walk you through what I've put together."

She started with the scope of work, moving through the building systematically. Roofing first, sealing the envelope, addressing the flashing failure, and any secondary damage from the backstage leak. Then electrical: full rewiring, panel upgrade, code-compliant systems, and fire suppression. Then plumbing: gut renovation of all restroom facilities, expanded to meet ADA requirements, new supply and waste lines throughout. While the electrical and plumbing work was being handled by subcontractors, the work on the stage and the structural work on the balcony would be dealt with by her crew. Then the cosmetic and preservation scope: plaster repair, removal of the 1970s acoustic panels, seat reupholstering or replacement, trim restoration on the front windows, and the chandelier cleaning and rewiring.

Ethan listened with his full attention. He asked questions at natural breaks during Sarah's presentation, and every question told her he'd been thinking about this building with the same level of detail she had. He wanted to know her approach to the tin ceiling restoration. He asked about her sourcing options for the stage floor planks. He asked how she planned to handle the terrazzo floor repairs without disrupting the mosaic border.

"I know a designer who specializes in historic restorations," Sarah said, turning to the resources section of the proposal. "Her name's on the list here. She's done work on properties across east Tennessee, and she understands how to bring a space up to modern function without stripping it of character. I'd want to pull her in for the interior design elements: the lobby layout, the concession area redesign, and any decorative restoration decisions that go beyond structural." She paused. "I also have relationships with suppliers who carry replica materials for period-accurate restoration. Trim profiles, hardware, lighting fixtures, tile patterns. If we need it to look like 1952, I can get it."

"My father kept a list as well," Ethan said, and he pulled a folder from the stack beside his desk. "Preservation specialists, a muralist, and some material suppliers. I'd like to cross-reference what he put together with your contacts and make sure we're covering every base."

"Absolutely. That's smart."

She turned to the phasing plan and the timeline. "Here's where I want to be completely transparent with both of you. A project of this scope, with preservation compliance built into every phase, is not going to move fast. My best estimate is that we're looking at work extending through April, possibly May, of next year. That accounts for the phased approach, the inspection and documentation require-ments tied to the grant, weather delays during the winter months, and the reality that old buildings reveal things as you go. I've built a margin into the schedule, but I'd rather give you an honest timeline now than a pretty one that falls apart in December."

"I'd rather have honest than pretty every day of the week," Ethan said.

"I will also be upfront with you about the fact there will be times during this entire restoration that my crew will not be on site. Dealing with a grant and having to wait for approvals, it's just the nature of this business. During those waiting times, my crew will be working at other job sites. I have to keep my employees working; they depend on their paychecks. You have my word, though; the theater takes precedence over any other jobs I schedule for my crews."

"Understood."

Maggie, who had been listening with the quiet attentiveness of a woman who had spent decades sitting in on meetings in this very building, leaned forward slightly. "Sarah, the grant has specific mile-stones tied to the timeline. Is your phasing plan aligned with those?"

"Yes, ma'am. I built the phases around the grant milestones specifi-cally. Each compliance checkpoint falls within a phase completion, so documentation and inspections can happen at natural pause points in the work. Your husband structured that grant very well, Mrs. Cole. It's clear he thought about how the work would actually flow."

Maggie nodded, and there was something in her expression that Sarah recognized. Pride. Not the loud kind. The kind that lived quietly in a woman who had watched her husband work diligently on some-thing worth being proud of and was still carrying the shape of that pride even after he was gone.

Sarah moved on to the financial section. She walked them through the cost estimates line by line, category by category, and she did it with the same straightforward clarity she brought to everything. Materials, labor, subcontractor fees, specialty restoration costs, and a contingency line for the unknowns that every old building kept in reserve. The grant covered the majority of the projected costs, and she said so. She also said, clearly and without apology, that overruns were possible and that she'd communicate any budget shifts immediately and in writing.

"My crew is experienced, and they work efficiently. All the subcontractors I employ are the same. No one works for me unless they've proven themselves to be capable and trustworthy," she said. "I don't pad hours, and I don't pad invoices. What you see in this proposal is what the job costs based on everything I know today. If that number changes, you'll know why, and you'll know before I spend a dollar over the estimate."

Ethan was leaning back in his chair now, and she noticed something about the way he was looking at her that she couldn't quite place. It wasn't skepticism. It wasn't the expression of a man checking her math. It was more like the expression of a man hearing a song he'd forgotten he liked and trying to remember where he'd heard it before. His focus drifted for a fraction of a second, landing somewhere near her hands where they rested on the paperwork, and then snapped back to her face with a blink that was just a beat too quick.

"When can you start?" he asked.

"Next Thursday. I've got crews finishing a project right now, and they'll be clear by the end of the day on Wednesday. I'll have my foreman, Tim Hargrove, on site at all times with the crew. Thursday we'll begin with the roof assessment and the electrical scoping. Those are our priority systems."

"That works for me," Ethan said. He looked at his mother. "Mom?"

Maggie turned to Sarah. "How many people will you have on-site?"

"It'll vary at times, but for the construction part of this project there will be six to ten workers from my crew, plus Tim. For the electrical and plumbing phases, I'll bring in my specialty subcontractors, which will mean three to six additional people on site. I also have several associates I work with regularly who I can pull in for the heavier structural work and the finish carpentry. Everyone I work with has been vetted, trained, and held to the same standard I hold myself to. I don't bring in anyone I don't trust."

Maggie studied her for a moment, and then she smiled. "Your father raised you right, Sarah. I can hear Bill Hartwell in every word you just said."

"Thank you, Mrs. Cole. That's about the highest compliment you could give me."

Sarah opened the separate folder and placed the contracts on the desk between them. Two copies, cleanly printed, with all terms, conditions, and scope of work clearly outlined. "This is the formal agreement. Take whatever time you need to review it. If you'd like your attorney to review it, I understand."

Ethan pulled a copy toward him and began reading. He was thorough; she noticed. He didn't skim. He read every clause, every line item reference, and every condition. Maggie leaned over to read alongside him.

"Your insurance coverage," Maggie said, looking up. "This lists both general liability and builder's risk?"

"Yes, ma'am. Both are current, and both cover the full scope of this project. I can provide certificates to you by the end of the day if you'd like."

"I would. Thank you."

Ethan finished reading, set the contract down, and picked up a pen from the holder on his desk. He didn't hesitate. He signed both copies with a steady hand, then slid them across to Sarah.

"We have a deal," he said.

Sarah signed the contracts and handed one back to Ethan. "We do indeed have a deal. I look forward to working with you on this project, Ethan."

She stood and gathered her binder, tucking the signed contract into the folder. The meeting had lasted just over an hour, and every minute of it had confirmed what she'd sensed from the beginning. This was the right project for her crew, the right building for their skills, and the right partnership for the work ahead.

She extended her hand to Maggie first. "Mrs. Cole, thank you for sitting in. It means more than you know. If you have any questions at all, don't hesitate to call me."

Maggie took her hand with both of hers and held it for a moment. "We're in good hands. I believe that."

Then Sarah turned to Ethan and offered her hand to him. "Thursday morning, then. I'll be at the Granville by seven."

"I'll be there," he said.

She gave him a look. "You're going to be that person who's always at the job site, aren't you?"

His smile shifted, and for just a second, the polished professional composure cracked open to reveal a flash of the boy who'd spent four years of high school finding new and creative ways to get under her skin.

"Probably," he said.

"I wouldn't expect any less from you, Cole."

She turned and walked out of his office, down the hallway lined with Phillip Cole's legacy, through the reception area, and out the front door into the Tennessee heat. The August sun hit her face, and she stood on the porch for a moment and reveled in the undeniable satisfaction of a woman who had just closed the deal she wanted.

Chapter 5

The idea had been Maggie's, floated casually in the church parking lot while Ethan was still shaking Pastor Warren's hand. Her voice had carried that particular lightness she used when she wanted something, but didn't want to look like she was asking for it. "Why don't we stop by the Granville on the way home?" she'd said, adjusting her purse strap on her shoulder, squinting against the noon sun. "Before the crews come on Thursday and it's not ours anymore."

So here they were, Ethan pulling his truck to the curb on Beech Street with his mother in the passenger seat. His navy sport coat was folded on the seat behind him, and his collar loosened against the August heat that didn't care what day of the week it was.

He cut the engine and looked at the building through the windshield. The Granville sat the way it always sat, brick-solid and patient, the faded gold lettering across the second story catching the midday light.

"Ready?" he asked.

Maggie was already looking at the theater, her hands resting in her lap, her expression carrying a quality he'd learned not to interrupt. "I haven't been inside since last December," she said. "Your daddy and I walked through the Saturday before..." She stopped. Recalculated. "The Saturday before he passed. He wanted to show me the sketches he'd been working on, and he wanted to show me in the building, not at his desk... it had to be inside the Granville. He said you had to stand inside a space to really understand what it could become."

"That sounds like Dad."

"It was exactly like your father." She smoothed the front of her dress, a floral print she'd bought two springs ago. "All right. Let's go in."

Ethan grabbed the keys from the center console and came around to open her door, offering his hand to help her down from the truck's cab. She took it without protest, which told him the heels she'd worn to church were bothering her feet, but she wasn't going to admit it. They crossed the sidewalk together, and he unlocked the heavy wooden doors with the same key ring his father had used, the brass handles turning smoothly beneath the tarnish.

The doors swung open, and the Granville breathed out an exhale.

That was how it felt every time, a long exhale of still air carrying the particular scent of this building, the dust and old wood. The sweetness that had soaked into every surface from decades of popcorn butter and caramel corn. Ethan had smelled it a hundred times, and it still brought a smile to his face.

Maggie stepped inside first. She stood in the center of the lobby and looked up at the pressed-tin ceiling, then down at the terrazzo floor, then across to the chandelier, every crystal still in place.

"She picked that chandelier out of a catalog," Maggie said quietly. "Your grandma. The year they opened. It took her three weeks to decide, and your grandfather told her to just pick the prettiest one and be done with it, and she informed him that the prettiest one wasn't always the right one, that you had to consider the scale of the room and how the light would move through the glass at different times of day." She smiled. "He said, 'Maggie, that woman could have run the Army Corps of Engineers if they'd had the good sense to ask her.'"

Ethan looked at the chandelier with fresh eyes. He'd noticed it during every visit, cataloged it for the restoration plans, noted the rewiring needs. He had never thought about his grandma standing in this lobby with a catalog, considering how light would move through glass.

"Did she get the prettiest one?" he asked.

"She got the right one. Which also happened to be the prettiest. She never let your granddaddy forget that."

Maggie moved toward the ticket booth, that octagonal glass enclosure with its peeling paint revealing layers of older color beneath. She rested her fingers on the narrow counter where generations of moviegoers had slid their money across. Her touch was careful. The way a person touches something they know is fragile, not the glass, but the memory attached to it.

"I sold tickets here," she said. "Friday and Saturday nights, the summer I was sixteen. Your granddaddy hired me because I was dating your daddy, and he figured if I was going to be around anyway, I might as well be useful." She laughed, a sound that came out warm and a little surprised, as if the memory had snuck up on her. "The line used to go all the way out the door and down the sidewalk for the church Christmas play. Every year. Standing room only. Your grandma would be backstage managing the whole production, and your grandpa would be up in the projection booth pretending he was doing something technical, so he didn't have to help with costumes."

Ethan leaned against the lobby wall and listened. He'd heard pieces of these stories before, but now they meant more. Before they'd always been background noise, the kind of family lore you absorb without really hearing. In this building, standing on the floor where it all happened, the stories had a different weight. They had an address.

Maggie moved through the lobby the way a woman moves through her own house, with a sureness that had nothing to do with the building's current condition and everything to do with the map she carried inside her. She pointed to the wall beside the concession stand. "That's where the community bulletin board used to hang. Right there. Every local event, every lost dog, every church bake sale. Your grandma insisted on it. She said the theater wasn't just a business; it was the town's living room, and a living room needs a bulletin board."

He made a mental note. The restoration plans didn't include a bulletin board. Maybe they should.

She ran her hand along the brass wall sconces near the auditorium entrance, the tulip-shaped frosted glass fixtures that lined the hallways. Her fingers moved over the metal with a gentleness that made Ethan's throat tighten.

"Your granddaddy chose these," she said. "Had them shipped from a company in Chattanooga. He wanted them to match the ones in the old courthouse downtown. He said if the courthouse was the town's head, the theater was its heart, and they ought to look like they belonged to the same body."

"I didn't know that," Ethan said.

"Well, now you do. And I hope these stay." She looked at him, and there was nothing casual about the way she said it. The words were gentle, but the request beneath them was not.

"The original fixtures are a priority, Mom. Preservation is the whole point of this project."

"Preservation is the point," she repeated and nodded once, as if she were filing that promise somewhere she could find it again later.

She looked at the terrazzo floor beneath their feet, the mosaic border tracing the lobby's perimeter in muted blues and burgundy. "Your great-grandmother chose this tile pattern. Did you know that?"

He didn't.

"She and your grandfather's mother went to Knoxville together and spent an entire day looking at samples. This was 1952, remember. Two women in a tile showroom, and the salesman kept trying to steer them toward something simpler, something cheaper. Your great-grandmother told him she wasn't paying for simple; she was paying for beautiful, and beautiful was worth it."

Ethan crouched and looked at the tile with new appreciation. Hairline cracks, a film of grime, but the pattern was intact, the craftsmanship visible even under decades of neglect. Sarah had noted this floor during their walkthrough and had identified the repair approach without hesitation. He'd agreed because it was the right call architecturally. Now he agreed because his great-grandmother had driven to Knoxville for it.

"This floor stays exactly as it is, Mom. This won't change," he said.

"The floor stays," Maggie said.

They pushed through the double doors into the auditorium, and the space opened around them. The ceiling soaring overhead behind its decorative plasterwork. The faded murals. The rows of worn velvet seats sloped toward the stage. The smell was stronger in here, older, layered with the particular stillness of a room that hadn't heard applause in nearly two decades.

Maggie walked halfway down the center aisle and lowered herself into one of the old theater seats. The cushion sagged beneath her, and the hinges protested with a creak that echoed in the empty room. She folded her hands in her lap and looked at the stage.

Ethan sat beside her. The seat groaned under his weight, and he shifted carefully, the iron frame solid beneath the worn upholstery.

"Your grandparents fell in love up there on that stage," Maggie said. "Senior year. The high school was putting on 'Our Town,' and your grandmother had a speaking part, and your grandfather had been roped into building the set in addition to a small part in the play. He told me later that he'd agreed to do it because he'd seen her in the hallways at school and couldn't figure out any other way to be in the same room with her for more than five minutes." She paused, and a softness entered her voice that belonged to a younger version of herself. "One night during a dress rehearsal, your grandma walked out from behind the curtain in a white dress, and your grandpa was standing in the wings with a paintbrush in his hand, and he just stopped. That was the word he always used when he spoke about that moment. He said he just stopped. Everything stopped. And he knew."

"Grandma's version was better," Ethan said.

Maggie's mouth curved. "Your grandmother's version involved him dropping the paintbrush into a bucket of gray paint and splattering the stage manager's shoes. She enjoyed that detail."

"She sure did."

The silence that followed was not empty. It was full of the room, the dust, the stage where a boy with a paintbrush had fallen in love with a girl in a white dress, and three generations later, the building still stood. Still held the story. That was the thing about structures built with care. They outlasted the people who built them, and they carried what those people left behind.

"Your daddy proposed to me on the balcony," Maggie said. "After a Saturday matinee. He said he'd been carrying the ring for two weeks, waiting for the right moment, and I told him two weeks was a long time to keep a secret, and he said it wasn't a secret, it was a plan." She pressed her lips together. "He always had a plan."

Ethan watched his mother's hands in her lap, the way her fingers turned the wedding ring she still wore. She turned it slowly, absently.

"The weekend after we got married," she continued, "your dad spent the whole Saturday up on the stage rewiring the lighting system. The old one kept flickering during shows, and it drove your grandpa crazy. Phil came home covered in dust and completely worn out, and I told him most men take their new wife somewhere nice the first weekend after the honeymoon, and he said, 'Maggie, that theater is somewhere nice. Now go get dressed; we're going out for dinner, and then we're gonna catch the show at the theater'" She smiled at that, but the smile had a fracture in it. "He was right... this theater was somewhere nice... it was grand and elegant."

She told him about the afternoon Phil had spotted a crack in the balcony railing and insisted on repairing it himself that same day. Ethan had been just a baby, small enough to ride on Maggie's hip while she held the flashlight and Phil worked, his sleeves rolled up, his toolbox open on the balcony floor. "You slept through the whole thing," Maggie said. "I was worried you'd wake up and start crying, and he'd lose his grip on the railing, but you just slept. Your daddy said you were already a natural on a job site."

There were other stories. The summer his grandmother ran a classic film series, and families came from three counties away, folding chairs set up in the aisles when the seats ran out. The night a thunderstorm knocked the power out during a showing, and his dad stood on the stage and told jokes for forty-five minutes, holding a flashlight until the lights came back on. The audience clapped harder for him than they had for the movie. The way the lobby used to smell on Christmas Eve, when the concession stand served hot cider and the whole building glowed with candles in the windows.

Ethan listened to all of it. He made mental notes, the kind a person makes when he's learning the language of a building, because these stories were as much a part of the Granville's structure as the brick and plaster. But he was also watching his mom, the way he'd watched her every day for the past month since he'd moved home with the careful attention of a son who knew the difference between a good day and a performance. She was animated in a way he hadn't seen since before his dad passed. Her hands moved when she talked. Her voice had color and rhythm. This building was doing something for her that the house and the office and even the church couldn't do. It was giving her a room where Phil was still alive within these walls.

And that was the thing that settled into Ethan's chest like a stone he'd have to carry, because he understood that the restoration was going to cost his mother something he couldn't calculate on a spreadsheet. Every change would be a small erasure. Every update, every code-required modification, every surface that had to be stripped or replaced would take something from the version of this building that Maggie carried inside her. He could preserve the chandelier. He could save the floor tile. He could keep the brass fixtures. But he could not keep the Granville exactly as it was, because a building that stays exactly as it was is a building that dies.

He thought about what Pastor Warren had said that morning during the sermon, about the difference between holding on and holding open. He hadn't been paying close attention at the time, his mind already sorting through the week's project schedule. But sitting here beside his mother in this room full of ghosts she loved, the words came back with an uncomfortable precision. *Holding on closes a fist around what was. Holding open creates space for what could be.*

His mother's fist was closed around this building. And he couldn't blame her for it, because the man she'd loved for thirty-five years had touched every surface in this room, and letting go of the surfaces felt like letting go of the man.

He didn't know how to fix that. He'd spent thirty years in a family that believed problems had solutions, that the right plan and enough hard work could carry you through anything. His father had believed that. Ethan had built a career on it. But watching his mom turn her wedding ring in the half-light of this empty theater, he understood that some things couldn't be fixed with a plan. Some things just had to be carried.

"About a year and a half ago," Maggie said, "Your dad stood right up there on that stage and told me he was going to bring this place back. He had the grant application nearly finished. He had the sketches in his head. He stood up there, and he said, 'Maggie, I'm going to make this building sing again.' And I believed him, because when that man said he was going to do something..." She stopped. Her chin dipped. Her hand came up and pressed against her mouth, and the sound she made was small and contained and devastating.

Ethan reached over and took her other hand. She gripped his fingers, and she cried.

Ethan said nothing, because there was nothing to say. He adjusted and put his arm around her shoulders, and she leaned into him. They sat like that in the dusty quiet of the Granville Theater while the August afternoon pressed against the high windows and the dust moved slowly through the light.

After a while, Maggie straightened. She pulled a tissue from her purse and pressed it to her eyes, then folded it neatly and squared her shoulders.

"I'm sorry, sweetheart," she said.

"Don't you dare apologize to me."

She almost smiled at that. Almost. "You sound like your dad when you talk like that."

"Good."

She smoothed her dress. Took a breath and set her hands in her lap again.

"What do you say we go get some lunch... maybe Minnie's diner?" Ethan said.

Maggie shook her head. "I don't want to go out. I'm not in the mood to sit in a restaurant and smile at people who want to ask me how I'm doing." She looked at him, and her honesty was the kind that only comes after tears have burned away the effort of pretending. "I just want to go home. We've got bread and deli turkey in the fridge. I'll make us sandwiches."

"Sandwiches sound perfect," he said.

He stood and offered her his hand, and she took it, rising from the old seat with the careful grace of a woman who was tired but wouldn't let it bend her posture. They walked through the lobby, past the chandelier and the tile floor and the ticket booth where a sixteen-year-old Maggie had counted change on Friday nights. Ethan held the door, and she stepped out into the sun, and he locked the Granville behind them.

Thursday, Sarah's crew would be here. The building would fill with people and noise and the necessary violence of renovation. Walls would be opened. Surfaces would be stripped. Systems exposed and replaced. The Granville his mother had just walked through, the one that still held the fingerprints of every Cole who had loved it, would begin to change.

He helped his mother into the truck and closed her door. Then he stood on the sidewalk for a moment, his hand resting on the warm metal of the cab, looking at the building that was about to ask more of him than blueprints and budgets.

His father had stood on that stage and made a promise. Ethan was going to keep it. He just hadn't considered how much the keeping would cost.

Chapter 6

Olivia Hartwell's kitchen smelled heavenly. The chicken was roasting in the oven with fresh rosemary from the garden box on the back porch. The green beans were cooking on the stove. Sarah stood at the sink peeling potatoes.

Rebecca Hartwell was at the island, slicing tomatoes and cucumbers from the garden and arranging them on a plate with the care of a woman who treated food presentation the way she treated hair styling, as something that deserved attention even when nobody was watching.

Anna Hartwell sat cross-legged on the counter stool across from them, tearing romaine lettuce into bite-sized pieces and telling a story about a vendor who had called the Chamber of Commerce office on Friday to ask if the Harvest Festival permitted live peacocks.

"Live peacocks... can you believe that?" Anna repeated. "He said, and I am quoting him directly, that they would add 'an element of visual sophistication' to the craft tent area."

"Lord have mercy," Olivia said from the stove, where she was stirring gravy in a cast-iron skillet. "Can you imagine Minnie Whitfield's face if a peacock wandered into the pie contest?"

"I can imagine it perfectly," Rebecca said. "And I would pay money to see it."

"I told him we appreciated his enthusiasm, but that livestock of any variety was outside the scope of the festival's vendor guidelines. He asked if peacocks technically counted as livestock. I told him I'd get back to him."

"Did you?" Sarah asked.

"I absolutely did not."

Sarah laughed. Sunday meant family time, and it was a day each week she looked forward to. The hum of her mother's kitchen, her sisters' voices winding around each other the way they had since childhood. The smell of a meal being built from scratch by women who knew each other's rhythms well enough to move around that kitchen without bumping elbows.

Sarah rinsed the last potato under the tap and cut it up, then carried the pot to the stove.

"You look rested today," Olivia said.

"I slept in until seven. Felt like a vacation," Sarah said.

"Seven." Olivia shook her head with a smile. "My daughter thinks seven o'clock is sleeping in. My goodness."

"I think seven o'clock is sleeping in too," Rebecca said, "and I don't even have to be on a job site at dawn."

"You don't have to be at the salon until nine," Anna pointed out. "That's practically retirement hours."

"Says the woman who works in an office with central air and a break room." Rebecca arranged a tomato slice and stepped back to admire her work. "Some of us are on our feet all day with a blow dryer in one hand and a conversation in the other."

"And loving every second of it," Sarah said, because it was true. Rebecca Hartwell was born to own a salon the way some people are born for a stage. She could talk to anyone about anything, and by the time they left The Fluff & Curl, they'd had a haircut, a therapy session, and at least three pieces of town news they hadn't walked in knowing.

"Every single second," Rebecca confirmed without a trace of apology.

Olivia moved between the stove and the counter with the quiet efficiency of a woman who had been orchestrating these Sunday meals for years. She didn't rush. She didn't need to. Every dish had its place in the rotation, and every daughter knew her assignment without being told.

"So," Olivia said, in the particular tone that meant the casual portion of the afternoon was about to shift, "tell me about the week ahead for you girls. What's everybody got going on?"

Anna went first, launching into a rundown of Harvest Festival logistics that involved tent rentals, parking coordination, and an ongoing negotiation with the high school marching band about their performance slot. Rebecca mentioned she had a full book of appointments through Thursday, two bridal consultations, and a color correction that was going to take most of Wednesday afternoon.

"Sarah?" Olivia asked.

Sarah leaned her hip against the counter. "Big week. We start renovation work at the Granville Theater on Thursday."

The shift in the kitchen was small but real. Anna looked up from the lettuce. Rebecca's hands paused on the tomato plate. Even Olivia turned from the stove, wooden spoon still in hand.

"The Granville," Olivia said. "That's wonderful, sweetheart. Tell us more."

"It's a full restoration, funded by a historic preservation grant that Phil Cole secured before he passed. His son, Ethan, took over the project when he moved back to town. We did a walkthrough last week and signed the contract I drew up, and on Thursday we bring the crew in."

"Ethan Cole," Rebecca said. "I vaguely remember him. Handsome, right? He was on the football team in high school, right?"

Sarah picked up a dish towel and dried her hands. "He's an architect now."

"Mama, did you see Maggie at church this morning?" Rebecca asked.

Olivia nodded, and something tender crossed her face. "I did. I spoke with her after the service. That sweet woman is carrying such a weight. She's putting on a brave face, but you can see it in her eyes, the way grief just settles into a person and changes the way they hold themselves." She turned back to the stove and adjusted the flame under the gravy. "Phil Cole was the love of her life, and his death has changed her world. He was a good, good man. The whole town misses him. I can only imagine what Maggie is walking through. We should invite her and Ethan to Sunday dinner soon."

The kitchen was quiet for a moment, the kind of quiet that happens in a family that has known loss at close range when one of their own went through a difficult time. Mike, Sarah's brother, had lost his wife, Jenny, three years ago, and the Hartwells understood grief all too well.

"I'm glad Ethan came home to be with her," Anna said softly.

"So am I," Sarah said as she draped the towel over the oven handle and reached for the bag of flour. "You know, it's funny how people change. I remember Ethan from high school, and he used to get on my last nerve. Every class, every project, every student council meeting. He had an opinion about everything, and he delivered it like the rest of us should be taking notes. Oh, my goodness... he used to drive me crazy."

Rebecca turned to face her fully. "So what's he like now?"

Sarah measured flour into the mixing bowl and thought about the question with more care than she'd expected to give it. The walk-through at the Granville came back to her, the way Ethan had moved through that building with a respect that had nothing to do with ego and everything to do with the structure itself. The way he'd listened when she talked about the foundation work. The way he'd mentioned his father's sketches with a slight waver in his voice.

"He's different," she said. "Deeper, maybe. More settled. And yes, Rebecca, he's still handsome." She reached for the shortening and cut a measure into the flour. "He was nice-looking in high school too, but he was so caught up in himself you couldn't really see past it. Now he's just... different. Like he's actually paying attention to the world around him instead of expecting the world to pay attention to him."

"Handsome and paying attention," Rebecca said. "That's a yummy combination."

"It's a professional observation," Sarah said.

"If you say so," Anna said.

"I'm serious." Sarah worked the shortening into the flour with her fingers, the way Olivia had taught her when she was nine years old. "He seems like a good architect. He knows the building. He respects the history of it, and he respects the work that restoration requires. That's what matters."

"Of course it is," Rebecca said.

Olivia had been quiet through the exchange, moving between the stove and the refrigerator with the unhurried grace of a woman who was listening to every word and choosing her moment. She pulled the butter dish from the shelf and set it on the counter beside Sarah's mixing bowl.

"A project that size is going to need good partnership," she said. "The kind where both people bring something the other one needs."

"Maybe. As long as he does his job and doesn't interfere with my crew... we'll get along just fine," Sarah said, turning the dough out onto the floured board. "These biscuits will be ready for the oven in about five minutes. Is the table set?"

"Anna and I will get right on it," Rebecca said.

Sarah rolled the dough and cut the biscuits with the round cutter that had a nick in the rim from the time Jim dropped it in the garbage disposal when he was twelve. Every biscuit came out with a tiny notch on one side. Olivia had never replaced the cutter. Sarah had asked her about it once, and her mother had said, "It still cuts biscuits, doesn't it? And it reminds me of your brother's face when he realized what he'd done. Some things are worth more slightly damaged than perfect."

From the living room, the muffled sound of a football game broadcast filtered through the doorway, and she could hear the low rumble of her father's voice, then Dave's measured reply, then Mike's quiet laugh. The men had been out in the garage earlier working on Bill's old table saw that had been making a noise he didn't like. They'd come inside sometime in the last hour, settling into the living room with the ease of men who knew exactly which chair was theirs and how the remote control hierarchy worked in this house.

Olivia pulled the chicken from the oven, golden and fragrant, and the scent rolled through the kitchen like an announcement. Sarah slid the biscuits in and closed the oven door.

"Dinner's about ready, boys... fifteen minutes or so," Olivia called toward the living room.

The transition happened the way it always happened, with the gradual migration of Hartwell men from their chairs to the dining room. Bill came first. Dave followed, phone tucked into his back pocket, his expression carrying the particular contentment of a man who had spent an afternoon doing absolutely nothing productive and felt no guilt about it. Mike came last, and his daughter Lizzie was with him, perched on his hip with her arms around his neck.

"Aunt Sarah!" Lizzie announced, as if Sarah's presence in this kitchen on a Sunday afternoon was a development that required exclamation.

"Hey, sweet girl." Sarah reached out and squeezed Lizzie's bare foot as Mike carried her past. "Did you catch any frogs when you were outside earlier?"

"Three," Lizzie said with enormous satisfaction. "But I let them go because Daddy said they had families."

Mike set her down in her chair and tucked a napkin into her lap. "They do have families," he said. "Somewhere."

"Probably," Dave said, pulling out his chair.

Bill said grace after everyone was seated, his voice low and steady, thanking God for the food and the hands that prepared it, for the health of his family and the blessing of another Sunday spent in each other's company. He kept it short. Bill Hartwell talked to God the same way he talked to everyone else, directly and without filler.

"Amen," everyone said, and the chicken platter started its journey clockwise.

"Jim and Grace are with her family today, right?" Bill asked, passing the potatoes to Dave.

"Yes, it's her mama's birthday," Olivia said. "They'll be here next week. Grace told me Jim complained all week about missing my chicken."

"Smart man," Bill said. "He may be marrying a good woman, but he still knows where the best chicken is."

"Bill Hartwell." Olivia pointed her fork at him across the table, and the corners of her mouth were doing something they only did when she was trying not to laugh. "Are you comparing my future daughter-in-law's cooking to mine?"

"I am not comparing anything. I'm stating a fact."

Dave looked at Mike. Mike looked at Sarah. Nobody intervened because this particular exchange between their parents had been happening in some form or another for as long as any of them could remember. It always ended the same way, with Olivia shaking her head and Bill grinning and looking pleased with himself.

"Their wedding is sneaking up on us," Olivia said. "I still need to find a dress. Grace showed me pictures of what her mom is wearing and the bridesmaid dress. She showed me several dresses she thought I might like, and they were all lovely, but I want to see things in person. Rebecca, would you come to Knoxville with me one Saturday?"

"Name the date," Rebecca said, brightening. "I'll clear the whole day for you."

"Anna, you should come too. We'll make a day of it."

"I'm in," Anna said. "But I'm picking the lunch spot."

"You always pick the lunch spot," Rebecca said.

"Because I always pick good ones."

"Sarah, you should come with us too," Olivia said.

"I'm in. Just let me know when."

Sarah listened to them plan, the easy negotiation of schedules and preferences, her mother's quiet pleasure at having her daughters available for something as simple as a shopping trip. The wedding was still weeks away, but it had already become a current running beneath every family gathering, a happy undercurrent that surfaced in small details:

seating charts mentioned between bites of potato, flower arrangements debated over dessert, the question of whether Lizzie would scatter petals or freeze in the aisle, which Mike handled by saying, "She'll do whatever she wants to do in the moment, and it'll be perfect either way."

"Dad," Dave said, reaching for a biscuit, "you should hear about Sarah's new renovation project."

Bill looked at Sarah.

"The Granville Theater," Sarah said. "Full historic restoration. We start Thursday. How did you know about that, Dave?"

"Ethan told me all about it," Dave said as he buttered his biscuit. "He came into my office Friday afternoon. He just brought his business accounts over to my firm a couple of weeks ago, and we met to go over his projections for the quarter. He mentioned the renovation project and that he'd hired your crew."

Sarah looked at her brother. "You're Cole and Associates' accountant."

"I am." Dave took a bite of his biscuit. "He's organized. I'll give him that. He's an interesting character. He was telling me how he took over his dad's firm and about how he's not personally taking on any clients until sometime next year. He said his focus will be on the Granville and nothing else. He's not one bit concerned about it either. I like him. He seems like a good person."

"How's that building holding up, Sarah?" Bill asked.

"The bones are solid. The original construction is exceptional. The brick exterior is in good shape; the foundation needs some targeted repair but nothing catastrophic. The interior is where the real work is. Plaster walls, the original hardwood stage, all the decorative millwork and ceiling medallions, and the old mechanical systems. Everything needs to be restored to period accuracy while bringing it up to current code. It's going to be the most complex project we've taken on in quite some time."

Bill nodded. "I remember when Phil talked about getting that grant. He came by the mill, must have been maybe a year ago now, and we stood in the yard for an hour talking about the timber he'd need for the stage restoration. He wanted to match the original heart pine." Bill paused, and the pause had the quality of a man remembering a friend. "Good man, Phil. That building meant the world to him."

"It means the world to his son too," Sarah said.

"Your mother and I used to go to the Granville every Friday night when we were first married," Bill said. "Before you kids came along, we couldn't get out the door without a diaper bag and a car seat. They'd show movies on Friday nights, and the church put on their Christmas play there every December. Standing room only for that play. The whole town showed up."

"I remember going as a little girl," Rebecca said. "The popcorn with all that extra butter, and we'd sit in the balcony."

"The balcony was the best," Anna said. "You could see everything from up there."

"It'll be nice to have it open again. I have plenty of good memories of that place," Olivia said quietly.

Bill looked at Sarah again. "What's the structural condition of the stage?"

"The framing is sound. There's some water damage where a roof leak went unrepaired, but the structural members are solid. Heart pine doesn't give up easily."

"No, it doesn't." Bill set his napkin on the table and leaned back in his chair. "Listen, I've got some time on my hands these days. The mill practically runs itself since we brought on the new shift manager. If you need an extra set of hands out there on any of the detail work,

I'd be glad to help. I haven't swung a hammer on a real project in too long, and something like the Granville..." He trailed off, but his eyes had a light in them that Sarah recognized, the particular brightness that came over Bill Hartwell when he was looking at a piece of work worth doing.

Sarah smiled at her father across the table. "Daddy, you can stop by the theater any time. Come Thursday if you'd like. This project is going to stretch out for months, and we can always use an extra pair of hands." She reached for her glass of sweet tea.

Bill picked up his fork again and nodded once, and that single nod from Bill Hartwell was worth more than a standing ovation from anyone else at the table. Across from Sarah, Olivia caught her husband's eye and winked. Something slightly charged passed between them that thirty-six years of marriage had made wordless and complete. These were the moments Sarah enjoyed, her parents' subtle flirting after years of marriage.

Lizzie chose that moment to announce, with the absolute conviction of a six-year-old, that she also wanted to help at the theater and that she was very good at hammering.

"You are very good at hammering," Mike confirmed. "Especially things that don't need to be hammered."

The table erupted, and Sarah laughed with them, surrounded by the noise and warmth and gentle chaos of the people who had known her longest and loved her most. This was her reset every week, and she cherished her time with her family. This was the solid ground beneath everything else she built for herself.

Chapter 7

The trail curved north along the ridgeline, and Ethan settled into the rhythm of it, his feet finding the packed dirt and exposed root patterns that his legs had been relearning over the past month. The air was cooler up here, carrying the particular sharpness of a Smoky Mountain morning in late August. Mist hung in the low spots between the ridges, and the forest on either side of the trail was dense and green and close, the kind of canopy that turned early light into something filtered and cathedral-like.

He'd run this trail back when he was in high school, when running was about conditioning for football season. In Nashville, he'd run on city streets and paved greenways, and it had served its purpose, keeping his body moving and his mind clear. But there was no comparison to running on a trail in the mountains. Pavement gave you nothing back. A mountain trail gave you the smell of nature and peace. The sound of water moving from the river below and the occasional flash of a whitetail deer disappearing into the laurel.

He rounded a bend where the trail narrowed between two large oaks, their root systems creating a natural step-down that required a hiker's attention but a runner's instinct, and nearly collided with someone coming from the other direction.

He sidestepped hard to the right. The other runner did the same, and for one startled second they were both off balance on the trail's edge, and then he saw who it was.

Sarah Hartwell.

Her hair was pulled back in a ponytail that was starting to lose its grip, dark strands falling around her face, and she was wearing running shorts and a fitted athletic tank. This was a long way from the work jeans and steel-toed boots he'd seen her in every other time they'd been in the same room. She had earbuds in, one of which she pulled out as she caught her balance, and the expression on her face cycled through surprise, recognition, and something that looked like mild irritation at having her solitude interrupted. All in about two seconds.

"Ethan," she said.

"Sarah." He put his hands on his hips and caught his breath. "I almost took you out."

"Almost." She pulled the other earbud out and looped the cord around her hand. "What are you doing out here?"

"Running. Same as you, apparently."

"I've been running this trail for years. I've never seen you out here."

"I've only been back a month, and I usually run the other direction." He gestured behind him, toward the stretch of trail that wound in the opposite direction and eventually connected to the road that led out past his mother's property.

Sarah looked at him. "I didn't know you were a runner."

"I didn't know you were either."

"Well, apparently there's a lot we don't know about each other nowadays, Cole."

She said it matter-of-factly, without edge, and Ethan registered the use of his last name. Cole. The professional distance she kept between them was maintained even on a mountain trail at six-thirty in the morning, when neither of them had any reason to be professional about anything. He noticed, too, that she was barely winded. Whatever pace she'd been keeping, her recovery was fast. She was in serious shape, and he filed that away with the growing catalog of interesting things about Sarah Hartwell that contradicted the one-dimensional portrait he'd carried since high school.

"Fair point," he said. "So how far do you usually go?"

"Depends on the morning. Today I've got about a mile left. I want to get home and eat something before I head into the office. Long day ahead."

"What's on the schedule?"

"Finalizing the crew assignments for Thursday. Tim and I are mapping out the first two weeks of phased work in more detail, and I need to confirm the electrical subcontractors." She said it with the same ease another person might describe a trip to the grocery store. This was her world, organized and moving forward, and she lived inside it the way he lived inside blueprints.

"Sounds like you've got it handled."

"I do." She tucked the earbuds into a small pocket at her waistband and looked back down the trail in the direction she'd come from. "All right, I'm going to finish my run. I'm starving, and there are eggs at my house with my name on them."

"Mind if I join you? For the run, not the eggs." He said it before the sentence had fully formed in his head, and the slight surprise on her face told him she hadn't expected it either. "I'm in no rush this morning."

Sarah tilted her head and looked at him for a beat. Then something in her expression eased, just slightly, and she shrugged one shoulder.

"Sure. Try to keep up."

She turned and started back the way she'd come, and Ethan fell into step beside her. The trail was wide enough here for two runners side by side; the surface packed hard by years of foot traffic, and their pace settled into something comfortable, a steady jog that allowed conversation without gasping.

"How long have you been running trails?" he asked.

"Since I was about twenty. I started on the roads near my house, but the pavement got boring. Switched to trails and never went back." She navigated a section of exposed roots without breaking stride, her footing sure and instinctive. "Out here is where my brain actually shuts off. On the road, I'm still thinking about work. Out here, the trail takes enough attention that everything else goes quiet."

"I understand that."

"So... you ran in Nashville?" she asked.

"Every morning, rain or shine. But it was pavement and greenways. Flat. Predictable." He ducked a low-hanging branch that Sarah had cleared easily. "Coming back to these trails was like remembering a language I'd forgotten I spoke."

She glanced at him sideways, briefly, and then back to the trail.

Ethan was aware of her beside him in a way that had nothing to do with architecture or the Granville or the professional boundaries of their working relationship. She moved with a natural athleticism that was efficient and unselfconscious; her stride smooth and her arms relaxed, and he noticed that Sarah Hartwell off the job site and out of her work boots was a different composition entirely. Not a different person. A fuller version of the same one.

The trail opened into a wider section where it followed a creek bed for about a quarter mile, the water low and clear over smooth stones, and the ground here was flat.

"I have to tell you something," Sarah said, and her tone had shifted, lighter and carrying a quality he hadn't heard from her before. Almost playful.

"What's that?"

"I was a sprinter in high school. Did you know that?"

"Cheerleading and sprinting... I vaguely remember you ran track."

"Cheerleading, track, and a competitive streak, my mother says I inherited directly from my father." She looked at him, and there it was, a grin that changed her whole face, that cracked the professional composure and let something younger and freer flash through.

She took off.

There was no countdown, no warning. One second she was jogging beside him, and the next she was gone, her stride lengthening into something that was absolutely not recreational, her ponytail swinging, her feet barely touching the trail. She was fast. Not just in good shape fast. Actually, genuinely, blazingly fast.

Ethan watched her pull away for about three seconds of pure disbelief, and then something in his chest that had been sleeping since high school woke up. He dug in. His legs protested the shift from steady jog to full sprint, and the trail surface was not ideal for this kind of thing, but his body remembered what competition felt like. The competitive muscle that had once thrown footballs at defensive lines that outweighed him kicked into gear.

She had a twenty-yard lead and the terrain advantage of knowing every inch of this trail. He closed the gap to fifteen. Then ten. She was not slowing down. He could hear her laughing ahead of him, actually laughing while sprinting. He was running as hard as he had in years, and Sarah was still ahead of him.

He caught her at a fork in the trail, where two paths diverged around a massive old hickory. She had stopped, hands on her knees, breathing hard but grinning with the unguarded satisfaction of a woman who had just proven a point she hadn't needed to make but enjoyed making, anyway.

Ethan pulled up beside her, his lungs burning pleasantly, his shirt damp with sweat. "Okay," he managed between breaths. "You're fast."

"I know." She straightened up and pushed the loose strands of hair back from her face. "You're not bad yourself. For an architect."

"For an architect." He shook his head, and he was smiling in a way he hadn't smiled in a long time, the kind of smile that comes from being surprised by joy in the middle of an ordinary Tuesday morning. "You sandbagged me, Hartwell. You set that up."

"I did not set anything up. The flat section presented an opportunity, and I took it." Her eyes were bright with the energy that physical exertion brings to the surface, and she was enjoying this, the competition and the victory and the fact that she'd caught him completely off guard. "I have to go left here. This fork leads to the trail that runs behind my property."

"You live out here?" He looked down the left trail, which curved away through the trees and sloped gently downhill.

"About a quarter mile that way. I built my house on two acres where the residential streets give way to the foothills."

"You built it?"

"Designed it and built it." She said it plainly, but there was a pride underneath the words that she didn't try to hide, and Ethan heard it clearly. She had built herself a home. With her own hands, on her own land, from her own design. That was not a small thing.

"I'd like to see it sometime."

"Maybe."

She turned to head down the left path, and Ethan spoke before the moment could close.

"Sarah."

She turned back.

"You wanna grab breakfast at Minnie's? We could talk through the Thursday start plan. I'll buy."

She tilted her head, and the expression on her face was one he couldn't quite read, a mix of surprise and something that looked like she was running a quick internal calculation, weighing variables he couldn't see. She was quiet for a moment, and in that moment Ethan realized his pulse hadn't come down from the sprint and probably wasn't going to. The breakfast invitation, while it had a professional justification attached to it, was not entirely professional, and he knew it.

"Minnie's," she repeated.

"Minnie's. Scrambled eggs, bacon, biscuits, coffee, and a conversation about roof phasing. Nothing complicated."

She studied him for one more second. "All right. Give me an hour. I need to shower."

She turned and jogged down the trail toward her home, her ponytail catching the light that was breaking through the canopy in earnest now, and Ethan stood at the fork in the trail and watched her go.

He turned back toward his own path eventually after he lost sight of her. His legs had that good, wrung-out feeling that comes after a hard effort, and his mind was racing.

Sarah Hartwell was a runner. She was fast. She laughed when she sprinted. Furthermore, she built her own house on two acres at the edge of town. And she'd just agreed to meet him at Minnie's breakfast.

Not a bad start to the day... not bad at all.

Chapter 8

S arah parked beside a mud-splattered farm truck she recognized as belonging to one of the families out on County Road 14. She checked her reflection in the rearview mirror and then wondered why she'd done that. She looked fine. Hair down, still slightly damp from the shower. Clean jeans, a fitted cotton top, and her work boots.

She walked into Minnie's Diner, and the smell of coffee and the sweetness of Minnie's cinnamon rolls made her stomach grumble. Nearly every booth was taken, the counter lined with the usual morning regulars who treated this place the way other people treated church. This was to say they showed up faithfully, sat in the same seats, and expected to be fed.

Ethan was sitting in a booth by the front windows. He had a coffee in front of him and his phone on the table. He was wearing a button-down with the sleeves rolled to his forearms and jeans.

He stood up when he saw her approaching, and the gesture registered with Sarah. Men didn't stand up when she walked into rooms. They waved. They nodded. They called out from across a job site.

"You beat me here," she said, sliding into the booth.

"I had just sat down and glanced out the window and saw you parking. Minnie's already informed me that I look like I've lost weight and need to eat more." He sat back down and pushed a second coffee mug across the table toward her. "I took the liberty. She said you take it with cream, no sugar."

Sarah looked at the coffee, then at him. "She told you how I take my coffee?"

"She volunteered that information rather enthusiastically."

"Of course she did." Sarah pulled the mug toward her and took a sip. It was good. It was always good. Minnie's coffee wasn't fancy or artisan or anything that would impress someone from a city. It was strong and hot, and it tasted wonderful.

"Well, well, well." The voice arrived before the woman did, warm and laced with a sweetness that had nothing innocent about it. Minnie Whitfield appeared at the end of their booth with a coffeepot in one hand and a pair of menus tucked under her arm. She was looking at the two of them with an expression that Sarah recognized immediately as the opening move of something Sarah was not going to enjoy.

Minnie was sixty-two years old and had been running this diner for more than thirty of those years. She was a compact woman with silver hair she kept pulled back and neat, reading glasses on a beaded chain around her neck, and an apron that was always clean at the start of the shift and never clean by the end of it. She had the kind of face that made people want to tell her things, which was convenient because Minnie wanted to be told things. She had buried her husband, Walter, ten years ago and still wore his wedding band on a chain under her blouse. She believed in love with the stubborn faith of a woman who had lost the best version of it and refused to stop believing it existed. And because she believed so deeply in love, she always attempted to be a matchmaker. No single person in Serenity Crossing could avoid her covert missions; most had come to expect it.

"Well, now… if it isn't little, miss Sarah Hartwell," Minnie said, setting the menus on the table and topping off Ethan's coffee without asking. "And Ethan Cole. In my diner. Having breakfast." She said this as if she were narrating a nature documentary about a rare species sighting. "Together."

"Mornin', Minnie," Sarah said.

"And it's a good one, too. The Lord gave us all another beauty to enjoy, that's for certain." Minnie beamed as she turned to Ethan. "Honey, you really do need to eat more; I wasn't kiddin' when I said that earlier. Men need meat on their bones, sugar. Your mama told me last week she can't get you to sit still long enough for a proper meal. She worries about you, you know."

"She worries about everyone," Ethan said. "It's her primary form of exercise."

Minnie laughed, a bright, delighted sound that carried across the diner and turned a few heads. "Oh, you are your daddy's son. Phil used to say the same kind of thing in that exact same tone of voice." She patted Ethan's shoulder. "Now, what can I get you two? And don't tell me you're just having coffee, because I will not allow it."

Sarah ordered scrambled eggs, sausage, toast, and a side of fruit. Ethan ordered the same, plus a short stack of pancakes, which made Minnie nod with approval.

"Now you're talkin' Ethan… Good down-home food; we don't serve any of that city stuff you're used to." She collected the menus and pointed her coffee pot at both of them. "You two enjoy yourselves. It's good to see young people taking the time for a good breakfast instead of running around like the world's on fire." She looked at Sarah with a pointed expression. Then she turned and made her way back toward the kitchen, stopping at three other tables on the way to refill cups and collect intelligence.

"She's going to tell everyone that walks through those doors that we were here together," Sarah said.

"She's going to tell everyone beyond those doors, too," Ethan said.

"By noon, my mother will know and she'll be calling me to get all the details. Rebecca will know because one of her customers will fill her in. Minnie's information network makes the internet look slow."

"I'm aware." He picked up his coffee. "I grew up here too, remember?"

"How could I forget?" she said, setting the folder she brought with her on the table between them. "Thursday. Let's get down to business."

The conversation that followed was professional and thorough and exactly the kind of exchange Sarah was comfortable having. She walked him through the first-week plan: roof and electrical assessment on Thursday and Friday, with Tim coordinating the crew on the exterior while she and the electrical subcontractors began scoping the interior wiring. The original knob-and-tube system needed to come out entirely. They'd run new service to the panel and branch circuits through the building in a sequence that allowed other trades to follow without delay.

"The roof is our first priority because everything else depends on it," she said. "We can't start interior plaster work or ceiling restoration with water intrusion still a possibility. Tim's already been up there once, and his assessment matches what the roofer you hired stated. The main structure is sound, but there's damage along the northwest section where the flashing failed. We'll address that first, then work across the full surface."

"What about the stage floor?" Ethan asked.

"I'm starting on that tomorrow actually... well, not in the theater, just off-site. My dad and I are driving out to a reclaimed lumber supplier east of Knoxville. They have heart pine salvaged from an old lumber mill that closed last year, and if the grading is right, it'll be a near-perfect match for the original stage planking." She took a sip of her coffee. "Your dad talked to my dad about this. My dad told me he wanted to match the original heart pine as closely as possible. We're going to try to make that happen."

"Thank you," he said. "For taking that seriously."

"Of course. It's the right material for the job. Heart pine is harder and more dimensionally stable than anything new we could source. It's the smart choice, not just the sentimental one. If the salvaged wood I look at tomorrow isn't good enough, I have another source I can look into."

"That's very Sarah Hartwell of you," he said. "Practical and meaningful in the same sentence and, of course, always with a backup plan. You're an interesting woman."

She looked at him. The comment had landed somewhere between a compliment and something else, something warmer, and she wasn't sure which one he'd intended. His expression gave her nothing. He was just looking at her across a diner table with his coffee in his hand and the ease of a man comfortable in his own skin.

"Whatever, Cole. I'm not quite sure how to take that comment...so," she said, steering the conversation back to the folder. "Let me show you the electrical routing plan."

They talked through the details for a few minutes, and the conversation was good. It was the kind of professional exchange Sarah valued most, two people who knew their respective crafts well enough to speak in shorthand, to anticipate each other's questions, to disagree without drama, and agree without flattery. Ethan understood restoration architecture at a level that made the conversation efficient, and he asked the right questions at the right moments, questions that told her he'd been thinking about the Granville's systems with care and specificity.

Minnie brought their food, and the plates were generous. Sarah moved the folder aside and picked up her fork. The eggs were hot and perfectly scrambled and seasoned with whatever Minnie's cook put on them that nobody had ever been able to replicate at home.

"Can I ask you something that isn't about the Granville?" Ethan said, buttering a pancake.

"You can ask. I reserve the right not to answer."

He smiled at that. "Fair enough. How did you start Hartwell Construction? I'm curious about the beginning. How does a twenty-something-year-old start a construction company?"

"Stubbornness, mostly," she said. "And a dad who owns a lumber mill, which gave me a materials advantage nobody else in the region had. But the rest of it was just hard work. I never wanted to go to college. I liked working with my hands and helping Dad with odd jobs... I don't know. I just knew what I wanted to do with my life. I wanted to build things. I apprenticed in every trade I could get my hands on after high school. Framing, electrical, finish carpentry, plumbing basics. I got my contractor's license at twenty-two and started bidding jobs at twenty-three with a crew of three guys and a truck that burned oil."

"Three guys?"

"Tim was one of them. He was working for a regional firm and hated it. I offered him a job, and he said yes before I even told him what it paid." She smiled at the memory. "He's been with me for seven years now, and I'd be lost without him. He's my right-hand man; I trust him with everything."

"The first two years were brutal," she continued, and she wasn't sure why she was telling him this much, except that he'd asked and he was listening. "Clients who wouldn't look at me. Suppliers who quoted me higher because they assumed I didn't know any better. Men on job sites who talked over me or went around me to speak to my crew. I had to prove myself on every single project, every single time, and it took years before the quality of my work started to do the talking for me."

"But it did."

"It did. And now Hartwell Construction is one of the most respected firms in the region." She picked up her coffee and took a sip. "What about you? You left Serenity Crossing after graduation and didn't look back. Nashville, architecture school, your own firm. Those aren't small thing either."

Ethan set his fork down and leaned back in the booth. "I was in such a rush to get out of this town. I thought Serenity Crossing was too small for me. I wanted to see the world and make a statement. Architecture school was everything I hoped it would be. The adaptive reuse and preservation work lit something in me that I'd never felt before, this idea that a building's past doesn't have to be erased for it to have a future."

"That's a good way to think about it."

"I had my own firm in Nashville by twenty-five, and by twenty-eight it was doing well. High-end clients, complex projects, the kind of work that gets written up in trade publications." He paused. "I was also working twelve-hour days, living in a condo that looked like a showroom, and going to industry events where every conversation felt like a transaction. I built beautiful things for people I would never see again, and I told myself it was enough because the work was excellent."

"Was it? Enough?"

He looked at her, and something in his expression shifted, opened a fraction, like a door left ajar on purpose. "No. It wasn't. It was a cold and lonely existence. I was a workaholic... I didn't know anything but work. The firm came before everything else in my life. But I didn't figure that out until my dad died, and I suddenly had to ask myself what I'd actually built with my life besides a portfolio."

The honesty of that landed in Sarah's chest in a way she hadn't braced for. She knew grief. She'd watched her brother carry it for three years and seen it settle into the empty spaces at the family dinner table. Jenny had been one of her closest friends.

"Your dad would be proud of what you're doing with the Granville," she said. "That building meant everything to him, and you're honoring that."

"I hope so. That building meant a lot to him, and it still means a lot to my mom. I don't want to mess it up."

"You won't mess it up. You care too much to mess it up."

"That might be the nicest thing you've ever said to me, Hartwell," he said.

"Don't get used to it, Cole."

He laughed, and the sound was easy and warm and genuinely surprised.

The conversation loosened after that. He told her about Nashville, the parts that were good and the parts that hollowed him out. She told him about the early years of the company, the project that almost broke her, and the first time a client specifically requested Hartwell Construction by name. They discussed the town, how it had changed and how it hadn't, the businesses that had closed and the ones that had held on. They talked about running, about the trails, and about the particular peace of being in the mountains before the rest of the world wakes up.

"You know what surprised me this morning?" Ethan said, finishing his last pancake. "How fast you are. I played quarterback for four years, and I haven't been outrun like that since Tyler Webber caught a pick-six against us junior year."

"Tyler Webber. I forgot about him." Sarah shook her head. "He was fast."

"He was fast. You're faster."

"I know."

Ethan grinned, and something about the grin and the ease of it and the way he was looking at her made Sarah's stomach do that flip thing again. She reached for her coffee and took a long sip.

Minnie appeared to clear their plates. "Can I get y'all anything else? More coffee? A slice of pie? We've got pecan this morning that'll make you want to cry."

"I'm good, Minnie, but thanks," Sarah said.

"I might just have to come back for lunch and take you up on that pie," Ethan said with a grin.

"All right then, you do that and bring your mama with you." Minnie stacked the plates with practiced speed and placed the check on the table. "Y'all have a wonderful day now, and I expect to see you both in here more often...together."

Sarah rolled her eyes and reached for the check, but Ethan's hand was already there. He picked it up and slid it to his side of the table without ceremony.

"I'm buying...I told you that this morning," he said.

"Ethan, you don't need to do that."

"I know I don't need to. I want to. You can get the next one."

Sarah looked at him. He was pulling his wallet out, relaxed and unbothered, as if he hadn't just implied that this was going to happen again.

"If there is a next time," she said.

"Oh, there will be. Don't forget, we have months of working together ahead of us."

Sarah didn't know how to respond to that.

He left cash on the table, enough for the meal and a tip that would make Minnie's morning even better, and they slid out of the booth and walked toward the door. The diner was still full, still noisy, still the beating heart of a small town on a Tuesday morning. Sarah was aware, in a way that irritated her slightly, that at least three people she recognized had noticed her walking out of Minnie's Diner beside Ethan Cole. The gossip mill was going to be in full swing before the sun went down.

They stood in the parking lot in the warm morning air, and Ethan had his keys in his hand and Sarah had hers, and the day was waiting for both of them.

"Thursday," she said. "Seven o'clock at the Granville. Don't be late."

"Have I ever been late?"

"We've known each other professionally for about two weeks. I'm still collecting data."

He smiled, and the smile was the kind that started slowly and reached his eyes before it reached his mouth. "I'll be there at six-forty-five."

"Show-off. I may just show up late to irritate you."

She turned and walked to her truck, and she could feel him watching her go the same way she'd felt it on the trail that morning, a quiet awareness that sat on her skin like a change in temperature. She got in, started the engine, and pulled out of the parking lot.

Chapter 9

Tim had the crew lined up on the sidewalk in front of the Granville by the time Sarah finished pulling the last of the site plans from the tube. She walked toward them with her clipboard in one hand and her hard hat in the other, already talking before she reached the group because the morning was already warm and the day was long. There was no reason to waste the first fifteen minutes of it on pleasantries.

"All right, here's what today looks like." She stopped in front of them on the sidewalk, the Granville's brick facade rising behind her, and looked at each face in the half circle. Tim, solid and patient, his arms folded, his expression carrying the calm readiness of a man who had heard a thousand morning briefings and would hear a thousand more. Brian and Luke flanking him on one side, and Melvin and Dan on the other, tool belts on and coffee thermoses in hand. The two electricians, Liam and Art, she'd brought on for the job today stood slightly apart from her crew the way subcontractors always did on the first day. They were close enough to be part of the team but not yet woven into its rhythm.

"Tim, you're taking Brian, Luke, Melvin, and Dan to the roof. The northwest section is our priority. That's where the flashing failed, and that's where we've got the most significant damage. I want a full assessment of that section first. Anything you find that changes the scope of what we discussed, you come find me before you start cutting or pulling. I need to know what we're dealing with before we commit to a repair approach."

Tim nodded once.

"The rest of the roof is secondary today, but I want eyes on it. Check every seam, every penetration, and every flashing joint. I want to know exactly what condition we're in before we bring any materials up. If the structure under the northwest damage is worse than what I assume, we deal with that first, and everything else adjusts."

She turned to the electricians. "You two are with me inside. We're starting in the lobby. The original knob-and-tube has to come out entirely, and today we're mapping the existing routing against the original blueprints, locating the main panel, and planning the new service entry. I've got the building's original electrical layout, and we'll work from that as our baseline. The goal today is assessment and documentation, not demo. I don't want anyone pulling wire until we know exactly what we're looking at and we've photographed every-thing for the grant compliance file."

Art, the lead electrician, a quiet, competent man she'd worked with on numerous previous projects, gave her a thumbs-up.

"Questions?" Sarah looked around the group. Nobody spoke. "Good. Let's get to work. Tim, do you need anything from me before I head inside?"

"I'm good, Boss," and he turned and led his four men around the corner of the building toward the back, where the fire escape and the roof access ladder would take them up. Sarah watched them go for a moment, confirming in her mind the mental map of the building's exterior, the roof pitch, the access points, and the safety considerations she'd reviewed with Tim earlier this week already. He knew what he was doing. She trusted him with her life, which, on a construction site, was not a figure of speech.

A truck pulled to the curb behind her. Ethan climbed out of his truck dressed for a job site, work boots and jeans and a henley that fit him in a way that was completely irrelevant to the task at hand, but she noticed anyway. He caught her eye across the sidewalk and gave her a nod. Just that, no wave, no greeting shouted across the distance, no attempt to walk over and insert himself into her conversation. He just acknowledged her, pulled a leather portfolio and a camera bag from his truck, and walked to the Granville's front doors. He unlocked the doors, propped them open with the rubber doorstops, and went inside.

Sarah put her hard hat on and turned to the electricians. "That man was Ethan Cole. He's the architect on this project. Now let's get to work."

The Granville's lobby looked different with people in it. Not better or worse, just different. The stillness that had defined every previous visit was gone, replaced by the energy of a building that was about to be opened up and worked on and changed. Sarah could feel it in the air, that shift that happens on the first day of every project, when a dormant space becomes an active one.

She spread the original building blueprint across the marble concession counter, anchoring the corners with her plan weights, and the two electricians flanked her on either side. The blueprint was a reproduction of the 1952 original that she'd sourced from the county records office, and the electrical routing was drawn in the hand of whatever engineer had designed it years ago. Neat, precise, and completely obsolete by current code, but invaluable as a roadmap for understanding where the original wiring ran and how the building's electrical skeleton was structured.

"Main panel should be here," Sarah said, tapping the blueprint. "Back wall of the utility corridor behind the concession area. That's where the original service entry came in. We'll need to verify that the panel location makes sense for the new service or if we're better off relocating it to give us a cleaner run to the auditorium and the stage."

The lead electrician leaned in and studied the routing. "If the conduit runs are still accessible through this corridor, we can probably keep the panel location and just upgrade everything in place. Saves us from cutting into the lobby walls."

"That's what I'm hoping. But let's get eyes on it before we commit. I don't want to plan around a panel location and then find out the corridor is blocked or the wall behind it has been modified." She pulled a flashlight from her belt. "Let's start with a walk. I want to trace every run we can find in the lobby and document what's there before we touch anything."

They worked through the lobby methodically, moving from the concession area to the ticket booth to the main entrance, tracing visible wiring runs where they emerged from walls and ceilings. They photographed junction boxes, noting the condition of every fixture and outlet they could find. Sarah kept her own notes alongside the electricians' documentation. Ethan would need copies of everything they documented today, and she made a mental note to coordinate that with him before the end of the day.

The work was not glamorous. First days on a restoration project never were. This was the necessary, painstaking groundwork that made everything that followed possible, the careful cataloging of what existed before anyone could decide what needed to change. Sarah loved this part of the process, even when it was tedious, because it was where the building told you its secrets. Every wire run revealed a decision someone had made decades ago. Every junction box told a story about how the building had been used and modified and adapted over the years.

They were about forty minutes into the lobby survey when Ethan came through the auditorium doors and walked toward the concession counter, where Sarah was reviewing a section of the blueprint with the electricians. He moved with the easy awareness of a man who understood job sites well enough to know where to stand and where not to. He stopped at a respectful distance until there was a natural break in the conversation before stepping up beside her.

"How's it going in here?" he asked.

"Good. We've traced about seventy percent of the lobby routing, and it's tracking with the original blueprint. The panel location looks viable, but we won't know for sure until we open up the utility corridor." She glanced up from the blueprint. "How's the auditorium?"

"I've been documenting the ceiling condition and the plasterwork for the grant file. There's more detailed work in the medallions than I realized from the walkthrough. The original craftsmanship is remarkable." He paused and grinned. "How did the trip to Knoxville go yesterday? The lumber?"

Sarah straightened up from the counter. "It went well. Really well, actually. The reclaimed heart pine from that closed mill is exactly what we need. The grading is excellent, the grain is tight, and it's a near-perfect match for the original stage planking. We brought about a quarter of the load back yesterday, and it's stored at Dad's mill. The rest is being delivered here tomorrow afternoon."

"That's great. You must have been pleased with the find."

"I was, and so was Dad. He was in his element. He spent about thirty minutes inspecting every plank, and he only found two he didn't like, which for Dad is practically a standing ovation." She smiled at the memory of her father in the reclaimed lumberyard, running his hands over the wood with the attention of a man who had spent his life reading grain and density the way other people read books. "It's the material your dad would have wanted, I'm sure of it. Heart pine and period-correct. It's going to be beautiful on that stage."

"Would your dad mind if I stopped by the mill to see it?" he asked.

"I don't think he'd mind at all. In fact," she looked at the electricians, who were documenting a junction box near the ticket booth and didn't need her standing over them, "we could head over now if it works for you. I can show you the lumber and hook up the trailer and bring it back with us. No reason to let it sit at the mill when it could be acclimating to the building's interior climate. The sooner we get it inside the Granville, the better for the wood."

"Let's go then."

Sarah turned to the lead electrician. "I'm going to run to the mill and back. It should be about an hour. You two good here?"

"We're good. We'll finish the lobby survey and start on the utility corridor."

"If you open that corridor and find anything unexpected, don't touch it. Just document it and wait for me."

"Got it."

Sarah pulled her hard hat off as she headed for the door. The August heat met her on the sidewalk, immediate and heavy after the

Granville's cool interior. She walked to her truck, with Ethan falling into step beside her.

She unlocked the driver's side and climbed in. Ethan walked around to the passenger side and got in. She started the engine and pulled away from the curb, and the Granville receded in her mirrors.

"Your crew really respects you," Ethan said as she turned onto Main Street.

"They should. I pay them well, and I don't ask them to do anything I wouldn't do myself."

"That's not what I mean." He was looking at her from the passenger seat. "The way Tim listens and respects you. The way the whole crew listens. That's not paycheck loyalty. That's something else."

Sarah drove for a moment without answering, because the comment had landed in a place that was closer to personal than she usually let professional conversations get, and she needed a second to decide how to respond to it.

"Tim was the first person who believed in me when I didn't have a track record to prove anything," she said. "He left a stable job at a bigger firm to come work for a twenty-three-year-old woman with a rundown truck and a contractor's license. I asked him why once, about a year in. He said he'd rather work for someone who cared about the work than someone who cared about the invoice. And because I went to church, and because I'm Bill Hartwell's daughter. Those were his reasons." She checked her mirrors and changed lanes. "I've tried to build a company that deserves the kind of loyalty Tim gave me on faith. If my crew respects me, it's because I earned it. Every day. I treat all my employees well, better than any other construction company owner I know. I pay them well. I don't require them to work more than an eight-hour day unless we absolutely have to. We never work on Sundays... never. Each of my employees gets four paid weeks of vacation time a year."

The truck was quiet for a beat, and then Ethan said, "That's exactly the kind of company my dad built. I know that now after being home for a month. Dad's company practically runs itself. He treated each of his employees with respect and considered each of them as family. I stepped into a well-oiled machine, and his employees respect me and get the job done."

"It makes life a bit easier when you have dedicated employees, wouldn't you agree?"

"I do. I'm thankful Dad ran a tight ship. I just wish he was still here today. I'd give anything to turn back time and just have him here with me and Mom. I've thought about that a lot lately."

"My brother Mike says that about Jenny every so often. You probably don't know this, but we lost Jenny, his wife, three years ago. She and Mike were a great pair. Jenny was one of my best friends. Mike still says he just wishes she were here. Not for anything specific. Just here." She paused. "But I honestly think the people who are no longer here with us would want us to keep going." She said it without looking at him, her eyes on the road, and she meant every word. The truck cab was quiet after that, and the road to the mill unspooled ahead of them through the green tunnel of trees that lined the road at this stretch. Sarah thought about fathers and the things they build and the children who carry it forward. She didn't say anything else because sometimes the truest thing you can offer a person who's grieving is just being there while they miss someone they loved.

Chapter 10

The Hartwell Lumber Mill announced itself before Sarah turned off the main road. The distant whine of the mill saws carried through the open truck windows first, then the diesel rumble of a loader working somewhere beyond the tree line. The gravel drive opened up and the whole operation spread out ahead of them like a map of one family's working life.

The lumber mill anchored the property on the right, a complex of connected buildings and open-air structures. Rows of lumber drying in graded tiers, organized with precision. A forklift idled near the kilns, and two workers in hard hats were guiding a load of timber onto a flatbed. Stacking yards stretched behind the main mill building. The scale of it registered differently through an architect's eye. This wasn't a small family operation running on sentiment. This was a serious commercial enterprise that employed dozens of people in a town of eight thousand, and it had been running long enough that the buildings themselves carried the patina of sustained use.

Sarah's workshop building sat to the left, separated from the mill by a gravel road. The workshop's bay doors faced the mill for easy material transfer. Her office sat where it could overlook both the yard and the drive. The staging area by the bay doors was positioned for efficient loading.

Sarah swung the truck around toward the back of the mill building, where a large flatbed trailer was parked. A heavy tarp covered the load, strapped down tight. She slowed, checked her mirrors, and put the truck in reverse.

The space she had to work with was narrow. The mill wall was on one side, a tall stack of milled lumber on the other. Ethan watched her hands on the wheel, steady and unhurried, making small corrections when needed. The truck eased backward through the gap without hesitation in one smooth, continuous motion. She put it in park and killed the engine.

Ethan got out and walked back to check the hitch. The ball sat directly under the trailer tongue. Dead center.

"You want to try that again just so I can watch?" he said when she came around to the back.

Sarah was already reaching for the trailer tongue. "I've been backing trailers since I was sixteen. Dad had me hauling lumber loads before I had my full license." She cranked the tongue down onto the hitch with the jack handle, the mechanical clicking as it locked in place. "You going to stand there being impressed, or are you going to help me with this tarp?"

"Both, if that's an option."

She looked at him for half a second, shook her head, and then turned to the tarp straps.

They worked from opposite ends of the trailer, unhooking the bungee straps that held the tarp edges to the flatbed frame. Ethan pulled his side free and walked it toward the center as Sarah did the same, and when they met at the middle to fold the heavy canvas back, his hand brushed hers where they both gripped the tarp's edge.

Sarah pulled her hand back and turned her attention to the trailer's load. "There's your lumber," she said, but she didn't look at him.

Ethan let the moment pass and turned his attention to the trailer.

The heart pine was beautiful in the late-morning light. He ran his hand along the top plank, feeling the slight roughness of the aged surface. The color was rich and the grain pattern was the kind of thing you could study like a fingerprint.

"This is exceptional," he said.

"That's what I thought when I saw it. Dad agreed. The grading is consistent across the entire lot. We got fortunate."

He walked toward the front of the trailer and crouched down to examine the end grain of a plank, studying the tight rings. His dad would have been running his hands over every plank, talking about growth rings and milling techniques and the irreplaceable quality of old-growth heart pine. Ethan stood up.

"It's perfect for the stage," he said.

Voices carried across the yard, and Ethan turned to see two figures coming around the corner of the mill building, walking toward them. Bill and Olivia Hartwell, moving at an easy pace, holding hands.

Ethan continued to watch them and felt envious. Years of marriage in the space between their palms. He wanted the kind of love that looked like that, steady and lived in and worn smooth by decades of ordinary days.

"There's my girl," Bill said as they reached the trailer. He released Olivia's hand to extend his own to Ethan. "Ethan. Good to see you."

"Good to see you, sir."

"Bill," he corrected. "Sir was my daddy."

Olivia stepped in and wrapped Ethan in a hug. She was a small woman with kind eyes and the kind of warmth that radiated from her like heat from a woodstove, immediate and impossible to stand near without feeling. "Ethan Cole, it is so good to see you again. How is your mama doing?"

"She's doing all right, Mrs. Hartwell. She has good days and harder days. But she's getting there."

"Please, honey, call me Olivia. And you tell her I said hello and I'm thinking of her. She and I need to have coffee soon." She released him and patted his arm once, a gesture that communicated more than a paragraph of words could have managed.

Sarah was watching the exchange with a look of mild surprise. "Mom, I didn't expect to see you out here."

"Your father left a stack of paperwork on the kitchen table this morning that he needs for a meeting this afternoon. I drove it out to him." Olivia smiled. "I needed to run by the quilt shop anyhow. I need more fabric for Jim and Grace's wedding quilt; I'm running low on options."

"She's been running low on fabric options for weeks," Bill said with a chuckle. "The quilt shop sees her coming from a mile away."

Olivia gave him a look that was part warmth, part warning, and entirely affectionate. "This is your son and your soon-to-be daughter-in-law's wedding quilt, young man; that's enough out of you."

Bill grinned and turned his attention to the trailer. He stepped up to the planks and ran his hand along them.

"Good stock," he said. "Tight grain. Heart pine like this doesn't come around much anymore."

"It's perfect for the stage floor," Ethan said. "You and Sarah did good."

Bill looked at his daughter and gave her a wink.

"We're bringing this load over to the Granville today," she said, working the safety chains through the hitch rings while she talked. Her hands moved through the process with the same unconscious competence she brought to everything. Ethan couldn't keep his eyes off her.

"Your mama and I were going to ride over there," Bill said, and then he turned to Ethan. "We haven't been in the Granville in years."

"You're welcome anytime," Ethan said.

Sarah connected the trailer's electrical plug to her truck and straightened up, wiping her hands on her jeans. "Then let's go."

Sarah put the truck in gear after Ethan got inside. The flatbed riding steady behind them, the heart pine strapped and secured, the weight of it settling the truck's rear suspension into a low, solid stance.

"Your parents are something special," Ethan said.

Sarah glanced at him. "They are."

"The way they are with each other. It's easy to see how much they love one another."

"They've always been like that. Mom says they still act like newlyweds, and Dad pretends he doesn't know what she's talking about, yet he holds her hand every time he gets the chance. I admire what they have. Thirty-six years and they still genuinely enjoy each other's company. That's rare in today's world."

The road wound through the green corridor of trees that connected the mill property to the main route back toward town, light filtering through the canopy in shifting patterns across the windshield.

"Dad wants to help at the theater," Sarah said. "Fair warning. He's going to find a reason to be there as much as possible, and I'm not going to stop him. He's been itching for a project that isn't mill work."

"Sounds good to me," Ethan said as he settled into the passenger seat and watched the road unspool ahead of them. He thought about

Bill and Olivia and the love they had for one another still to this day. He'd seen it between his own parents as well. He wondered, not for the first time, if he'd ever be so lucky as to be in a relationship like that.

Chapter 11

E than stood beside the lead electrician, tracing the lobby's electrical layout with his finger along the lines of the original blueprint while the second electrician stood nearby.

"I want additional capacity along this wall," Ethan said, marking the concession area on the blueprint with his pencil. "When this space is operational, they'll need outlets for equipment behind the counter. Commercial-grade dedicated circuits. And here," he tapped the ticket booth, "enhanced lighting. The booth is the first thing people see when they walk in. I want it lit properly."

Art studied the marks. "None of that's a problem within the scope of the rewire. We're pulling new runs through the whole lobby, anyway. Adding more outlets and lighting circuits is straightforward."

"Good. And the lobby entrance needs better fixture placement. The original design had wall sconces flanking the doors, which are beautiful but not sufficient for a working entrance. I want to supplement without competing with the originals."

"We can run a separate circuit for overhead fixtures and keep the sconce circuits independent. That way you can control ambiance and function separately."

"Perfect. That's what I want."

Sarah's voice carried through the auditorium doors. She was walking her parents around the building, explaining different aspects of the project.

Overhead, the roof crew's boots thumped across the decking of the roof in a steady rhythm, punctuated by the occasional ring of a hammer. The Granville was full of sound today. Full of people doing work that mattered.

Ethan finished his notes with the electricians and walked through the auditorium doors.

Sarah stood near the proscenium arch with Bill and Olivia, the three of them looking up at the ornate molding that framed the stage.

"The plasterwork in this arch is original," Sarah was saying as Ethan came down the center aisle. "The medallions in the lobby ceiling are the same vintage. Ethan's documenting all of it for the preservation grant, and we'll protect every piece during the renovation."

Bill had his hands in his pockets, studying the arch. "That molding's hand-applied," he said. "You don't see that anymore."

"No, you don't," Ethan said as he reached them. "The detail in the capitals is extraordinary. Whoever did this work was an artist, not just a plasterer."

Bill nodded.

Olivia had turned away from the arch and was looking out across the auditorium, her gaze moving over the rows of seats, the balcony above, and the old burgundy carpet with its faded gold pattern.

"Bill, do you remember when we brought the kids here to see that Easter play the church put on?" she said. "Sarah couldn't have been more than six or seven. Jim and Dave fought over the armrest the entire first act, and Mike fell asleep before intermission."

"I remember you cried at the end," Bill said.

"It was a beautiful play about the last week of Jesus' life. I couldn't help but cry. And Rebecca threw her popcorn at the boy in front of us because he wouldn't stop talking." Olivia laughed softly. "We were quite the crew."

Sarah shook her head. "I remember that clearly. Rebecca wouldn't stop fidgeting the entire time. Jim kept kicking me just to pester me. And Mike snored so loud after he fell asleep."

Olivia looked at Ethan. "I'm so glad you're dedicated to bringing this theater back to life. It meant the world to so many families in this town."

"It really did," Ethan said.

Bill checked his watch. "We need to get going, Sarah. I've got that meeting at two, and your mother needs her fabric fix."

"It's not a fix, dear. This is a fabric purchase for a special wedding quilt." Olivia corrected. "There's a difference."

"Not to my wallet, there isn't."

Sarah hugged her mother, then her father. Bill turned to Ethan and shook his hand. "Good to see the place again. You two will do right by it, I'm sure of it."

"I'll come help next week," Bill said to Sarah. "Tomorrow your mama and I are going to run some errands, so we'll be busy."

Olivia pulled Ethan into another hug. "You tell your mama I want you both at our table for Sunday dinner soon."

"Yes ma'am. She'd like that."

Bill and Olivia walked up the center aisle of the auditorium, hand in hand, their silhouettes moving through the light that fell from the high side windows. Ethan watched them go. Two people who had been walking side by side for thirty-six years, and you could see every one of those years in the easy way they moved together, unhurried, as if the world could wait.

Sarah turned to him. "Can I talk to you about something?"

"Of course."

She leaned against the edge of the stage, arms crossed loosely. "I overheard you in the lobby with Art and Liam earlier. Discussing additional outlets and lighting."

"I was. The concession area needs more electrical capacity, and the ticket booth lighting isn't sufficient for the—"

"Ethan." She held up a hand. "I'm not questioning the specifications. They're good calls. The concession area does need more capacity, and the booth lighting is on my list too. That's not the issue."

He waited.

"The issue is that those requests went directly to my electricians without coming through me first. Art and Liam are my subcontractors. I hired them, I'm managing their scope, and I'm responsible for how their work fits into the overall schedule and the budget."

"You're right."

"Every addition, even a small one, affects the phasing plan. It affects cost. It can affect the grant compliance milestones if we're not tracking it properly. I need to know about scope changes before my subs do, not after. If I lose control of the timeline or the budget because changes are happening around me instead of through me, that puts the entire project at risk."

She said all of this the way she said everything on a job site. Clear, direct, and without heat. She wasn't angry. She was establishing how things were going to work.

"I want us to work well on this project together," she said. "And I think we can. But I need all requests that modify my crew's or my subcontractor's work, their schedule, the scope, or the budget to come through me. Not through Art, not through Tim. Through me."

"Done," Ethan said. "And I owe you an apology. I should have brought those specs to you first. In Nashville, I was the only decision-maker on my projects most of the time. I'm used to working directly with subs because there was no one between me and them. That's not how this project is structured, and I should have adjusted sooner. I didn't mean to upset you. I apologize."

Sarah studied him for a moment. "You didn't upset me. I just wanted to get it on the table so we're clear going forward."

"We're clear."

"Good." She uncrossed her arms. "Now. How much are you planning to be on site? Because I need to know that for scheduling purposes."

"Most days," he said. "At least for the early phases. Probably through the fall."

"Most days."

"The preservation grant requires ongoing architectural documentation. Condition assessments, progress photography, and compliance reports at each milestone. That work has to happen in the building. And historic restoration doesn't follow a straight line. When your crew opens a wall or uncovers something unexpected, I need to be here to make design decisions in real time. If I'm working from an office across town, that means work stoppages while someone calls me and waits for me to drive over and look at it. That doesn't serve either of us."

"Yep, I understand all that. I've worked with many architects in the past. What else?"

"I want to start removing and cataloging the original fixtures in the lobby... I'm guessing next week, if that works for you. The brass sconces, the ticket booth hardware, and the chandelier. Those pieces are irreplaceable, and they need to come out carefully and be stored safely before any demolition gets close to them. I want to handle that personally."

Sarah nodded. That made sense to her.

"And my dad's drawings are preliminary. Conceptual. They're brilliant, but they're not construction documents. I need to be in this building measuring, adjusting, and developing those sketches into full working drawings your crew can build from. That's not something I can do from photographs."

"So you're essentially embedded in this project—I just want to make sure we're both on the same wavelength here."

"I am. But I want to be clear about something too. I'm not here to supervise your crew. I'm not here to look over Tim's shoulder or redirect your electricians. I'm here to do my own work, parallel to yours. You run the build. I handle the design, the documentation, and the preservation elements. The lines stay where you drew them."

"That's all I needed to hear," Sarah said. She pushed off from the stage edge and started walking away from him. "We'll make it work. I have faith. Now, I need to get back to work. "

"Sarah."

She turned back.

"Let me take you out for dinner tonight. To make up for overstepping today."

She tilted her head slightly. "That's not necessary."

"I know it's not necessary. I'm asking anyway."

"I appreciate the offer, but I have plans."

"Plans."

"Big plans. A pot of coffee, sweatpants, and a movie on Netflix. Very important evening. Can't be rescheduled."

Ethan put his hand over his chest. "Hartwell, you just wounded my pride. Turned down for a Netflix movie. I don't know how I'm going to recover from this."

"You'll manage."

"What movie?"

"Haven't decided yet. Something with zero construction, zero blueprints, and zero men asking me to dinner."

"So a documentary about penguins."

She laughed. It was sudden and real, and it changed her entire face. She shook her head, still smiling, and pointed at him.

"Goodbye, Cole."

"Come on."

"Nope. Netflix for the win. Try not to rearrange my electrical plan while you're out of my sight. "

She turned and walked up the center aisle toward the lobby, her boots steady on the threadbare carpet, and Ethan watched her go.

He sat down in the front row of the Granville Theater and looked at the empty stage and thought about a woman who turned down dinner for sweatpants and Netflix without a second of hesitation. A woman who set terms with the confidence of someone who'd earned the right to set them and who laughed like she didn't do it often enough.

He was in trouble. The good kind.

Chapter 12

Sarah had been staring at the same row of the scheduling matrix for five minutes, and the numbers weren't arranging themselves any faster for the effort. The marble concession counter had become her de facto desk, the surface cool and solid beneath the spread of papers she'd anchored with a cast-iron plan weight borrowed from her office. Her iPad was propped against it, the screen displaying Tim's preliminary notes on the northwest roof section. Beside that lay the original 1952 electrical blueprint she'd been annotating all afternoon with the findings from Art's assessment. Her handwriting filled the margins in tight, precise lines. Phasing notes. Circuit loads. Questions for Monday.

She had one earbud in, country music playing low enough that she could still hear the muffled rhythm of the electricians working somewhere deep in the auditorium and Tim's crew overhead on the roof.

Her ponytail had given up the fight around three o'clock. Dark strands hung loose around her face, and she tucked one behind her ear without looking up from the matrix. Friday afternoon. End of the work week, and the schedule for next week was the only thing standing between her and the weekend. She was close. Two more rows and she'd have the phased assignments locked.

A brown paper bag landed directly on top of her blueprint.

Sarah pulled her earbud out and turned to find Ethan standing behind her with his arms crossed and an expression that contained zero apology. The bag was large, and the smell hit her before she'd fully processed what had happened. Fried chicken.

"You turned me down for dinner yesterday," Ethan said. "So I brought dinner to you."

Sarah looked at the bag. Then at him.

"What is this?"

"Two of Minnie's Friday fried chicken specials. Mashed potatoes. Green beans." He nodded toward the bag. "And biscuits, because Minnie added those herself when she heard I was bringing food to the job site. She told me nobody should eat fried chicken without a biscuit on the side, and I wasn't about to argue with Minnie."

"Nobody argues with Minnie."

"Nobody wins an argument with Minnie. There's a difference."

Sarah looked at the bag again. The smell alone was doing things to her concentration that the scheduling matrix could not compete with. She'd skipped lunch. A granola bar at eleven-thirty and three cups of coffee since then, and her body was registering the presence of Minnie's fried chicken with the enthusiasm of a woman who had not eaten a real meal in nine hours.

"You didn't have to do this."

"I know."

She studied him for a second. He was still in his work clothes, the henley, jeans, and boots, and there was plaster dust on his left sleeve.

"All right," she said. "Help me move these papers."

They cleared the end of the counter together. Ethan unpacked the bag. Two Styrofoam containers, two sets of plastic utensils wrapped in paper napkins, and a smaller container that held four of Minnie's buttermilk biscuits, each one golden and the size of Sarah's fist. No plates. No formality. Just the food and the counter and the Granville settling around them.

Sarah opened her container, and the steam rose off the food in a way that made her close her eyes for a second and take in a deep breath. "Okay. This was a good call."

"You're welcome."

"I didn't say thank you yet."

"You closed your eyes and grinned as you enjoyed the scent of food—real food being brought to you, Hartwell. That's a thank you."

She picked up a drumstick and took a bite, and for a full thirty seconds, neither of them spoke because Minnie's fried chicken did not require commentary. It required attention. The breading was crisp and peppery, the meat tender. The green beans had been cooked with enough butter that they tasted like someone's grandmother had made them, which, in a manner of speaking, was exactly true.

"Tim's going to have a full report on my desk Monday morning," Sarah said between bites. "But he gave me the preliminary today. The northwest roof damage is contained. No structural compromise to the framing beneath it. The decking needs to be replaced in a twelve-foot section, and there's flashing work around the parapet that has to be redone, but the bones are solid."

"That's good news."

"It's excellent news. If that damage had reached the framing, we'd be looking at a different conversation entirely. Different timeline, different budget. We caught a break up there."

Ethan nodded, chewing. "I've been working through the auditorium with the camera again today. Photographing every original detail
for the grant compliance file: the molding, the plaster capitals, the seat
hardware, and the aisle fixtures. I found some hand-lettered signage
behind one of the acoustic panels on the east wall. The panels were
installed in the seventies, and whoever put them up just covered right
over it. Two signs. One that said 'Balcony' with an arrow and one that
said 'Gentlemen' for the old restroom. Both are hand-painted. The
lettering is beautiful."

"How's the condition?"

"Nearly perfect. The panels protected them. Seventy years behind
a wall, and they look like they were painted last month." He shook his
head slightly. "I spent forty-five minutes photographing them from
every angle. The grant committee is going to love it."

Sarah watched him talk about those signs the way she'd watched her
father talk about a particularly fine piece of old-growth timber, with a
specificity and a care that had nothing to do with money or deadlines
and everything to do with believing that some things were worth the
trouble of saving. This was the version of Ethan that kept catching
her off guard. Not the architect running calculations. Not the man
who'd overstepped with her electricians and had the sense to own
it. This version. The one who found seventy-year-old hand-painted
signage behind a wall and spent forty-five minutes making sure it was
documented properly because it mattered.

"How's your mama doing, Ethan?"

He set down his fork. The shift was immediate and quiet, the way
weather changes in the mountains.

"She's had a hard week," he said. "I brought her here last Sunday
after church. She wanted to see the building before the work got too

far along. It was good for her in the moment. She told stories. Laughed a little. But the days since have been quieter at the house."

"She's got countless memories in this building," Sarah said.

"She does."

Sarah reached for a biscuit and broke it in half. "Have you thought about bringing her in on some of the detail work? Not the construction. But you're going to be removing the original fixtures soon, the brass sconces, the chandelier, and the ticket booth hardware. That's careful, slow work. Cataloging. Labeling. Wrapping things for storage. Your mama knows this building better than anyone. She could help you with that."

Ethan looked at her.

"It might give her something active to do with the memories instead of just sitting with them," Sarah said. "Let her in, Ethan; invite her to come be a part of all this. Even a little. It might help."

He was quiet for a moment, turning the idea over in his mind. "That's an excellent idea," he said.

They ate in silence for a stretch after that, finishing the last of their meal.

"I've been running the same route every morning this week," Ethan said. "The same one where I nearly took you out on Tuesday."

Sarah reached for the last biscuit. "Okay."

"Haven't seen you once."

She took a bite. Chewed. Took her time with it. "I've been running in the opposite direction."

Ethan didn't say anything. He waited.

"I didn't want to crowd your space," she said.

"I wouldn't mind a running partner," he said. "The mornings are long when they're empty. I'd rather have company. The fork in the trail where the routes split is about a quarter mile from your property;

you said so yourself. If you happen to be running that direction some morning, I'll be there around five-thirty."

"I don't talk about work when I run."

"Fine by me… I'd prefer that."

"I run fast sometimes."

"I know. I did my best to keep up with you once already, remember? I barely managed it."

The corner of her mouth moved. Not a full smile. Close. "You didn't manage it. I beat you."

"You beat me soundly. I'm aware. I'm willing to suffer that humiliation again if it means the company."

She shook her head and started gathering the empty containers, stacking the Styrofoam and crumpling the napkins into a ball. She dropped everything into the trash bag hanging from the edge of the concession counter and wiped her hands on her jeans.

"That fried chicken was good," she said. "Hit the spot. That was really kind of you, Ethan. You didn't have to do that."

"I know I didn't have to. I wanted to." He looked at her. "There's a difference."

Sarah picked up her iPad and her stack of scheduling papers and tucked the plan weight into her bag. She walked toward the lobby doors, her boots quiet on the old terrazzo, and she could feel him watching her go the same way she'd felt it yesterday in the auditorium.

At the door, she turned back.

"I may or may not join you in the morning for a run. If you're at the fork in the trail when I get there, consider it an invitation to join me."

She pushed through the heavy wooden door and stepped out into the late afternoon. The air outside was warm and soft and smelled like fresh-cut grass and the particular sweetness of a small town on a Friday evening when the weekend is waiting. She put her things in the truck and sat behind the wheel for a moment before starting the engine.

Something was happening with Ethan Cole, and she was not as blind to it as she'd been pretending. The boy who had driven her crazy in high school had grown into a man who brought her fried chicken on a Friday afternoon and didn't ask for anything in return. She'd brushed him off more than once now, and it hadn't deterred him one bit.

She shook her head, and a grin spread across her face. She started the truck and drove home.

Chapter 13

Ethan had been at the fork in the trail for a few minutes, stretching his calves against a gnarled tree root. The morning was already warm, late August pressing in from every direction, but the shade beneath the tree felt perfect. Mist pooled in the low spots between the ridges, filling the valleys below the trail like someone had poured milk into a bowl and let it settle.

He'd left his house at five. The Cole property backed up to a network of trails that ran through the foothills, and this particular route wound south along the ridge before dropping to the fork where the paths split.

He drank from his water bottle. Stretched his other calf.

Sarah appeared around the bend eventually, running at a pace that had nothing casual about it. Ponytail swinging. Arms relaxed and stride smooth. She reached the fork where he waited and grinned.

It was the kind of grin that rearranged his entire morning.

"Morning," Ethan said.

"Let's get on with it. No time for chatter."

He fell into pace beside her.

The first mile was rhythmic. Matched stride, matched breathing, the trail opening ahead of them in sections of shade and brief clearings. Their feet found the packed dirt and occasional exposed root in sync. Ethan noticed that running with Sarah felt the way good architecture felt, like two systems designed separately that happened to work perfectly together.

"So what does Sarah Hartwell do on a typical Saturday?" he asked.

She glanced at him without breaking stride. "You really wanna know?"

"I really wanna know."

"Saturday mornings I go to my sister's salon. Standing appointment. She does my nails and my hair. It's me time. I let my sister pamper me, and I don't think about work the entire time." She navigated a section of trail where the ground dipped and rose again over a knot of tree roots. "It's my one non-negotiable. Every Saturday morning. Rain, shine, or the apocalypse."

"That's a serious commitment."

"What can I say? I like to be pampered every week. I deserve it. I work hard, I play hard, and I need me time. Besides, Rebecca would hunt me down if I skipped it. She's told me that my hair and my hands are an advertisement for her salon, whether I like it or not, and she's not wrong. I've had plenty of people stop me and ask where I get my nails done because they know I work construction. Rebecca's nails stand up against my work, and that's an advertisement you can't put a dollar amount on."

"Your sister gets referrals because of what you do for a living?"

"Rebecca gets referrals from everywhere... but yep, I'm a walking advertisement for her. You know construction work can be brutal." Sarah dodged a low branch. "After the salon, I run whatever errands need running around town, and then the rest of my Saturday is any-thing that has absolutely nothing to do with work."

"Such as?"

"Sometimes I watch movies and completely turn into a couch potato. Like, fully committed. Pajamas, blanket, every candle in my house lit so the whole place smells like a candle factory and sets the mood."

Ethan looked at her. "You a couch potato?"

"I am a person of layers, Cole."

"Apparently."

"Sometimes I'm on that couch with a book instead of the remote. Same commitment level. I will not move. I will not answer my phone. Jim called me six times last Saturday, and I let every single one go to voicemail because I was in the middle of a really good chapter."

"What do you read?"

"Romance novels."

She said it the way someone throws down a card they've been holding, with a touch of defiance and the clear expectation that the other person was about to say something stupid about it.

"I like the funny ones," she continued before he could respond. "Rom-coms where the dialogue is sharp and the characters are a mess, but you're rooting for them, anyway. And then sometimes I'll find one that's just, you know, the real deal. Where two people fall for each other and it's slow and it's sweet, and by the end of it you're sitting there with this big goofy feeling in your chest like love is the simplest thing in the world." She adjusted her ponytail without slowing down. "Which is, of course, completely and totally untrue. Love is not sim-ple. It's not even in the same zip code as simple. But that's the whole point, right? It's fiction. I get to make believe for three hundred pages that two people can just look at each other and know, and nobody has to get their feelings hurt or their ego bruised or spend three years rebuilding walls because some man decided they were too much to handle." She caught herself. Shook her head once. "Anyway. Romance novels. That's what I read. Go ahead and make fun of me."

"Why would I make fun of you?"

"Because most people do. My brothers give me grief about it constantly. Jim called them my fairy tales once, and I didn't speak to him for a week."

"My mom reads them," Ethan said. "She has an entire shelf in the living room. Three rows deep, paperbacks crammed in sideways because she refuses to get rid of a single one."

Sarah looked at him. "Your mama reads romance novels?"

"Religiously. And my dad used to buy her a new one every Friday on his way home from the office. He'd stop at the bookshop on Main, and whoever was working would recommend something, and he'd buy it and bring it home. He'd grab a mystery or a crime thriller for himself, and then Saturday afternoon and several evenings during the week, the two of them would just sit together in the living room and read."

"That might be one of the sweetest things I've ever heard."

"It was just what they did. Every week for years. My mom would finish hers first because she's a faster reader, and then she'd sit there pretending to read something else while she waited for my dad to finish his so they could talk about their books." He smiled at the memory. "He never read hers. She never read his. But they'd describe the plots to each other in detail, and my dad would try to guess the ending of her romance novel, and he was wrong every single time, and she loved it. She'd say, 'Phillip, you have no idea how love works in fiction,' and he'd say, 'I know how it works in this house, and that's good enough for me.' I remember those times so clearly from when I lived at home."

"Your parents had something really special."

"They did."

The trail curved north, and the shade deepened as the canopy closed overhead. A creek ran below them, the sound of water over stone carrying up through the trees.

"All right, your turn," Sarah said. "Tell me about Nashville. Not the work. I want to know what it was like to actually live there. Because I cannot imagine living anywhere but here. I'm curious what it's like to be somewhere that big and that loud and that fast all the time."

"You've never wanted to leave Serenity Crossing?"

"Never. Not once. I've visited places. I go to Knoxville for trade shows or shopping; I've been to Atlanta twice for supplier conferences. I spent a long weekend in Charleston, South Carolina, with Rebecca two years ago, which was beautiful, but after seventy-two hours I was ready to come home." She shrugged. "This is where I belong. I've known it since I was a young girl, and I've never wavered. The mountains, the people, the pace of life here... I know where I'm supposed to be."

Ethan was quiet for a moment, not because he didn't have an answer, but because her certainty struck him. He'd spent twelve years chasing something she'd already found.

"Nashville was electric for the first five years," he said. "The energy of it. The scale. I was twenty-three, and I had my own drafting table in a shared office space. I thought I was going to change the world. And for a while, it felt like I was. The projects kept getting bigger, and the clients kept getting more impressive, and every week there was something new—some gallery opening or industry dinner or networking event where everyone was sharp and ambitious and moving fast. I felt like I was living a dream, and I wanted more. Always more."

"That sounds exhausting."

"It was incredible. And then it was exhausting. You're right. Because eventually, the novelty wore off and what was underneath it was just noise. Loud restaurants where you couldn't hear the person across the table. Traffic that turned a ten-minute drive into forty-five. Neighbors I lived next to for three years and never learned their last names." He stepped over a fallen branch in the trail. "I had a condo with floor-to-ceiling windows and a view of the Cumberland River, and I spent more time at the office than I ever spent looking at that view. The city gave me everything I thought I wanted, and it took me years to figure out that what I actually wanted wasn't on the menu. I said before, my dad passing away was my wake-up call. My life came full circle. The impact of his death stopped my world, and I admitted to myself I was living a life I no longer enjoyed. Life changed in the blink of an eye."

"What was on the menu?"

"Success. Visibility. The kind of career that looks impressive on paper and from the outside in. And don't get me wrong, I'm glad I did it. I learned more in those years than I could have learned anywhere else. I became a better architect. I became a better businessman. But I did not become a better person. I didn't realize that until I came home." He looked at her. "You asked what it was like living in the city. It was like holding your breath and not knowing it until you stop."

"And now?"

"Now I'm here. I did the city thing. I'm grateful for it. But I'm not going back. I came home for my mom and to run my dad's company. I'm staying because this is where I'm supposed to be. Same as you, just took me a lot longer to figure it out."

Sarah smiled. "Better late than never, Cole."

They reached the overlook where the trail widened to a flat rock shelf with a view that stopped conversation cold. The Smokies were stacked in layers of blue and gray, ridge behind ridge behind ridge, the mist still clinging to the lower valleys. The light caught the tops of the nearest peaks in a way that made them look like they were glowing from the inside. The scale of it was absurd. No matter how many times Ethan stood at this spot, the view made him feel like he'd been looking at the world through a keyhole and someone had just opened the door.

They stopped and stretched. Sarah pulled her water bottle from the clip at her waistband and drank, then sat on the rock ledge with her legs stretched out in front of her and her face turned toward the valley. Ethan sat beside her, close enough that he could see the sheen of sweat on her collarbone and the way her ponytail had started to come loose again, dark strands sticking to the back of her neck. He turned his attention to the mountains for a distraction.

"Okay," Sarah said, capping her water bottle and setting it on the rock beside her. "I have to ask you something because it's been driving me crazy, and I need an answer."

"Ask away."

She turned to look at him, and her expression was equal parts curiosity and confusion. "Why did we go at each other so hard in high school? I have never understood it. We were in the same classes, the same activities. We spent four years driving each other nuts. What was that about? Because I've thought about it, and I've never been able to make it make sense."

Ethan looked at the valley. The mist was beginning to thin in the lower ridges; the sun working on it from above, and the layered blues were separating into greens and golds as the morning advanced.

"You really wanna know?"

"I really wanna know."

"I liked you."

Sarah went still.

"Sophomore year," he said. "Mr. Patterson's history class. We were covering the Constitutional Convention, and you stood up in the middle of a discussion and argued with me for fifteen minutes straight about the balance of federal versus state power. You were relentless. You had sources I hadn't read. You made points I hadn't considered. You didn't back down one inch, and the entire class was watching, and I was sitting there thinking two things at the same time. The first one was that I was losing the argument, which had never happened to me before in that classroom. And the second one was that the girl who was beating me was the most impressive person I had ever met."

He picked up a small stone from the rock shelf and turned it over in his fingers. "I was sixteen. I was the starting quarterback. I had friends who expected a certain version of me, and that version didn't include admitting that a girl had rattled me in a history debate and I liked her for it. I didn't have the words for what I was feeling. I didn't even have the framework. All I knew was that you were in every room I was in, and every time you walked in, the room got louder in my head."

"So I did what every sixteen-year-old boy does when he doesn't understand what's happening," he continued. "I turned it into a competition. Every debate, every group project, every student council meeting. I showed up wherever you were because showing up was the only way I knew how to be near you without admitting why. I let my friends set the tone for how I acted instead of figuring out how to be a better version of myself. I was the quarterback. I had a role, and I filled it, and the role didn't include being honest about the fact that the girl I was competing with was the girl I couldn't stop thinking about."

He set the stone down on the ledge between them. "That's what high school was about. For me, anyway. I was a teenage boy who was attracted to a girl who could out-argue him and out-study him in the same afternoon, and instead of doing anything useful with that information, I turned it into years of butting heads because that was the only door I knew how to walk through."

The silence that followed was full of twelve years of a story that had just been rewritten for the woman sitting inches away, trying to process it.

She stared at him. Her lips were slightly parted. Her hands had gone completely still. She blinked once, slowly, the kind of blink that takes a beat too long because the brain behind it is running a recalculation that isn't small.

Three breaths. Ethan counted them because he was watching her face and because he knew that the next thing she said was going to tell him everything about where they were.

She stood up and capped her water bottle, then clipped it back to her waistband with the precise, deliberate movements of a woman who needed to be doing something normal while the rest of her caught up.

"That's a lot for six-thirty in the morning, Cole."

Her voice was lighter than the moment deserved, and that was how he knew it had landed. The lightness was the tell.

She turned and started jogging back down the trail. "Come on. Keep up," she called over her shoulder.

He was on his feet and after her in three strides, and the pace she set was fast. Not the competitive sprint from their first run. Something different. This was a woman putting physical distance between herself and a conversation she wasn't ready to sit with, and her legs were doing what her words wouldn't.

"You're running away from what I just told you," Ethan said, pulling alongside her.

"Yep. That's exactly what I'm doing."

"Fair enough."

"Don't 'fair enough' me. You just dropped a twelve-year confession on a rock on a mountain before seven in the morning, and you expect me to have a response? I don't have one. I need to think about what you just said because it changes about a million things I believed were true, and I cannot do that right now, so we're going to talk about literally anything else right now."

"Okay."

"Okay." She pointed upward without breaking stride. "Red-tailed hawk. Two o'clock. Riding the thermals."

He looked up. She was right. The bird was circling in wide, lazy arcs above the ridge, wings barely moving, riding the warm air that was pushing up from the valley as the morning heated. "Beautiful."

"You're doing it," she said.

"Doing what?"

"Letting me deflect. Thank you."

"You're welcome." He pointed to a section of trail ahead where the edge had eroded, the dirt crumbling away toward a steep drop that was masked by undergrowth. "Someone needs to report that to the park service. That's going to give way completely in a matter of months. "

"I reported it two months ago. Called the ranger station, filed the form online, and followed up with an email. Nothing."

"You followed up with an email."

"I followed up with two emails and a phone call. The woman on the phone told me they had a maintenance backlog through November, and I told her that by November someone was going to step on that edge and end up in the creek bed twenty feet below it. She said she'd pass it along. Nothing has happened."

"That's unacceptable."

"That's government bureaucracy. Welcome home."

The trail wound down from the ridgeline through a section of older forest where the trees were tall enough to block most of the sky. The air was cooler here; the mist lingering in pockets that they ran through like curtains. Sarah pointed out a patch of wildflowers she'd been watching all summer, a cluster of black-eyed Susans that had spread along the trail edge and were blooming in a riot of gold. Ethan noticed a section of dry-stacked stone wall half-hidden in the undergrowth off the north side of the trail, remnants of a property boundary from a century ago. They talked about the wall and the flowers and a woodpecker that was hammering away somewhere above them with the persistence of a contractor on a deadline, and neither of them mentioned high school or confessions or sophomore year.

They neared the fork in the trail and slowed to a walk. Both of them were breathing hard from the pace Sarah had set. The air between them was different now, carrying something that hadn't been there an hour ago, something that neither of them was going to address while they were still catching their breath.

"What are you doing this weekend?" Ethan asked.

Sarah wiped her forehead with the back of her hand. "Why?"

"No particular reason. I just thought if you weren't doing anything, maybe we could do something together. Head to Gatlinburg and catch a movie. Or rent a boat on Hawthorne Lake."

She looked at him. "I'll think about it."

She turned toward her home and started jogging.

"I'm not letting you off the hook, Hartwell," Ethan called after her. "I'm going to keep asking until you go out on a date with me."

"I'd expect nothing less from you, Cole." She didn't stop. She didn't turn around. But her voice carried back up the trail, clear and warm and carrying the unmistakable edge of a woman who was smiling even if he couldn't see it.

Ethan stood at the fork and watched her disappear around the bend in the trail, her ponytail swinging.

She didn't say no...that's a move in the right direction.

He turned and headed toward home.

Chapter 14

The bell above the door of The Fluff & Curl Salon was still chiming when Rebecca spotted her from across the salon and let out the kind of greeting that turned every head in the room. "There's my favorite sister. Get over here and give me a hug."

Sarah crossed the black-and-white checkerboard floor, weaving between a stylist named Jenna, who was mid-blowout at station three, and a woman in foils reading a magazine near the window. She walked straight into Rebecca's arms. Her sister hugged the way she did everything, completely, both arms wrapped tight, rocking side to side for two full seconds before pulling back and holding Sarah at arm's length for inspection.

The salon was alive the way it always was on Saturday mornings. Every chair was occupied. Conversations layered over each other in that particular hum that belonged to a room full of women. Music drifting from the speaker Rebecca kept on the shelf behind the register, something folksy and warm that matched the mood she was building for the day. The exposed brick walls were lined with floating shelves holding more plants than a salon had any right to own, trailing ivy and succulents, and a fiddle-leaf fig in the corner that Rebecca talked to like a pet. The vintage turquoise cash register sat on the front counter like a piece of art, which it basically was, since Rebecca ran everything through the tablet beside it. The whole place smelled like coconut shampoo and fresh coffee from the pot Rebecca kept going for her clients.

Rebecca held her at arm's length and looked her over. This was the ritual. Every Saturday, without fail, Rebecca assessed her sister the way a mechanic assesses an engine, looking for anything that needed attention.

"Nails look decent," Rebecca said, turning Sarah's hands over and checking the pale pink polish. "Just a color change today. We'll do that after your hair." She tilted Sarah's head gently to the side, running her fingers through the dark waves that Sarah had let air-dry after her shower. "We're going to do a deep condition, just a little trim, and then I'm gonna work my magic on you. I just got this new big barrel curling iron, and it will do spectacular things for this gorgeous head of hair."

"I trust you."

"You'd better." Rebecca stepped back and gave her one more look, head to toe. The soft cotton sundress that hit above Sarah's knee, the wedge sandals, and the small cross necklace that sat in the hollow of her throat. Saturday Sarah. The version that had nothing to do with hard hats or construction work.

Rebecca's eyes narrowed. "You look different today. What happened? You've got this look like your world is confused or something."

"It's nothing."

"That is a lie, and you know it. Sit down."

Rebecca fastened a cape around her neck with the quick, practiced movement of a woman who did this fifty times a week and caught

Sarah's eyes in the mirror. She was wearing a floral blouse tucked into high-waisted jeans and a pair of boots that added three inches to her height. Sarah wondered again, not for the first time, how her sister spent eight hours on her feet in those things without a single complaint. Rebecca's own hair was flawless, because Rebecca Hartwell did not leave the house without looking like an advertisement for her own business. Soft waves, a little volume, every piece exactly where it belonged.

"Come on," she said, steering her toward the wash station at the back. "Let's get you started."

Sarah leaned back into the shampoo chair and closed her eyes as Rebecca turned on the water and tested the temperature against the inside of her wrist. The spray hit Sarah's hairline and moved through her hair in slow, thorough passes, and she felt the tension in her shoulders begin to release.

"So tell me about your week," Sarah said, because Rebecca's week was always a production.

Rebecca laughed and lathered the shampoo between her palms. "Where do I start? On Monday I had a consultation with the Henderson bride, and her mama came along, which I should have seen coming because that woman has opinions about everything. She brought a photo on her phone of a hairstyle she wanted me to recreate for the wedding. Sarah. It was from 1987. I'm talking full-on perm, big bangs, the works. She looked at me like I should be thrilled."

"What did you do?"

"I smiled. I complimented her taste. And then I spent forty-five minutes gently steering her toward something from this century." Rebecca worked the shampoo through her hair from scalp to ends, massaging in slow circles. "Then Tuesday I had a color correction that took four hours because a woman tried to go platinum at home with a box kit. Four hours, Sarah. I thought my hands were going to fall off."

"Was it salvageable?"

"She looked beautiful when I was done with her. The poor thing cried in the chair after I was finished, which always gets me." Rebecca rinsed the shampoo, and then the deep conditioner was next. "I'm also testing a new product line this month. All clean ingredients, locally sourced, and the deep conditioner is incredible. You're my guinea pig."

"Happy to serve."

Rebecca worked the conditioner through section by section, her fingers finding every strand with the thoroughness of someone who treated hair the way Sarah treated a building, with full attention and no shortcuts. The salon noise settled into a comfortable backdrop. Blow dryers humming, a burst of laughter from the waiting area, and the folksy music weaving through it all.

"Have you talked to Anna this week?" Rebecca asked.

"Tuesday. She called to vent about a Harvest Festival vendor application. Apparently, someone wants to sell homemade essential oils and claims they cure everything from back pain to bad luck."

"Lord have mercy."

"That's what I said."

"Did you hear about Jim and Grace? They finalized the flowers, the cake, and the dinner options for the reception. Grace went with a three-tier vanilla with buttercream, which is the right call. And Mama is still buying fabric for that quilt. I saw three new bolts of fabric in her sewing room yesterday, Sarah. Bolts, I tell you."

"Three?"

"Three. That quilt will be the size of a California king bed at the rate she's going."

Sarah smiled. Eyes still closed, warm water on her scalp, and her sister's voice winding around her in the comfortable, familiar rhythm of their Saturday morning routine. This was the version of her life that nobody at a job site ever saw. The version that existed in pretty clothes, perfume, and jewelry.

Rebecca rinsed the conditioner, then wrapped Sarah's hair in a towel and walked her back to the chair. Sarah settled in, and Rebecca began sectioning her wet hair, the comb moving in clean lines from crown to nape.

"So... how's the Granville coming along?"

Sarah watched her sister in the mirror. Rebecca's face was perfectly casual. Too casual. The kind of casual that took effort.

"You're doing that thing where you're digging and getting ready to pounce... I'll let you have your moment, though. The Granville... it's good. We're making progress. The roof work is coming together, the electrical is ahead of schedule, and everything is running like clockwork."

"That's wonderful."

"It is."

Rebecca unclipped a section of hair and combed it smooth. "How's the crew? Everybody doing well?"

"Crew's solid. Tim's got everything running smoothly."

"Good." Rebecca picked up her shears and began trimming the ends, small precise cuts that kept Sarah's layers shaped without losing length. "And how's working with the architect? What's his name again? Ethan?"

Sarah looked at her sister in the mirror. "And there it is... the real information you want. You darn well know his name."

"I do. Come on, sis, give me the details."

"Things are professional. We've found a good working rhythm. He's good at what he does, and he respects my work, which is more than I can say for some architects I've worked with."

Rebecca nodded and kept trimming.

"He's been different," Sarah said.

"Different how?"

"He's dropped a couple of comments that could be taken one way or another... like little bits of flirting... or maybe not. Then Thursday he asked me to dinner as a peace offering for overstepping with my electricians. I turned him down. He took it well, made a joke, and didn't push."

"Okay."

"Then Friday he brought Minnie's fried chicken to the Granville at the end of the day. Two dinners. We ate standing at the concession counter."

Rebecca's eyebrows lifted in the mirror, but she kept cutting. "So you turned down the dinner invitation, and then he brought dinner to you the next day."

"Yep."

"Smart man."

"Rebecca."

"I'm just stating a fact. Continue."

Sarah took a deep breath. "We bumped into each other out on the trails—I was out running Tuesday morning, and he was too, from the opposite direction. I've been running in the opposite direction since to avoid him. He called me out on it. He asked me to run with him instead."

"And?"

"This morning I met him at the fork behind my house."

Rebecca set the shears down and picked up the round brush, beginning the blow-dry at the back sections. The warm air moved through Sarah's hair as Rebecca pulled each section smooth and guided it around the barrel.

"What did you talk about?" Rebecca asked over the dryer.

"Everything. What I do on my weekends. My little romance novel luxury."

"You told him you read romance novels?"

"I did."

"And?"

"He told me his mama reads them, too. His daddy used to buy her a new one every Friday on the way home from work."

"Keep going."

"He told me about Nashville. What it was like living there, why he came home." Sarah picked at the edge of the cape. "Then I asked him about high school. Why we went at each other so hard back then? Because I've never understood it."

Rebecca set the dryer down and picked up the big barrel curling iron she'd been so excited about. She wrapped a section of Sarah's hair around the barrel. "What did he say?"

"He said he liked me back then."

Rebecca didn't move.

"Sophomore year. Mr. Patterson's history class. He said I beat him in a debate, and it was the first time anyone had, and he spent the rest of high school turning it into a competition because he didn't know what else to do with what he was feeling." Sarah stared at her reflection in the mirror.. "He told me all of it. Right there on the overlook, six-thirty in the morning, mist in the valleys, and he just laid the whole thing out, Rebecca. Years of rivalry that was apparently him not knowing how to handle the fact that he liked me."

Rebecca released the curl and let it fall. She picked up the next section and wrapped it around the barrel, and her movements were slow and deliberate, the way they got when she was thinking hard and didn't want to rush what came next.

"And then he asked me what I was doing this weekend. He said he wanted to spend time with me."

"What did you say?"

"I told him I'd think about it."

The salon hummed around them, blow dryers and laughter and the low strum of a guitar from the speaker, and Rebecca worked through another three curls before she spoke again.

"Can I ask you one question?"

"You're going to, whether I say yes or not."

"Do you like him?"

"I don't know what I feel," Sarah said. "I know he makes me laugh. I know he's not what I expected. I know he looks at me like..." She stopped and shook her head. "He's got me all confused, Rebecca. He looks at me like I'm the only person in the universe. He says things that throw me off track. And I'm all jumbled up inside. I don't know what to do with all this."

Rebecca finished the curl she was working on and set the iron down. She began separating the curls gently, running her fingers through them until they loosened into soft, effortless waves.

"What's holding you back?"

Sarah didn't answer right away. She watched Rebecca's hands in the mirror, working through her hair, shaping the waves into something that framed her face.

"You know what Daniel did to me," Sarah said.

"I do."

"You know what it took from me."

"I know what you let it take."

Sarah met her sister's eyes in the mirror. Rebecca held the look, steady and warm and unflinching, because Rebecca Hartwell was sunshine and sparkle and warmth until one of her people was hurting, and then she was steel.

"He hurt me, Rebecca. He told me I was the problem in the relationship. That I was too much. That my business, my ambition, and the fact that I had a bigger life than he was comfortable with made me less of what he wanted. He wanted me to shrink. Scale back. Be smaller, quieter, and easier to deal with. He wanted arm candy, not a partner." Sarah's voice was level. Controlled. The voice she used when she was managing the narrative of her pain. "He didn't want me. He wanted a version of me that didn't make him feel small."

"I remember," Rebecca said. "I remember all of it."

"So what I took from Daniel is that the real me, the whole me, is too much for a man to handle. And I haven't let anyone close enough to test that theory since. Once was enough. And now here's this man who shows up, and he's thrown my world out of order. He brings me fried chicken and tells me he liked me in high school. I'm waiting for the other shoe to drop. I'm waiting for the moment he decides I'm too much and not worth his time."

Rebecca put both hands on Sarah's shoulders from behind, her fingers pressing gently, and met Sarah's eyes in the mirror with an expression that was tender and serious.

"Sarah, have you considered the possibility that you're pushing a good man away because of what a bad one did?"

The words landed like a punch in the gut she didn't see coming.

She stared at her sister in the mirror. The salon noise faded to nothing.

She didn't have a response. For the first time in as long as she could remember, Sarah Hartwell, who had an answer for everything, who could argue a building inspector into submission and negotiate a contract in her sleep, had absolutely nothing to say.

Rebecca held her eyes for another beat. Then she squeezed Sarah's shoulders, picked up a comb, and went back to work. "Have you heard about the new scent at the candle store? Vanilla and cedarwood. Honey, I bought three. You need to go get yourself one because it smells like a dream, and you will love it."

Sarah exhaled. "Vanilla and Cedarwood?"

"It will change your life. I'm not being dramatic."

"You're always being dramatic."

"That is both hurtful and accurate. Now, what color lipstick do you want? Because you look gorgeous, and we need to make sure the whole package is right."

"I wasn't planning on lipstick today."

"You weren't planning on a lot of things today. Life is full of surprises." Rebecca winked at her in the mirror. "Is Anna bringing a date to Jim's wedding? Because I heard she's been talking to that new guy at town hall, and I need information."

"I don't have information."

"Then you need to get some, because I cannot be the last to know things in this family."

The conversation settled into the lighter current that Rebecca navigated with the skill of a woman who knew exactly when to press and when to let go. They talked about Anna and the wedding and whether Mike was going to wear a tie or if someone would have to physically force one around his neck. They talked about Lizzie's latest proclamation that she wanted to be a hairdresser like Aunt Rebecca, which had made Rebecca cry in the middle of the salon. They talked about the new bakery that had opened in Gatlinburg that Rebecca wanted to visit and whether the Harvest Festival was going to have funnel cake this year because Rebecca had strong feelings about funnel cake.

But beneath the wedding talk and the candle recommendations and the funnel cake debate, the weight of what Rebecca had said sat heavy in Sarah's chest. A question she couldn't un-hear, settling into the same space where Ethan's confession had landed hours ago on a mountain.

Have you considered the possibility that you're pushing a good man away because of what a bad one did?

Rebecca stepped back and turned the chair so Sarah faced the mirror head-on again. "Look at you."

Sarah looked. The waves were perfect. Soft and full, framing her face in a way that made her eyes look warmer and her cheekbones more defined. The sundress, the small cross at her throat, the tan on her shoulders from weeks of outdoor work. She looked like herself. Not the hard hat version. Not the job site version. The whole version. The woman who read romance novels on the couch and wore sundresses on Saturdays because she liked the way they made her feel.

She stood up from the chair and hugged Rebecca without warning, pulling her in tight.

Rebecca hugged back and laughed against her shoulder. "What was that for?"

Sarah pulled back and grinned. "Because I love you. Now let's do my nails."

Chapter 15

The frozen foods aisle of Valley Grocery was no place for a crisis, but Sarah was having one, anyway. She stood in front of the full-length commercial freezer, her eyes locked on the rows of ice cream. Her cart was half-full of groceries; most of her shopping was done. Boneless chicken breasts wrapped in butcher paper from the meat counter. A bag of fresh green beans, two bunches of asparagus, Roma tomatoes, a head of romaine, and sweet corn from the produce section. A loaf of sourdough from the bakery aisle, still warm. Three different bags of coffee because one variety was never enough, and she rotated flavors the way other people rotated seasons.

Two pints of ice cream were already in the cart. Salted caramel, because salted caramel was non-negotiable and had been since she was nineteen. Butter pecan, because butter pecan had earned its rotation this week in her ice cream addiction.

The problem was the new varieties sitting behind the glass door, lined up like contestants in some kind of frozen dessert beauty pageant, and every single one of them was calling her name.

Sarah pulled the freezer door open and felt the rush of cold air hit her bare arms. She leaned in slightly, studying the labels. Double Strawberry Cheesecake. Caramel with Espresso Flavored Chocolate Chips. Mint Dark Chocolate Chip. Cookie Dough with rainbow colored chips. She kept four varieties at home at all times. Two slots were filled. Two remained. The math was simple. The decision was not.

She picked up the Double Strawberry Cheesecake and read the description on the side of the carton. Set it back. Picked up the Caramel Espresso. Set that back too.

"That's the most serious expression I've ever seen on someone looking at ice cream."

Sarah jolted. The voice came from behind her right shoulder and she felt a flame of heat rush straight up her spine. She closed the freezer door and turned around.

"You have to stop doing that," she said. "You scared the daylights out of me. Again. This is getting to be a regular thing with you."

Ethan was standing in the aisle holding a hand basket with a half gallon of milk and a loaf of bread in it, wearing a black fitted t-shirt and jeans. His eyes moved from her face down the length of her sundress to her wedge sandals and back up again.

Sarah felt the full weight of what he was seeing. Not job-site Sarah. Not hard-hat Sarah. Not even Sunday-morning Sarah, who dressed well but dressed for church. This was Saturday Sarah. The version with salon hair and a dress that moved when she walked and sandals that added two inches and freshly painted nails the color of a blush rose.

She turned back toward the freezer, opened the door, and started fanning herself, enjoying the rush of cool air. She had walked into Valley Grocery feeling good, content with getting her grocery shopping done so she could go on and enjoy her day. But no, Ethan Cole had to appear once again and was standing six feet away, making her fan herself with a freezer door.

She let go of the door and let it swing shut. "You shouldn't sneak up on people in grocery stores."

"I wasn't sneaking. I was shopping." He tilted his head toward the freezer case. "You were the one having a staring contest in front of the ice cream case... I couldn't help but notice."

"I was not having a staring contest."

"You were making a face that belongs in a boardroom negotiation, not a dairy section."

Sarah crossed her arms. "I was deliberating."

Ethan walked over to her cart. He set his basket down on the floor, then he picked up one of the pints she'd already chosen, turning it over in his hands and reading the label like it contained architectural specifications. "Salted caramel." He set it back and picked up the other. "Butter pecan." He placed it back in the cart and looked at her. "What exactly were you so serious about when I walked up? It's ice cream. You looked like you were deciding who to vote for as the next president."

"I keep four varieties at home at all times," Sarah said.

"At all times."

"At all times. It's a system. Salted caramel is locked in. That one never changes. Butter pecan rotates in and out, but it earned its spot this week. The remaining two slots are open, and that's where it gets complicated."

"Complicated," he repeated.

"There's new flavors this week." She turned back to the freezer and pulled the door open again, pointing at each carton as she spoke. "Double Strawberry Cheesecake is the frontrunner, because who in their right mind would turn down double strawberries and cheesecake in ice cream? Mint Dark Chocolate Chip is like, oh my gosh... dark chocolate and mint flavor, and it's pulling at me, but I'm in the mood for something different, so it might have to wait a week. Cookie dough and rainbow chips... who doesn't love cookie dough, and that one is a new brand... but man, do I love cookie dough. I genuinely love it, Ethan. And then there's the Caramel with Espresso-Flavored Chocolate Chips, which sounds like someone designed it specifically for me."

She was walking him through the decision-making process with complete sincerity. As if the coming week depended on it.

Ethan laughed. A real laugh, the kind that came from somewhere below his chest and made the corners of his eyes crease.

Sarah looked at him. "How dare you! Ice cream is a serious matter."

He was watching her with an expression she could read clearly. Amused. Charmed. And making zero effort to hide either one. "Do you always put this much thought into ice cream?"

"I put this much thought into everything that matters. And ice cream flavors for the coming week matter very much, thank you."

He laughed again, shaking his head, and there was something in his face that was different from amusement. Something warmer than that. Something that looked a lot like a man watching a woman he liked being exactly who she was and enjoying every second of it.

He reached past her. She caught the faint scent of something clean, soap or maybe just laundry detergent and maybe cologne, and then his arm was in the freezer and he was pulling out cartons. Double Strawberry Cheesecake. Cookie Dough with Rainbow Chips. Mint Dark Chocolate Chip. Caramel Espresso Chocolate Chip. He placed all four in her cart beside the salted caramel and the butter pecan and straightened up.

"There," he said. "Debate settled."

Sarah looked down at her cart. Six pints of ice cream stared back at her.

"That's six pints."

"That's a solved problem."

She shook her head, but she was smiling. "I can't buy six pints of ice cream. That defeats the purpose of the system."

"The system had you paralyzed in front of a freezer case. I improved the system."

"You broke the system."

"I expanded it." He leaned one shoulder against the freezer case, arms folded, entirely too pleased with himself. "You're welcome."

Sarah looked at the six pints of ice cream and then looked at him leaning against a freezer in a grocery store on a Saturday afternoon. She thought about how few men in her life had ever responded to her being completely herself by moving closer instead of backing away.

"What about you?" she asked. "What's your favorite ice cream?"

"Vanilla."

She stared at him. "Vanilla."

"Vanilla."

"Vanilla is not a choice, Ethan. Vanilla is a surrender."

"Vanilla is underrated. People who dismiss it have never had the good kind."

"And what exactly is the good kind?"

"Real vanilla bean. The kind with the flecks in it. Made with cream that actually tastes like cream and not like whatever they put in the cheap stuff. Good vanilla is better than any of those six pints in your cart, and I will stand by that."

"You're wrong."

"I'm right, and someday I'll prove it to you."

They were arguing about ice cream in a grocery store aisle, and it was the most fun she'd had in weeks. She felt it settling into her ribs like something warm and familiar and slightly terrifying. The recognition that she was enjoying this man's company in a way she hadn't allowed herself to enjoy anyone's company in a very long time.

"What are you doing for the rest of the afternoon?" he asked.

Sarah's hands tightened on the cart handle. He'd asked this morning on the trail. She'd told him she'd think about it. Now he was asking again. Just a man asking a woman a question and being willing to wait for the answer.

The war inside her was familiar by now. She knew its geography, knew where the walls were, and knew the arguments on both sides. The part of her that had built defenses after Daniel, solid and load-bearing and designed to keep every man at a safe distance, was telling her to deflect. To joke. To say she had plans. The part of her that had sat in Rebecca's chair two hours ago and heard her sister say, *'Have you considered the possibility that you're pushing a good man away because of what a bad one did?'* was telling her something different.

"I was planning to take my kayak out to Hawthorne Lake. Paddle for the afternoon. Watch the sky change colors as the sun sets."

"Alone?" Ethan asked.

"That's usually how I do it."

He looked at her. "Spending a beautiful afternoon alone on a lake sounds boring. And watching the sunset by yourself sounds lonely."

"It's peaceful."

"It's alone. There's a difference." He paused. "I could rent a kayak, and we could enjoy the day together. Just me and you and a lake and a sunset."

Sarah looked at him. Six pints of ice cream in her cart. Salon hair. A sundress that hit above her knee. Wedge sandals. Pretty pink nails.

She felt good. She felt like a woman who built things and ran trails and argued about ice cream and looked beautiful doing all of it. Rebecca's question moved through her again, quieter now, less like a punch and more like a hand on her shoulder.

Have you considered the possibility that you're pushing a good man away because of what a bad one did?

Ethan Cole. A man who brought fried chicken to a job site because she turned down his dinner invitation. A man who confessed to a high school crush on a misty mountain trail. A man who was standing in a grocery store aisle looking at her the way no one had looked at her since she decided no one would be allowed to.

"Yes," she said.

Ethan blinked. Just once. Like a man who had prepared himself for another version of 'I'll think about it' and received something else entirely.

"Meet me at the lake in an hour," she said. She gripped the cart handle and pushed past him up the aisle before she could change her mind, before the walls could reassemble themselves. Before the voice in the back of her head could run the analysis, it so desperately wanted to run.

Three steps past him, she turned her head over her shoulder. "And don't be late." She was smiling when she said it.

She turned back and kept walking.

"You know, eventually you have to quit this cute way you end a lot of our conversations," Ethan called after her. "I'm not going to let you keep walking away from me. Sooner or later..."

Sarah stopped. She turned around so fast that her sundress swung against her legs, and she put her hands on her hips and grinned at him.

He hadn't expected that. She could tell by the way his mouth was still open on the last word he never got to finish.

"Sooner or later what, Ethan Cole?"

He stood there, not speaking. The man who always had an answer.

She watched the look on his face and liked it. Liked it more than she should have. She liked the way his jaw worked slightly, searching for the sentence that wasn't coming. And she liked that she had done that to him.

"One hour," she said. "Hawthorne Lake. Don't be late."

She turned around and walked up the aisle toward the registers, and she didn't look back again because she didn't need to. She could feel him watching her go. And for the first time in four years, she let herself be happy and look forward to a date on the lake with a man.

Chapter 16

Ethan was already in the parking lot when Sarah pulled in, his tailgate down, a tandem kayak leaning against the bed. He was leaning against the truck with his arms crossed, watching for her.

Sarah cut the engine and climbed out. Her single kayak was strapped into the bed of her truck.

Ethan straightened up and turned toward her. His eyes went to her truck bed, and he tilted his head toward it.

"Leave yours," he said. "We'll take this one."

She grabbed her dry bag from the truck bed, sunscreen, and water bottles and a towel stuffed inside, and slung it over her shoulder. "You planned this."

"I thought about it."

"That's the same thing."

"It's not. Planning is a blueprint. Thinking about it is hoping you'd really show up and being ready if you did. Besides, it's easier to talk when you're not fifty yards away pretending you can't hear me. "

Sarah walked past him toward the water. "You're something else, Cole."

He hoisted the kayak with an ease that told her this was not his first time handling a boat. He carried it toward the launch point, a gentle slope of packed dirt and smooth stones where the grass gave way to the water's edge.

He set the tandem at the water's edge and held the bow steady while she climbed into the front seat. The hull rocked gently beneath her weight, and she settled in, adjusting her feet against the foot pegs, her paddle across her lap. Behind her, Ethan pushed the boat forward into the shallows and swung himself into the rear seat in one fluid motion. And then they were floating, the shore falling away, the water opening up ahead of them like an invitation.

Sarah dipped her paddle and pulled. The first stroke was muscle memory, the same motion she'd made hundreds of times on this lake. But the tandem moved differently than her single. Heavier. Steadier. She felt Ethan's stroke behind her, matching her rhythm almost immediately, and the boat glided forward with a smoothness that her solo kayak never quite achieved. Two paddles instead of one. Shared momentum.

Hawthorne Lake spread out ahead of them, flat and blue and ringed with pines that ran straight up to the shoreline and reflected in the water like a mirror image of themselves. The Smokies rose behind the tree line, layered in the haze that gave them their name. Each ridge was a slightly paler shade of blue than the one in front of it until the farthest peaks dissolved into the sky. The breeze came off the water in a warm current that Sarah felt on her bare arms and across the back of her neck.

Families dotted the main shore to the north. Children on the public dock, legs dangling, somebody's golden retriever shaking water across a towel. A couple in a green canoe paddling slowly along the far bank. An older man in a folding chair with his fishing line in the water and a thermos beside his foot. Saturday afternoon at Hawthorne Lake, the kind of scene that made a person want for nothing more in life.

This was normally her time alone on the lake. The place she came to when the weight of being Sarah Hartwell, business owner, crew leader, construction worker, Hartwell daughter, and community fixture, got heavy enough that she needed to set it down somewhere. On the water, she was nobody's boss. Nobody's sister. Nobody's competitor. She was a woman in a kayak watching the mountains, and nobody needed a single thing from her.

Ethan, being here, changed the math. She was aware of him behind her. His paddle strokes were steady and confident. She could hear his breathing, even and unhurried.

"You handle a kayak like you've done this before," Sarah said, breaking the silence.

"I grew up on this lake. My parents used to bring me out here when I was a kid. We'd paddle for hours, the three of us. My dad loved the water. My mom would pack a cooler, and we'd find a spot on the bank and enjoy a lazy afternoon." She heard the smile in his voice, the particular warmth that entered his tone whenever he talked about his parents. "In high school, me and my buddies were out here every chance we got. Fishing, kayaking, swimming off the dock. We practically lived on this lake from May to September."

"I didn't know that about you."

"There's a lot you don't know about me, Hartwell. When I moved back, the trails and this lake were the first things I came looking for. The first morning I put a kayak on the water after being gone all those years, I sat in the middle of the lake and just breathed." His paddle lifted and entered the water again, and she felt the pull of it through the hull. "I had forgotten how much I needed this. The quiet. The mountains. Being outside and letting the outdoors settle everything that's going sideways inside."

Sarah kept her eyes on the water ahead of them. She knew exactly what he meant.

They paddled in rhythm for another minute, and then Ethan's voice came again, quieter this time.

"Can I ask you something?"

"You just did."

"Can I ask you a real something?"

"Go ahead."

"You come out here alone. You run alone. You kayak alone. I'm not challenging it. I just want to understand why. Why alone so much?"

Sarah's paddle stopped mid-stroke. Water dripped from the blade in slow drops that hit the surface and sent tiny ripples outward, and she watched them spread and disappear. Behind her, Ethan waited. He was good at that. Waiting. Giving her the space to find the words instead of rushing to fill the silence himself.

She started paddling again. Three strokes. Four. The rhythm steadied her, the way running steadied her, something for the body to do while the mind decided how honest it was willing to be.

"I love being around people," she said. "I love my family, I love my crew, and I love Sunday dinner at my parents' house with everybody talking over each other. I am not a person who avoids people."

"I know you're not."

"But sometimes I need a reset. A place where I don't have to be strong for anyone. Where I don't have to be Sarah Hartwell, the business owner, or the female construction worker. Where I don't have to carry the Hartwell name or the business or anyone's expectations. I run alone. I kayak alone. I sit on my porch alone. Not because I don't want company. Because sometimes my alone time is how I think through what's going on in my life and decide what I want on my terms. To sit and not be strong for anyone. Not carry anything. Not build or fix anything."

"That makes sense. Was it always like that? The solo everything. Or did something change that made you need it?"

"The something's name was Daniel," she said. "Daniel Mullins. Loan officer at the bank. Polished, well-liked, the kind of man this town approves of. My parents liked him. My friends liked him. Everybody liked Daniel." She pulled the paddle through the water and felt the resistance in her shoulders. "I was twenty-five. My business was two years old and growing. I was working hard and loving every minute of it, and Daniel walked into my life with a good smile and a steady job and told me I was impressive. And I believed him."

She heard Ethan stop paddling.

"At first, he loved my ambition. Loved telling people his girlfriend owned a construction company. It made him interesting at parties and gave him something to brag about to his colleagues. He was proud of me the way someone is proud of a nice car or a good watch. Something that reflected well on him. Not something that existed for its own sake."

The tandem drifted slightly, carried by its own momentum. Sarah kept her voice steady and practical, the way she talked about a load-bearing wall or a foundation issue. These were facts. This was the structural report on the worst two years of her adult life.

"But my business kept growing. My name started showing up in places. Business roundtables. Town leadership meetings. I was getting attention that had nothing to do with him, and he didn't know what to do with that." She dipped her paddle and pulled. "The shift was slow enough that I almost missed it. Little things at first. Reasonable-sounding things. 'Do you really need to be on-site Saturday?' 'You work too much.' 'You never make time for me.' Concern, right? That's what it sounded like. That's what I told myself it was."

A fish jumped somewhere off to their left, a quick silver flash and a splash, and Sarah watched the ripples spread across the surface.

"Then the concern stopped sounding like concern. 'You don't always have to be the one in charge.' 'I don't need you to prove something all the time.' What he wanted was for me to scale back. Step away from the hands-on work. Stop crawling under buildings and climbing scaffolding. Stop ending my work days with dirt under my nails and sawdust on my collar. He wanted a girlfriend who sat behind a desk and looked polished, not a woman who physically worked alongside her crew." She gripped the paddle shaft. "He picked the restaurants we ate at. He chose our weekend plans. Dinners with his bank friends where the conversation was about money and status and nothing that mattered to me. He liked me on his arm. He liked showing me off. But the version of me he wanted on that arm was the version he could manage, not the one who managed a construction company."

"Wait... so he didn't want you to stop being successful," Ethan asked from behind her.

"No. He wanted me to stop being visible the way I was. He wanted the success without the sweat. The woman without the work boots. He wanted to be the provider, the decision-maker, the one at the top of whatever hierarchy he thought a relationship was supposed to be, and I didn't fit that picture. In a nutshell, he basically wanted to manage me." She lifted her paddle and rested it across the cockpit rim, letting the tandem drift. "We dated for two years. And for two years, I kept telling myself the friction was normal. That couples compromise. That I was being too rigid or too independent or too something. I kept trying to find the version of myself that would make him stop asking me to shrink."

"The night it ended, he said something I've never been able to get rid of. He looked at me, and he wasn't angry. That's the thing I think about. He wasn't yelling. He was tired. Tired of me. And he said, 'You're just too much, Sarah. All the time. You're too much.'" She swallowed. "Like I was a problem he'd spent two years trying to solve and had finally given up on."

The lake was quiet around them. No sound but the water lapping against the hull and a breeze moving through the pines on the nearest shore.

"I ended it that night. I drove to my parents' house and sat on the porch with my mama and didn't cry because I was too angry. Not heartbroken. Angry. Because I had given that man the real me. Every part of me. The boots and the painted nails and the business and the ambition and the woman who laughs too loud and argues about ice cream and reads romance novels and gets up early in the morning to run trails because she loves the way the mountains look before the world wakes up. I gave him all of it, Ethan. Everything I had. And he looked at it and said 'less, please.'"

She picked up her paddle and started stroking again, because she needed the motion, needed the rhythm, needed something for her arms to do while the rest of her sat exposed.

"But the thing that scares me isn't what he did. It's that I didn't pay attention to what my gut was telling me." She shook her head. "I allowed myself to stay with him for way longer than I should have. I allowed him to mess with my head. And I've spent the last four years trying to figure out how to trust myself again."

"That's why I come out here alone. That's why I run alone. That's why I do everything that matters on my terms, on my own clock."

She kept paddling, kept her eyes forward. "This lake doesn't have an opinion about whether I'm too much. The trail doesn't tell me to slow down. And when I'm out here by myself, I don't have to worry about whether my judgment is going to lead me somewhere that costs me another piece of who I am. Out here or out on the trails, it's just me and God. It's my time with Him."

She dug the paddle in and pulled hard, and the tandem surged forward. She gripped her paddle tighter and kept her eyes on the mountains.

Behind her, Ethan was quiet. The silence lasted long enough that Sarah could feel the weight of what she'd said settling between them, filling the space in the tandem like a third passenger.

When he finally spoke, his voice was lower than she'd ever heard it. "I'm trying to find the right words, and I don't think there are any," he paused. "What that man told you... that you were too much. That is the opposite of everything I see when I look at you. And I'm angry, Sarah. I am actually angry that someone made you believe that and that you've been carrying this lie for four years, as if it were the truth."

Sarah kept paddling. Her throat was tight and her hands were steady, and she let his words sit where they landed, somewhere behind her ribs where she wasn't ready to examine them yet.

They moved through the water in silence for a long stretch, and the silence was different from every silence they'd shared before. Not competitive. Not cautious. Not the loaded quiet of two people circling each other. This was the silence of a woman who had just emptied herself and a man who was holding what she'd given him carefully, the way you hold something valuable and fragile that someone trusts you not to drop.

"What you told me on the mountain this morning," she said. "About high school. It threw me, Ethan. Completely. Twelve years I spent believing that what was between us in high school was mutual hostility. That you disliked me and that the whole rivalry was exactly what it looked like. And then you sit on a rock at six-thirty in the morning and tell me you liked me since sophomore history, and I'm supposed to process that while sitting on a mountain with you inches away from me."

"I didn't plan the timing," he said.

"I know you didn't. That's what made it worse. I asked you a question, and you answered me. You just stated your truth, like it was the easiest thing in the world to say, and I've been carrying around a twelve-year-old version of you that doesn't match the man who said it." She pulled the paddle through the water. "I went to my sister's salon this morning. My normal standing appointment. I sat in her chair and told her everything. The trail, the confession, the way you looked at me when you said it. And my sister asked me a question I haven't been able to shake."

"What question?"

"She asked me if I'd considered the possibility that I'm pushing a good man away because of what a bad one did. I sat there looking at myself in the mirror, and I couldn't tell her she was wrong."

"I spent twelve years thinking you couldn't stand me, and then you rewrote the whole story in five minutes on a rock at dawn, and I'm supposed to just fold that into everything else I'm dealing with right now. You got to me. You changed something I thought was settled, and I don't know what to do when the ground moves like that."

"And today," Ethan said, "you were going to come out here alone. What did you need to think about?"

Sarah stopped breathing for a full second. She turned in her seat; the hull shifting beneath her and looked at him.

He was sitting in the rear cockpit with his paddle across his knees, his forearms resting on the shaft, watching her with an expression that held nothing back. No calculation. No strategy. Just a man on the water with honest eyes asking a woman a question he already knew the answer to.

"You," she said.

"Why?"

"Because you are becoming important to me. And I don't know what to do with that."

The words left her mouth, and she watched them land on his face. Watched the way his jaw went still. Watched the way his eyes held hers without blinking.

Sarah turned back around and picked up her paddle.

She paddled. He paddled. The cove she always ended up in appeared ahead of them, a curved inlet on the southeastern shore where the tree line pressed close to the water and a strip of sandy bank created a natural landing. Her spot. The place she came to at the end of every solo paddle, the small private shore where she sat and watched the sunset and let the world get quiet enough to hear her own thoughts.

They beached the tandem on the bank; the hull scraping against sand and smooth stones, and climbed out. Sarah pulled the towel from her dry bag and spread it on the bank above the waterline, and they sat. Side by side. Close enough that she could feel the warmth radiating from his arm next to hers.

The cove was sheltered from the breeze, the air warm and still, the water lapping at the hull of the tandem in a soft, rhythmic pulse. The light was changing. Late afternoon doing what it did in the Smokies in August, going soft and warm, turning everything it touched into something richer. The mountains across the lake were catching shadow on their western faces, and a dragonfly skimmed the surface of the water near the bank, wings catching the light.

Ethan leaned back on his elbows and looked at her. "I wanna know more about you."

"You know plenty."

"I know the builder. I know the business owner. I know the woman who argues with herself about ice cream and outruns architects on mountain trails." He was watching her with an ease that she envied. "I want to know the rest. Tell me about your house. Not the specs. I know you're good at specs. Tell me why you designed and built it the way you did."

Sarah looked out at the water. This was a question she hadn't expected and the one that would cost her the most to answer, because her house was not a house. It was a confession she'd built out of wood and stone and the kind of longing she didn't let herself think too deeply about.

"I designed the porch first," she said. "Large enough for several rocking chairs and a porch swing. Enough room for my whole family on a Saturday evening, my parents and all five siblings, and still have space left over." She pulled her knees up and wrapped her arms around them. "But that's not the only reason I designed it so large. I did it because I wanted room for a family of my own to sit out there someday. A husband. Children. I wanted my entire home to feel the way my parents' home felt when I was growing up. Open, warm, and full of people who belonged there."

"I oriented my kitchen windows to face east. I wanted to cook breakfast with the sun coming through the glass and the mountains visible from the sink. I pictured mornings like the ones I grew up with, quiet and slow, the kind of morning where the light itself feels like company." She rested her chin on her knees. "The master bedroom is at the back of the house, facing the mountains. I wanted the last thing I saw before I fell asleep to be moonlight on the Smokies. A room made for peace. For rest. For the end of a day, that mattered."

The water lapped at the bank. The dragonfly made another pass.

"I built my house for a life I haven't lived yet, Ethan. I have a porch where I sit alone most evenings. A kitchen where I drink my coffee by myself every morning. I designed and built a home for the family I hope to have one day." She paused. "And I've been living in it alone for years."

She didn't look at him when she said it. She looked at the lake and the mountains and the late afternoon light turning everything to amber, and she let the admission sit in the air beside the other admissions she'd already given him today. Another piece of herself added to the pile.

"What about you?" she said. "Tell me something. Any dreams? Hopes? Past girlfriends who changed your world the way Daniel changed mine?"

Ethan sat up and pulled his knees up the way she had, mirroring her posture without seeming to notice he was doing it, and he looked at the water for a long time before he spoke.

"Her name was Kelly Davidson. Interior designer. Smart, creative... an all-around great person." He picked up a smooth stone from the bank and turned it over in his fingers. "We were together for three years in Nashville. She loved my work. She loved my ambition. She loved me. And I loved her back. For a time, we were happy."

He turned the stone again. Sarah watched his hands.

"But my firm grew, and my hours grew with it. Weekends disappeared. Dinner plans got canceled. She didn't ask me to be less successful. She never asked for that. She asked me to be more present. Close the laptop. Be here. Choose us." He tossed the stone toward the water, and it skipped once before sinking. "And every time she asked, I told myself, 'After this project.' 'After this quarter.' 'After this client.' I believed, with everything in me, that if I built the firm perfectly now, there would be time for everything else later."

A fish surfaced near the cove's edge, a quick circle of ripples, and then stillness.

"Kelly got offered a position in Chicago. A big opportunity. She asked me to think about restructuring, maybe relocating. I couldn't do it. Not because I didn't love her. I did. But I couldn't let go of what I'd built. Letting go felt like losing control, and control was the only thing that made me feel safe." He picked up another stone and held it without throwing it. "She left. I stayed. And in the quiet that came after, I started to understand that I hadn't chosen work over Kelly. I'd chosen control over vulnerability. I'd chosen the thing I could manage over the person I couldn't."

Sarah sat very still beside him.

"But that's not the worst part. The worst part is that I had the example of a good man, a good husband, and a good father. Right there, in front of me my whole life. My father came home every night. Every night, Sarah. Not because business was slow. Because his family was what mattered most. He was at the dinner table. He was in the yard on Saturday mornings with me. He was on the porch with my mother every evening. He didn't talk about being present. He just was. He lived it the way he lived everything, steady and quiet, without anyone needing to ask."

He turned the stone in his fingers, and Sarah watched the way his jaw tightened.

"I went to Nashville and became the opposite of the best man I've ever known. I built a firm and lost a good woman because I couldn't do the one thing my father did every single day without thinking about it. Show up." He tossed the second stone. It skipped twice. "When he died, the grief hit me, but it wasn't just grief for my dad. It was grief for the years I wasted not paying attention to what he was teaching me. I had the best example of a man who knew how to love. Years of watching him do it right. And I spent a decade proving I hadn't learned a thing. I messed up. I hurt Kelly. I own that. I know I was the one at fault in our relationship."

Sarah looked at the profile of his face against the mountains, at the way his hands had gone still in his lap, at the man sitting beside her on a towel on a bank at Hawthorne Lake, his guard down. His history spread out between them like an offering that matched her own.

"I hear you," she said. "And I want you to hear what I'm about to say."

He turned his head.

"Daniel wanted me to be less. You made Kelly feel like she wasn't enough of a priority because you wanted to be more. Think about that."

"I admire you for owning what you did, Ethan. A man who names his failures instead of blaming the woman who left. That means something to me. Daniel never once admitted he was wrong. Not once. He walked away, believing I was the problem."

Ethan's jaw shifted, and she saw the muscle work beneath his skin.

"But I also hear the risk in what you're telling me. You're saying you have a pattern. Work, control, choosing the manageable thing over the vulnerable thing. And I'm sitting here with a pattern of my own. Walls. Independence. Refusing to let anyone get close enough to test whether the next man will do what Daniel did." She looked at him, and the look was not soft. It was direct, clear-eyed, the look of a woman who evaluated load-bearing structures for a living and was now evaluating something far more important. "I've spent four years alone because I stopped trusting my own judgment after Daniel. And the fact that I'm sitting on this bank telling you all of this either means my judgment is finally right, or I'm about to make a big mistake."

She paused. The light shifted. The water caught it and held it.

"I'm choosing to believe it's the first one."

Ethan didn't move. He held her gaze, and what she saw in his face wasn't relief or triumph or any of the things she might have expected. It was recognition. The look of a man who understood exactly what that sentence cost her and was not going to waste it.

After a stretch of quiet, he shifted beside her on the towel.

"You asked me about dreams," he said. "I want what my parents had. Sunday mornings with someone who's still interesting after thirty years. A kitchen full of laughter and good coffee and something cooking on the stove. A porch where two people sit at the end of the day and don't say a word because the quiet between them is full, not empty."

"I watched my parents build that kind of life. My father came home every night. My mother had dinner waiting, not because she had to, but because she wanted to. The table was where we were a family. And when my dad died, that love didn't disappear. It's still in the house. It's in everything my mother does. She still sets two coffee mugs on the counter every morning. Two. And then she catches herself and puts one back."

"My parents' love is the only thing I've ever seen that outlasts the person who built it," he said. "And it's the only thing I've ever wanted badly enough to be terrified of never having it."

She looked at Ethan. Not at the architect. Not at the high school rival. Not at the man who brought to-go bags and asked too many questions and pushed past every deflection she'd offered with patience and humor and a stubbornness that matched her own.

Just Ethan. Sitting on a bank beside a lake, his eyes on the mountains, and his heart on his sleeve.

She saw him clearly. The recognition was quiet and enormous at the same time, and Sarah realized she was afraid of what wanting him meant. Because wanting Ethan Cole meant believing that the real Sarah Hartwell, all of her, the steel-toed boots and the ambition and the painted nails and the loud laugh and the woman who read romance novels on a quiet evening, was not too much. It meant believing that Daniel was wrong, really believing it instead of acting like she did.

Ethan opened his mouth to speak, and Sarah lifted a finger to her lips.

He looked at her, a question on his face.

"Hush. Just be still," she said. "Let me sit with everything for a minute. Watch the sunset with me."

He studied her. "Is this another deflection? Because I can feel what's happening between us, and I know you can, too."

She shook her head. Not a denial. Not a retreat.

"Just let me breathe, Ethan. Everything I've said today, everything you've said, I need a minute to sit inside it." Her voice was warm. Steady. Not pushing him away. Holding the space. "Watch the sky with me. Just for a little while."

She leaned back on the towel, her shoulders against the sand, the sky opening up above her. After a beat, Ethan lay back beside her. The sky stretched from horizon to horizon, shifting from blue to amber to rose, the clouds catching color at their edges. The first stars were not visible yet but were coming, gathering somewhere behind the brightness, waiting for the light to make room.

Ethan extended his hand toward her. Open. Unhurried. Not grabbing. Offering.

Sarah looked at his hand, strong and capable. She looked at the lines across his palm and the strength in his fingers.

She took it.

Her fingers closed around his, and his closed around hers, and the fit was solid and warm. His hand was large enough that hers settled into it completely, and she felt the strength in his grip. A man holding a woman's hand because she let him, because she chose to, because she reached across the space between them and decided that the distance was no longer the thing she wanted.

They lay there in the fading light, side by side, on a towel on a bank at Hawthorne Lake, watching the sky turn colors while holding hands. The quiet between them wasn't absence. It wasn't avoidance. It was full. Full of every word they'd said today.

The sky deepened. The first star appeared above the mountains, faint and steady, and Sarah continued to hold Ethan's hand as she watched it blink into existence. She thought about how a star only becomes visible when the surrounding light steps back far enough to let it through.

She wondered what else might become visible now that she'd started letting go.

Chapter 17

Ethan pulled his truck into the Serenity Crossing Community Church parking lot, his mom beside him in the passenger seat. The parking lot was already half full, and a cluster of men in pressed shirts stood near the front steps, speaking with their hands in their pockets while their wives moved ahead through the double doors.

He parked, came around, and opened Maggie's door. She took his hand as she stepped down, her purse already looped over her arm, her hair perfectly styled the way she'd worn it for as long as he could remember. She smoothed the front of her dress and looked toward the church.

"Helen Porter told me she's bringing her banana bread to fellowship today," Maggie said. "I've been thinking about that banana bread since Wednesday."

He offered her his arm, and they walked across the lot, joining the steady stream of families, couples, and older folks making their way toward the entrance. Ethan felt the familiar rhythm of Sunday settle around him. The particular warmth of a town where church wasn't just a building but a weekly gathering of people who genuinely wanted to be with each other and listen to Pastor Warren preach.

Inside, the sanctuary smelled like fresh flowers. Arrangements of white daisies and greenery sat on the altar. The plain glass windows let in the full force of the late August light, filling the room with a brightness that turned the wooden pews honey-colored. Hymnals were lined up in their racks. Bulletins were being passed hand to hand down the rows. The organ played something quiet and familiar as people found their seats. The low hum of conversation filled the space the way it did every Sunday, unhurried and overlapping, neighbors catching up, mothers settling children.

Ethan guided Maggie to their pew. Right side, five rows back. Maggie set her purse on the pew beside her and opened the bulletin, scanning the announcements with the interest of a woman who liked knowing what was happening in her community.

The Hartwells were on the left side, two pews from the front. Bill sat at the aisle end, solid and upright, his arm resting along the back of the pew behind Olivia. Jim and Grace beside them. Dave next. Mike, with Lizzie tucked against his side. Rebecca and Anna. And at the far end, Sarah.

She was wearing a pink summer dress, and her hair was down, falling past her shoulders in dark waves that caught the light from the windows. She was turned slightly toward Rebecca, listening to something her sister was saying, and her face was open and relaxed. She was in her element. Surrounded by the people she loved most, in the place where she'd grown up. She looked beautiful.

Pastor Warren stepped to the pulpit at ten o'clock sharp, and the sanctuary settled. Warren Davis was a man who looked like he belonged exactly where he was standing. Sixty years of living and thirty-five of pastoring had given him the kind of face that put people at ease without trying, lined around the eyes and soft at the mouth. The face of a man who had heard everything and judged nothing. He wore a simple navy suit and an open-collared shirt, no tie.

"Good morning, church family," he said.

"Good morning, Pastor," came the reply, a chorus of voices that varied in volume and enthusiasm.

Warren smiled. "I was sitting on my back porch yesterday evening, watching the light change over the mountains, and Mary brought me a glass of sweet tea and said, 'Warren, you've been staring at those mountains for twenty minutes. Are you preparing your sermon or having a conversation with God?' And I told her, 'Sweetheart, most of the time those are the same thing.'"

Laughter moved through the sanctuary. Comfortable. Familiar.

"I've been thinking about seasons," Warren said. He rested his hands on either side of the pulpit and looked out over the congregation the way a father looks across a dinner table. Then his gaze went to his wife in the front pew, and he smiled. "We're sitting here at the end of August, and every one of you knows what's coming. You can feel it in the mornings already, can't you? That first cool edge in the air before the sun gets high. The way the light hits the valley a little different. We haven't seen a single red leaf yet, but something's turning. You know it in your bones. Fall's coming."

He paused and let the room hold the thought.

"The Smokies don't do sudden change. That's not how these mountains work. Spring doesn't arrive on a Tuesday all of a sudden. Fall doesn't walk in and announce itself fully. The change happens gradually, slowly, one degree at a time, until one morning you step outside and realize that the world around you looks completely different from how it looked a month ago. And you can't point to the exact day it changed. You just know that it did."

He opened his Bible to the page he'd marked, but didn't look down at it.

"I think God works the same way in our lives. We want the road-to-Damascus moment. We want the burning bush, the parting of the waters, the unmistakable sign that tells us exactly where to go and what to do. And sometimes God gives us that. But more often, in my experience, God works the way fall works in these mountains. Gradually. Quietly. One small shift at a time. A conversation that plants a seed. A moment of kindness that softens something hard. A person who walks into your life, and you don't realize until much later that everything started changing the day they arrived."

Ethan's hands went still on the bulletin in his lap.

"Ecclesiastes tells us there is a season for everything. A time for every purpose under heaven. And I've always loved that passage, but I think we sometimes read it as a list when it's really a rhythm. Seasons aren't items to check off. They're patterns to trust. God doesn't skip seasons. He doesn't rush the turning. He lets the change come at the pace it needs to come, because He knows that growth that happens slowly is growth that lasts."

Warren looked out across the pews, and his gaze was the gaze of a man who knew every face in this room and cared about every story behind them.

"If you're sitting here this morning and you feel like something in your life is shifting, something you can't quite name, something that feels different from how it felt a month ago or a year ago, I want you to trust that. Don't rush it. Don't fight it. Don't try to skip ahead to the next season because you're uncomfortable in the turning. Sit in it. Let God do what God does. The leaves will change when they're ready."

The sermon continued, moving into scripture and story and the particular kind of wisdom that comes from a man who has lived long enough to mean what he says. Ethan listened. He listened the way he listened to things that mattered, fully and without trying to manage what he was hearing.

Something in his own life was turning. He knew it. He knew it the day his mama called and could barely speak, could barely whisper the words, 'He's gone, Ethan. I need you. Come home.' He'd known it since the morning he put a kayak on Hawthorne Lake and sat in the middle of the water and breathed. He'd known it since the day he walked into Sarah Hartwell's office and felt something in his heart rearrange. He'd known it yesterday on a bank at the lake, holding her hand while the sky changed above them. The turning wasn't sudden or dramatic. It was the slow, accumulating shift of a man finding his way back to the life he was supposed to be living.

Pastor Warren closed the service the way he always did, with a benediction that sounded less like a formal pronouncement and more like a man sending his family out the door with love. The organ played. The congregation stood. Hymnals were returned to their racks, and bulletins were folded and tucked into purses and jacket pockets, and the slow migration toward the center aisle began.

Ethan stood and offered Maggie his arm. They joined the stream of people moving toward the back of the church, where Pastor Warren and Mary stood at the double doors, greeting everyone as they filed out. Warren shook Ethan's hand with both of his and held it an extra beat.

"Good to see you, Ethan. How's the Granville coming along?"

"Slowly and well, Pastor. The way good work should be done."

Warren smiled. "That's exactly right." He turned to Maggie and took her hand. "Maggie, you look beautiful today. Mary and I are thinking of you always and praying for you."

"Thank you, Warren." Maggie squeezed his hand.

They stepped out into the late morning. Most of the congregation was already flowing across the parking lot toward the fellowship hall, the practical, plain building that sat beyond the church like a younger sibling who didn't need to be fancy to be useful.

The fellowship hall was full of conversation when they arrived. Folding tables lined the far wall, covered in white paper tablecloths and loaded with plates of baked goods that the women of the church brought every Sunday with a consistency that bordered on competitive. Ethan spotted the banana bread his mom craved immediately, a dark, glistening loaf on a ceramic plate near the end of the table. Beside it, a tray of lemon squares dusted with powdered sugar, a plate of oatmeal cookies, a coffee cake with a crumb topping, and a platter of brownies cut into careful squares. The coffee was already brewed, steam rising from two large percolators, and the Styrofoam cups were stacked in towers beside a bowl of sugar packets and a carton of half-and-half.

Maggie went straight for the banana bread.

Ethan poured two coffees and brought one to his mother, who was now standing near the windows speaking with Helen Porter and Frank Dawson, a retired contractor who had known Ethan's father for years. The conversation was the kind that happened in this room every Sunday, warm and surface-level, catching up on the week, commenting on the sermon, making plans that might or might not materialize. Ethan stood beside his mom and sipped his coffee, and let the hum of the room settle around him. Children weaved between table legs. A boy of about eight was trying to sneak a second brownie without his mother noticing. Two older women were deep in a conversation near the coffee percolators that involved animated hand gestures and occasional bursts of laughter. Somebody's baby was making a sound that was either contentment or a warning.

Across the room, Sarah stood with Rebecca and Anna near the lemon squares. She had a small paper plate in one hand and was talking to Rebecca. Her posture was loose, her weight shifted to one hip, and she laughed at something Rebecca said with a quickness that told Ethan the joke had been good.

Ethan turned his attention back to his mom just as Olivia Hartwell arrived.

"Maggie," Olivia said as she set her coffee cup down on the nearest table and opened her arms to hug her. When she stepped back, she kept one hand on Maggie's arm.

"How are you, my friend?"

"I'm good. I'm managing," Maggie said. "Some days are better than others."

"I know they are." Olivia's hand stayed on Maggie's arm. "Bill and I were talking about you the other day. He said to tell you that if you need anything around the house, any yard work, or anything heavy moved, you should call him. Don't wait for us to ask."

"That's so kind. I'll remember that."

They talked for a few minutes about the week, about the sermon, and about Helen Porter's banana bread, which Olivia declared criminal in its quality. Ethan stood beside them and drank his coffee.

"Listen," Olivia said. "You two should come to dinner today. I've got a roast in the crock pot that's been going since this morning, and the girls and I will handle the sides. Don't bring a thing. Just come. Please?"

"Oh, Olivia. That sounds wonderful. I would love that."

"We eat around two. Come early if you want. Bill and the boys usually kick a ball around in the yard or do something in the garage while we girls finish getting dinner ready. You can join us in the kitchen, and we can talk and enjoy ourselves for a bit before we eat."

"I'll be there," Maggie said. "Ethan?"

"Yes, ma'am. We'll be there."

Olivia squeezed Maggie's arm once more, then picked up her coffee and moved on.

Ethan took a sip of his coffee and turned to see where Sarah was.

She was standing just a couple of feet away with Rebecca and had probably heard the entire exchange. He hadn't noticed them approach during the conversation.

Sarah looked at him. He looked at her. The fellowship hall hummed around them, oblivious.

Then Sarah stepped forward and walked past him, straight to his mom, and wrapped her in a hug.

"I'm glad you're coming today, Maggie. We'll have a full table, and that's exactly how Sundays are supposed to be."

"Thank you, sweetheart. Your mama is one of the kindest women I've ever known. I cherish her friendship."

"She is a very kind person." Sarah said and then turned to Ethan. "Come dressed comfortably. My brothers have been itching for a game of flag football."

She delivered this with a slight tilt of her head and a smile that was equal parts warmth and warning.

She turned and started walking away. Ethan set his coffee cup down and followed her, closing the distance in two strides. He caught her arm, his fingers circling her wrist, and she stopped and turned.

"You want to fill me in a little more?" he said. "Flag football? What exactly are you getting me into?"

Sarah looked down at his hand on her arm, then back up at his face.

"I'm not getting you into a thing," she said. "Mom invited you to dinner. You're coming. I just stated a fact, which is that my brothers have been itching for a good game of flag football, and wouldn't this be the perfect time to give them one?" The smile widened. "With you coming and Grace being there for dinner, we'll have a decent number of players." She paused. "Game on, Cole."

Ethan let go of her wrist. "And whose team am I on?"

"No clue. I'll let my brothers know you're coming."

She grinned and started backing away from him. She didn't turn around. She just moved backward, one step and then another, that grin on her face and her eyes on his, and Ethan stood in the middle of the fellowship hall watching her retreat.

"Game on, Hartwell," he said.

She pointed at him, still backing away, and then she turned and walked toward her mom, who had been watching the entire exchange over the rim of her coffee cup.

Ethan walked back to where his mom was standing with Helen Porter, and she looked at him with a small, knowing expression of her own.

"Flag football?" she said.

"Apparently."

Maggie took a bite of banana bread and looked across the room toward where Sarah was standing with Olivia. "Well, now... isn't this Sunday turning into a rather interesting day?"

"You can say that again." He drank his coffee. It had gone cold. He didn't care.

Chapter 18

"I keep thinking about Pastor Warren's message this morning," Anna said from her stool at the island, trimming the end of a carrot stick and adding it to the veggie tray beside a line of sliced cucumber. "About the mountains and how you can't point to the exact day the season changed. You just know it did. That's such a Warren thing to say."

"Because it's true," Olivia said from the stove, where she had a watchful eye on three things at once. The potatoes were boiling in the large pot, nearly soft enough to drain. The green beans simmered in the smaller pot with a piece of fatback that had been seasoning them for the last hour. And the gravy in the cast-iron skillet was thickening slowly under the steady motion of her spoon. Olivia Hartwell cooked the way she did most things, with a calm that made complicated look simple. "I've lived in these mountains my whole life, and I still can't tell you exactly when summer ends and fall begins. It just happens around you. One day the air is different, and you realize it's been different for a while."

"I loved the way he opened with that story about Mary and the sweet tea," Rebecca said from the far end of the counter, where she was putting the finishing touches on a large bowl of chef salad, tossing the lettuce and tomatoes and cucumbers and sliced turkey and cheese with two wooden spoons. "The look on his face when he told the story, looking at his wife in the front pew. They've been married forever, and he still looks at her like she hung the moon."

"The part that got me," Sarah said, pressing the biscuit cutter into the rolled dough and placing each circle onto a baking sheet. "Was the part about not rushing the turning of seasons in your life. About trusting the pace of it."

"I thought about that," Maggie said. She placed a ring of red bell pepper slices around the edge of the tray and sat back to look at her work. "Phillip used to say something similar about buildings. He'd say you can't rush a foundation. You pour it, and then you wait. And the waiting is the hardest part because you want to start building, but if you skip the cure, nothing you put on top of it will hold."

Olivia reached over and squeezed Maggie's hand on the counter. "Phillip was a wise man."

"He was," Maggie said. She picked up another piece of cauliflower and placed it on the tray. "He also burned every piece of toast he ever made in that kitchen of ours, so his wisdom had its limits."

Rebecca laughed first. Then Anna. Then the whole kitchen was laughing, and Maggie was laughing too. Sarah watched Maggie and saw something there that she recognized from her own mother's expressions over the years, the particular brightness of a woman who was choosing joy because the people around her made it safe to choose.

"What about the part where Warren said a person walks into your life and you don't realize until much later that everything started changing the day they arrived?" Rebecca said. "That's what tugged at me. I can't tell you how many times in my life I've experienced things like that."

"I thought that was a beautiful line," Grace said. She was leaning against the counter near the refrigerator with a glass of sweet tea, her dark hair pulled back in a low ponytail. Grace Bennett had become a natural part of the Hartwell kitchen in the months since she and Jim had started dating. "It reminded me of something my grandmother used to say. That God doesn't send you a telegram. He sends you a Tuesday."

"Ohhhh! I love that," Olivia said. "Your grandmother sounds like a woman I would have enjoyed knowing."

"She would have loved you, Olivia."

Sarah pressed the cutter into the last section of dough and then lifted the final biscuit onto the baking sheet. She opened the oven door and slid the sheet onto the middle rack, then closed it and set the timer for ten minutes.

Through the open window above the sink, the sound of the men carried into the kitchen in the warm afternoon air. Her dad was on the front porch in his favorite rocking chair. Out in the yard, Jim's steady baritone moved through a sentence she couldn't quite catch, followed by Dave's measured reply, then Mike's laugh, and then Ethan's voice, easy and unhurried.

They were talking football. Tennessee Volunteers football and the upcoming season, who was starting at quarterback, and whether the offensive line had improved enough to matter. Sarah could hear just enough to follow the shape of the conversation without catching every word, and what struck her was how naturally Ethan moved inside it. He was holding his own with her brothers, matching Jim's knowledge, engaging Dave's analysis, and laughing at something Mike said.

She leaned against the counter and continued to listen. Ethan's voice through the open window, low and relaxed, mixed with her brothers' voices and the sounds of a football being tossed back and forth as they stood in the yard. No competition. Just men throwing a ball and talking about the upcoming football season.

"Hey you." Sarah turned, and Rebecca was standing beside her at the counter. "You're smiling."

"I'm not."

"You absolutely are. Enjoying the view?"

Sarah turned away from the window. "For your information, I am. Is the salad done?"

"The salad's been done for five minutes. You didn't notice because you were too busy watching someone way more interesting than lettuce."

"Rebecca."

"Just stating facts, sis. You know I love giving you a hard time." Rebecca turned and grabbed the salad bowl, carrying it to the dining room table and coming back, still smiling, and she had the good grace not to say another word about it.

Olivia tested the potatoes with a fork, nodded to herself, and carried the pot to the sink. She drained the water carefully, steam rising in a cloud around her face, then carried the pot back to the stove and added a generous amount of butter and a splash of milk. She picked up the masher and went to work, her arm moving in the steady up-and-down rhythm that Sarah had watched a thousand times. The potatoes yielded under the pressure, turning from firm chunks into something smooth and thick, and Olivia added another pinch of salt and kept mashing until they were exactly right.

"Maggie, would you grab the serving bowls from the cabinet beside the refrigerator?" Olivia said. "The big white ones on the second shelf."

"Of course." Maggie slid off her stool and crossed the kitchen.

Anna finished the veggie tray and carried it into the dining room. Olivia transferred the mashed potatoes to one of the white serving bowls and spooned the green beans into another, then checked the gravy one final time, adjusting the heat and giving it a slow stir. The roast had been in the crock pot since before church, and when Olivia lifted the lid, the smell filled the kitchen even more, rich and warm.

The oven timer went off. Sarah pulled the biscuits out, golden on top and soft in the middle, and transferred them to a cloth-lined basket.

Olivia wiped her hands on the dish towel draped over her shoulder and walked to the window above the sink. She leaned forward and called through the screen.

"Dinner's ready, boys. Come wash up."

The response was immediate. The football conversation stopped mid-sentence. Sarah heard boots on the porch steps and the screen door opening, and then the kitchen was full of men, lining up at the kitchen sink.

Sarah carried the biscuits to the dining room.

The table was full after everyone had been seated. Twelve people in chairs that had been pulled from every room in the house to make the seating work. Bill sat at the head. Olivia at the other end. Jim and Grace on one side, with Dave beside them. Mike and Lizzie next, Lizzie in a chair with a cushion that raised her high enough to reach her plate. Rebecca, Anna, and Sarah were across from them. Ethan sat beside Sarah. Maggie beside Ethan, near Olivia's end of the table.

Bill bowed his head, and the table followed.

"Lord, we thank You for this food and for the hands that prepared it. We thank You for the health of our family. We thank You for the friends at our table today. Bless this meal and bless this time together. Amen."

"Amen," twelve voices said, and the roast platter started its journey clockwise.

The noise began immediately. Serving spoons clinked against bowls. Plates were passed and filled. The biscuit basket made its way around with a speed that suggested everyone at this table had opinions about biscuits and intended to act on them before the supply ran out. Lizzie wanted potatoes but not green beans, and Mike negotiated this with the quiet diplomacy of a single father who had learned to pick his battles. Grace passed the salad to Jim, who took a portion and passed it to Dave, who looked at it the way Dave looked at most things that weren't numbers or baseball, with polite skepticism.

"Jim, are you watching the Vols game Thursday night?" Dave asked, reaching for a biscuit.

"Course I am. First game of the season. I've been waiting all summer."

"Their offensive line worries me," Dave said.

"Their offensive line worries everyone. That doesn't mean they can't win."

"It means they can't protect the quarterback, which means they can't sustain drives, which means they'll be relying on the defense to keep games close."

"Dave. It's the first game. Can we at least let them take the field before you start the autopsy?"

Anna turned to Rebecca, Grace, and Sarah. "So there's a new yoga studio coming to town. It should be opening in about a month. Over on Maple, in that space where the old bookshop used to be."

"I heard about that," Rebecca said. "Who's running it?"

"A woman named Claire, who moved here from Asheville. I met her at the Chamber office last week. She's really nice. I think we should all join once it opens."

"I'd try it," Grace said.

"I would too," Rebecca said. "Sarah?"

"Maybe," Sarah said, which in Hartwell sister language meant yes, but she wasn't going to commit out loud until she'd thought about it for at least three days.

Olivia leaned forward from her end of the table. "I think that sounds like fun. Maggie, what do you think? We could all go together on Saturdays. Make it a girls' thing."

Maggie's face brightened. "I think I'd like that. I used to do yoga years ago. It might be nice to start again."

"Then it's settled," Anna said. "Saturday. All of us. Girl time it is."

Rebecca looked at Grace. "How are the wedding invitations coming along?"

"They're done," Grace said. "Jim and I spent last week addressing them. My hand is still recovering."

"Mine too," Jim said from across the table without looking up from his plate.

"When do I get to pick out my flower girl dress?" Lizzie asked.

Grace smiled at her. "Soon, sweetheart."

"I want it to be pink," Lizzie said.

"We'll see what we can find."

At the other end of the table, Ethan and Bill had leaned toward each other in a conversation that had its own gravity.

"How's the stage work shaping up?" Bill asked as he cut a piece of his roast.

"I believe we'll start dismantling it this week," Ethan said. "The documentation on the original planking is complete. Sarah and I have mapped every section, marked the water damage areas, and identified which boards can be preserved and which need to come out. The reclaimed heart pine should be acclimated and ready to go."

"That heart pine is beautiful material," Bill said.

"It is."

Bill nodded. "I'd like to be there this week when you dismantle the stage. I want to help pull those old planks and lay the new ones."

"I'd welcome that," Ethan said. "And if I'm being honest, I'd like to be part of it, too. Not just documenting. Working alongside the crew on the actual install."

"Good," Bill said. "That's how it should be done. A man should have his hands on the work that matters to him."

Ethan picked up his glass and took a drink.

Dave leaned back in his chair and looked toward Ethan. "You follow the Braves?"

Ethan turned. "Since I was ten."

Something shifted in Dave's posture. Dave Hartwell, the quietest of the Hartwell siblings, the man who could sit through an entire Sunday dinner contributing exactly six sentences, leaned back and crossed his arms and said, "Explain to me how they justify keeping that bullpen together after what happened in the second half of last season."

"They can't justify it," Ethan said. "The numbers don't support it. Their relief ERA after the seventh inning was the worst in the division, and the front office acted like a couple of deadline acquisitions were going to fix a structural problem."

Dave's eyebrows went up. "Structural problem. That's exactly what it is."

"You don't fix a bullpen by adding arms. You fix it by changing the philosophy of how you use them. The Braves have been burning through their middle relievers by June every year because the starters can't go deep enough into games."

"I've been saying that for two years," Dave said. "Nobody in this family listens to me about baseball."

"Because you turn every conversation about baseball into a spreadsheet," Jim said.

"Because baseball is a spreadsheet."

The debate continued for several minutes, which Sarah watched and listened closely to because she had never in her life heard Dave volunteer that many consecutive sentences at a dinner table. Ethan matched him point for point, stat for stat, and the two of them went back and forth with the intensity of men who had finally found someone who spoke their particular language.

Mike watched the exchange with amusement and then turned to Ethan during a pause. "You've got Dave talking. That might be the most impressive thing anyone's done at this table in years."

"The man knows his baseball," Ethan said. "I respect that."

Dave took a bite of his biscuit and said nothing, but the faintest trace of a smile crossed his face. And for Dave Hartwell, that was practically a standing ovation.

Lizzie, who had been working through her mashed potatoes with single-minded focus, looked up at Ethan from across the table. "Are you the one building the old movie theater?"

The table quieted.

"I'm helping bring it back to life," Ethan said as he turned in his chair to face her fully. "But your Aunt Sarah is the one doing the real building. I just draw the pictures."

Lizzie considered this. Her fork was suspended halfway to her mouth, and her face had the focused expression of a child processing new information against her existing understanding of how the world worked.

"Drawing pictures is important too," she said. "Because you have to know what something's going to look like before you build it."

"That's exactly right," Ethan said.

Lizzie nodded, satisfied that the matter was resolved, and returned to her potatoes.

Sarah watched all of it. She watched Ethan talk to her father about the stage with the respect of a man who understood that Bill Hartwell's knowledge was earned over decades and worth listening to. She watched him engage Dave in a conversation that drew more words out of her reserved brother than most people managed in a week. She watched him answer a six-year-old's question with the same patience and directness he gave to everyone else. She watched him sitting at her family's table, eating her mother's roast and passing the biscuits, talking and laughing, and the thing she couldn't look away from was how naturally he fit. Not like a guest performing politeness. Not like a man trying to make an impression. Like a man who belonged here.

Eventually, she turned her attention to Maggie, who was telling a story.

"Phillip decided, when Ethan was about eight years old, that he was going to build a birdhouse," she said. She set her fork down and folded her hands in front of her, and her voice had the particular warmth of a woman settling into a memory she'd told before and loved telling again. "Now, you have to understand. My husband was a brilliant architect. He could design anything. But Phillip Cole could not build a birdhouse to save his life back in those days."

"Mama," Ethan said.

"Hush. I'm telling this." Maggie waved him off without looking at him. "He went to the hardware store. He bought the wood, the nails, the little perch, everything. He set up in the backyard with his tools and his plans, because of course he drew plans for a birdhouse, and he started building."

Bill leaned back in his chair with his arms crossed, and the corners of his mouth were doing something that suggested he either knew this story or could already see where it was going.

"The first attempt fell apart before he got the roof on," Maggie said. "He blamed the wood. The second attempt lasted about an hour before the whole thing collapsed sideways. He blamed the nails. The third attempt, he got the walls up and the roof attached and he stepped back to admire it and the front wall just slowly, gently, fell off. Like it was tired."

The table was laughing. Rebecca had her hand over her mouth. Anna was leaning into Grace's shoulder. Jim was grinning into his plate.

"Little Ethan was sitting on the back steps watching all of this," Maggie continued. "Eight years old. And after the third collapse, Phillip stood there looking at the pieces on the ground and said, very seriously, 'I am an architect, not a carpenter, son. And there is a diff erence.'"

Ethan covered his face with one hand, and the table erupted. Bill laughed his quiet, chest-deep laugh. Olivia wiped her eyes with her napkin.

"But he didn't give up," Maggie said. "He went back out the next morning. Early, before Ethan was awake. And he built that birdhouse. It wasn't pretty. It leaned a little to the left. But it held together."

"Did the birds move in?" Lizzie asked from her chair, her eyes wide.

"They did not," Maggie said, turning to her with a smile. "But the squirrels did. A whole family of them. And Phillip declared it a success because at least someone was using it."

Lizzie considered this with the gravity of a philosopher evaluating a moral argument. "Squirrels need houses too," she said.

"That's exactly what my husband said."

"Dad was something else. After the birdhouse debacle, he went on to learn a lot about building and construction. I learned a lot working alongside him as I grew up," Ethan said.

"He was a good daddy. I have so many fun memories of you two building projects together. I cherish each and every one of them. God surely blessed me with a good man," Maggie said.

"That he did, Mama," Ethan said as he placed his arm around her shoulders, leaned over, and kissed her forehead.

The meal wound down slowly. Plates were pushed back. Olivia's peach cobbler was served. The conversations continued over empty plates and full stomachs, overlapping and interweaving, the sound of a family that had nowhere else to be on a Sunday afternoon and no desire to be anywhere else.

Olivia and Maggie started clearing the plates. Grace stood to help. Rebecca and Anna gathered the serving bowls. Sarah pushed her chair back and stacked the plates nearest to her, carrying them to the kitchen where the counter was already filling with dishes.

In the dining room, Jim turned to Ethan. "So. You ready for this game?"

"I've been ready since your sister informed me at church this morning that I didn't have a choice."

Jim grinned. "She has a way of doing that."

Dave and Mike were already discussing teams. Mike leaned forward with his elbows on the table. "Eight players. Jim, Dave, me, Sarah, Rebecca, Anna, Grace, and Ethan."

"I'm playing," Lizzie announced from her chair.

"Lizzie... are you sure?" Mike asked.

"Yes, Daddy... duh... I'm sure."

Bill appeared in the doorway between the kitchen and the dining room. He looked at Olivia, who was rinsing a serving bowl at the sink. "Leave all that, honey," he said. "Come sit on the porch with me and Maggie."

Olivia turned off the faucet and dried her hands. "That sounds like a mighty fine idea."

Bill held the front door for Olivia and then for Maggie, and the three of them settled into the porch rockers.

Sarah stood in the kitchen doorway and watched her brothers pulling on old sneakers in the mudroom, Jim lacing up fast because Jim did everything fast, Dave sitting on the bench and tying his with the methodical precision he brought to every task. Mike helped Lizzie change into her play shoes. Rebecca was in the hallway pulling her hair up into a messy bun and telling Anna, with considerable emphasis, that she was not playing quarterback under any circumstances.

"I'll play receiver," Rebecca said. "I'll play defense. I will not throw the football."

"Nobody asked you to throw the football," Anna said.

"I'm establishing this early, so there's no confusion later."

Sarah grabbed her sneakers and sat down on the bench to put them on. Jim pulled a bin of flag belts off the shelf and tossed one to Sarah. She caught it one-handed.

"Whose team do you want to be on?" Jim asked.

Sarah stood up and looked out the back door. Ethan was in the yard already, crouched beside Lizzie, helping her adjust a flag belt around her small waist. He cinched it carefully and tugged the flags to make sure they hung right.

Sarah grinned. "Whichever team is opposite of Ethan."

Jim looked at her. Then he looked out at the yard where Ethan was standing up and Lizzie was testing her flags by spinning in a circle.

He handed her a flag belt. "Game on, then."

Chapter 19

Jim pointed at Dave, then Grace, then Sarah. "You three. With me."

Mike crossed his arms. "Fine. Rebecca, Ethan, and Anna, you're with me."

"And me," Lizzie said, looking up at all of them like a general waiting for her battalion to fall in line.

"Of course, sweet pea," Mike said.

"I'm not on a team," Lizzie clarified. "I play with whoever has the ball."

Mike looked at Jim. Jim looked at Mike. Neither argued.

Ethan stood at the edge of the yard, adjusting his flag belt, and took in the field. The Hartwell front yard was a wide, flat stretch of mowed grass that ran from the wraparound porch to the tree line at the edge of the property. The grass was thick in most places but worn thin in others, the particular wear pattern of a yard that had hosted decades of exactly this kind of afternoon. A basketball hoop stood on a pole near the edge of the driveway. A stone fire pit sat at the far end near the trees. Two mature oaks marked what would serve as the end zones.

On the porch, Olivia had brought out a pitcher of sweet tea and a stack of glasses on a wooden tray. Maggie sat forward in the rocker beside Olivia, a glass of tea in her hand, watching everyone in the yard with interest.

Ethan looked across the field at Sarah. She had pulled her hair back into a ponytail and was stretching her calves near one of the oaks, talking to Jim about something that involved hand gestures. She was pointing at positions on the field. Jim was nodding. Dave stood beside them with his arms crossed, listening with the expression of a man receiving a tactical briefing.

Ethan watched Sarah roll her shoulders and bounce on her toes twice, testing her footing on the grass. He knew he was in trouble and was ready for it.

"Alright," Mike said, pulling the four of them into a loose huddle near the driveway. "Here's what I know. Jim is fast, and he's competitive. Dave is quiet, but he's accurate. Grace is an athlete. And Sarah..." Mike paused and looked at Ethan. "Sarah is going to come after you personally, so be ready for that."

"I'm aware," Ethan said.

Rebecca adjusted her ponytail. "I'm not throwing the football."

"Nobody is asking you to throw the football," Mike said.

"I just want it on the record."

"It's on the record. Anna, you're fast. I need you running routes. Rebecca, block whoever Jim sends at me. Ethan, you're my primary receiver."

"Got it."

Mike clapped once. "Let's go."

The first drive belonged to Jim's team, and it became clear within thirty seconds that Jim Hartwell had been thinking about this game since sometime around the second helping of cobbler. He took the snap from Dave, faked a handoff to Sarah that froze Rebecca for a full second, and fired a pass to Grace, who was running a clean route along the left sideline. Ethan cut toward her and had the angle, and then Jim stepped into his path with a forearm across the chest that was technically legal in the loosest possible interpretation of flag football rules. This sent Ethan sideways just long enough for Grace to pull the ball in and cross the end zone line.

"Touchdown!" Jim called.

"Good play," Bill said from the porch.

"Jim, don't hit so hard," Olivia said.

"Mama, it's flag football, not a pillow fight."

Olivia gave him a look that contained decades of maternal authority compressed into a single expression, and Jim had the good sense to turn around and jog back to his huddle without another word.

Grace held the football up with both hands, grinning. Dave gave her a small nod that, from Dave, was the equivalent of a standing ovation. Sarah slapped Grace's hand as she jogged past.

Ethan rubbed his chest where Jim's forearm had landed as Mike pulled the team into a huddle.

"New plan," Mike said. "Designed misdirection. I'll take the snap and carry left. Draw Jim and Dave with me. Ethan, you run a crossing route to the right. Anna, sell the block, then sneak out to the flat. Rebecca, just stand somewhere and look threatening."

"I can do that," Rebecca said.

They lined up. Mike took the snap from Rebecca at the center, tucked the ball, and ran hard to the left. Jim bit on it. Dave followed. Anna sold the block and then drifted right, but Mike had already pulled up and thrown the ball across his body to Ethan, who was running the crossing route wide open on the right side. Ethan caught it in stride and turned upfield. Sarah was the only defender between him and the end zone, and she came at him from an angle, fast and low, reaching for his flag belt. He juked left. She adjusted. He cut right. Her fingers found the flag and yanked it free three yards from the line.

"Got you," she said, straightening up.

"Three yards short."

"Still got you."

She tossed his flag back to him, and the look on her face was pure competition. No pretense. No performance. Just a woman who had pulled a flag and wanted him to know she'd enjoyed it.

Mike's team scored two plays later when Anna caught a short pass and outran Dave to the corner of the yard. Dave, to his credit, did not appear to have expected this outcome. He stood near the midfield line, looking at the spot where Anna had blown past him with the bewildered expression of a man recalculating an equation that had not produced the expected result.

The score was tied. The yard was noisy. Olivia was commentating from the porch with the calm authority of a woman who had watched enough football to have opinions and the confidence to share them with anyone within earshot. Bill rocked in his chair and watched. Maggie leaned forward and clapped when Anna scored.

"Lizzie's drive," Jim announced.

Ethan watched Sarah crouch down and hand the football to Lizzie with both hands. Lizzie wrapped her arms around it and looked up at Sarah with an expression of absolute readiness.

"When you get the ball, you run as fast as you can," Sarah said. "Straight ahead. Don't stop. Are you ready?"

Lizzie nodded once and handed the ball to Jim, who was standing beside her..

Jim snapped the ball to Sarah, and she pivoted and placed it in Lizzie's arms on a direct handoff. Lizzie took off. All eight adults parted. Jim stepped left. Dave stepped right. Mike backed away with his hands up. Rebecca moved aside. Anna cleared the lane. Grace drifted to the sideline. Ethan stepped back and watched a six-year-old girl in a purple T-shirt sprint the length of the Hartwell front yard at full speed, clutching the football with both arms. Her flag belt bouncing, her sneakers pounding the grass with the urgency of a child who believed this was the most important run in the history of the game.

She crossed the end zone line near the oak tree and spiked the football. It bounced once and rolled onto the roots. Then she did a dance that involved spinning in a circle with both arms raised.

The porch erupted. Maggie was clapping. Olivia was on her feet. Bill put two fingers to his mouth and let out a whistle that cut across the yard and echoed off the tree line.

Mike jogged to Lizzie, scooped her up, and set her on his shoulders. She grabbed his hair with both hands and looked out at the yard from her new vantage point, with the satisfaction of a conquering hero surveying her territory.

"Greatest play I've ever seen," Jim said.

"She's faster than Dave," Rebecca said.

"Everyone is faster than Dave," Anna said.

Dave said nothing, but the corner of his mouth moved a fraction of an inch into his kind of grin.

The score was tied at some number that depended on who was counting. The game was everything a Sunday afternoon game should be. Competitive enough that people cared. Loose enough that Lizzie could score a touchdown. Loud enough that whoever lived down the road knew the Hartwells were having a good day.

Ethan lined up for the second half, and something had changed on the other side of the field. Sarah was no longer playing for fun. She was talking to Jim with her hands on her hips. Jim was nodding the way a man nods when his sister is telling him exactly how the next drive was going to work, and he knows better than to argue. Dave had moved to the line. Grace was set wide right. Sarah took the snap from Jim, and the air around the game shifted. She wasn't smiling anymore. She was playing to win.

Her team ran three straight plays that moved the ball the length of the yard. Dave threw a short pass to Jim on an out route that gained fifteen yards. Sarah scrambled left on the next play and found Grace for another ten. Then Jim ran a draw play straight up the middle that Mike didn't read until it was too late. Jim crossed into the end zone and pointed at Mike and said, "Pillow fight that," which made Olivia shake her head on the porch.

Mike's team answered. Anna was fast and smart, and ran routes that kept Jim guessing. Rebecca, despite her firm position on not throwing the football, turned out to be a surprisingly effective blocker. Ethan caught two passes from Mike and turned both into long gains, and the game tightened.

The play that mattered most to Ethan happened on the next drive.

Sarah took the snap, and the pocket collapsed immediately. Dave and Jim were both covered. Grace was tangled up with Rebecca on the left side. Sarah scrambled right, tucking the ball, looking downfield for anything open. Ethan was shadowing Grace on the left, but when Sarah broke to the right, he read the play and cut back across the middle of the field, angling toward her.

Sarah planted her back foot and threw. The ball came off her hand clean, but it was slightly behind where Ethan was moving. He reached back, turning his body, stretching for it. At the same moment, Mike came from Sarah's blind side and pulled her flag. The momentum of her throw and the sudden tug at her waist sent her stumbling forward, unbalanced, feet tangling over the uneven ground.

Ethan caught the ball. He pulled it in against his chest and turned upfield, and Sarah's forward momentum carried her directly into him.

They went down. Ethan landed flat on his back with the football pressed against his ribs and the full force of Sarah on top of him. The grass was cool against his neck. The sky was a wide, cloudless blue. And she was braced on her hands above him, looking down at him with an expression that was equal parts startled and mortified, her ponytail hanging down beside her face, a blade of grass caught against her cheek.

"Well," Ethan said. "This is interesting."

Sarah laughed. Not a polite laugh. A real one, sudden and bright, the kind that came before a person had time to decide whether to let it out.

Lizzie appeared beside them. She looked at him, then at Sarah, then back at him.

"Does this mean Aunt Sarah tackled you? Because that's not how you play flag football."

Everyone lost it. Jim doubled over. Mike had his hands on his knees. Rebecca was holding onto Anna's arm. Grace covered her mouth. Dave turned away, and his shoulders were shaking. On the porch, Olivia had her hand pressed to her chest, and Bill was laughing his low, deep laugh.

Sarah dropped her forehead against Ethan's shoulder for one second, her laughter shaking through both of them, and then she pushed herself up and off him and stood, brushing grass from her knees. She reached down and offered him her hand.

He took it. Her grip was strong and warm as she pulled him to his feet and let go.

"For the record," Ethan said, holding up the football, "I caught it."

"For the record," Sarah said, "I want a rematch."

The game ended minutes later when Lizzie walked to the middle of the field and announced that she needed a drink and she was tired, and could they please have popsicles? She said it with the calm authority of a child who understood that her request was not a suggestion.

The final score was in dispute. Jim claimed his team had won by one. Mike claimed there was a scoring error on his third drive and the game was tied. The argument carried across the yard and up the porch steps and continued in the space between the rocking chairs. Bill, who had been watching both of them with the patient expression of a man who had been settling arguments between his sons for three decades, raised one hand.

"Game's a tie, boys," Bill said. "Both of you stop arguing and drink your tea."

Jim opened his mouth.

"Tie," Bill said.

Jim closed his mouth. Mike wisely said nothing. Dave sat down in a rocking chair and looked satisfied, which was his default response to any situation in which his brothers were told to be quiet.

The family settled onto the porch, spreading out across the steps and the railing, and the grass below. Mike went inside and came back with an armful of popsicles from the kitchen freezer, passing them around. Lizzie took a grape popsicle and sat on the top porch step, eating it with the slow, deliberate concentration of a child making something good last as long as possible, turning it carefully between licks so it melted evenly.

Sarah sat on the porch railing, a glass of sweet tea in her hand. Rebecca walked over and leaned close to her sister's ear.

Ethan was standing near the steps, close enough to see Rebecca's mouth moving and Sarah's immediate reaction. Sarah's jaw tightened. Her cheeks colored. She turned to Rebecca.

"Hush."

Rebecca grinned, wide and unapologetic, and walked away without looking back.

Ethan waited. He finished his tea and then walked toward Sarah, taking his time. He leaned against the porch railing beside her.

"So," she said. "You survived Sunday dinner with the Hartwells."

"I did."

"Football included."

"Football included."

She took a sip of her tea. "You held your own out there. I'll give you that."

"Coming from the woman who tackled me, that means a lot."

"I did not tackle you. I collided with you. There's a difference."

"There really isn't."

She tried not to smile. She failed.

Ethan turned and looked out at the yard for a moment, at the long shadows and the worn patches in the grass and the football still sitting near the oak tree where someone had left it. Then he looked back up at Sarah, and he said quietly, just for her. "Same time next Sunday?"

Sarah held his eyes. "You're assuming you're invited back."

"I'm assuming you'll want a rematch."

She looked away, out across the yard, and the corner of her mouth pulled up in a way that answered his question.

"We'll see, Cole."

Chapter 20

The pry bar caught the edge of the first plank, and Sarah leaned into it with her full weight, working the flat end beneath the nail heads that had held the board in place for over seventy years. The wood resisted, then gave with a groan that echoed through the auditorium like a voice the building had been holding back. Dust rose in a slow cloud from the gap where the plank separated from its neighbor, carrying with it a smell that was older than anything else in the room, the dry, sweet, almost tobacco-like scent of heart pine. Tim was three feet to her left, running the same process on the next section, his movements steady and unhurried, the pry bar an extension of his arm. Brian and Luke worked the far side of the stage. The old, heavy velvet curtains had been removed, and the stage was open to the auditorium, wide and exposed under the work lights Sarah's crew had rigged up.

"Easy on this one," Tim said, pausing. He tapped the plank with the flat of his hand. "She's got a split running about eighteen inches. If you force it, you'll lose the whole board."

Sarah set her pry bar down and crouched beside him. She could see the hairline fracture running along the grain, a crack that had likely started as a stress point decades ago and widened with every season of heat and cold and the weight of a thousand performances. She traced it with her finger.

"Can we save it?"

Tim tilted his head. "If we pull it slow. Work from the ends in. I'll hold the split side while you lever the nails."

They repositioned, and Sarah worked the pry bar beneath the nail heads at the far end of the plank. The nails came up one at a time with short, metallic shrieks that cut through the larger noise of the demolition. When the last nail was released, the board came free in one piece, and Tim lifted it carefully and turned it over in his hands, inspecting both sides.

"She'll live," he said. He carried the plank to the growing stack where they were sorting the salvageable boards from the ones too damaged to keep. The salvage pile was already taller than the discard pile.

Sarah stood and looked at the progress. They'd been at it since eight that morning; it was past two now, and roughly a third of the stage floor was open. Where the planks had been removed, the subfloor was visible, a layer of rough-cut boards laid perpendicular to the finished floor above. Beneath that, the joists ran in parallel lines the length of the stage.

"Subfloor looks solid on this section," Sarah called to Ethan, who was kneeling near the center of the stage with a flashlight aimed between two exposed joists. He had his sleeves rolled to his elbows, sawdust on his forearms, and a pencil behind his ear. His camera sat on the subfloor beside him, the lens cap off. He'd been photographing every layer as it was exposed, documenting the original construction for the grant compliance file.

"Joists are clean here too," Ethan said. He rapped his knuckles against the nearest timber. The sound was solid, no hollowness, no give. "No rot. No insect damage. The framing is in excellent condition." He sat back on his heels and looked up at her. "The original builders did this right."

"They did."

Bill was working stage left, near the edge closest to the auditorium seating, pulling nails from a section of planking. He didn't use the pry bar the way the younger crew members did, muscling the tool with speed and force. Bill worked the bar with precision, finding the exact angle where leverage did the work instead of effort, and the nails came up clean every time, straight enough to drop into the coffee can beside his knee without bending.

Ethan moved to the section adjacent to Bill's, and Sarah watched the two of them fall into a working rhythm. Bill pulled a plank free and turned it over, running his thumb along the edge.

"This grain," Bill said, holding the plank at an angle to the work light. "You don't find this anymore. This is old-growth. A hundred, maybe a hundred and fifty years when this tree was cut."

Ethan took the board from him and studied the end grain. "The density is remarkable. I feel the weight of it compared to modern pine."

"There is no comparison," Bill said. "Modern pine grows fast and mills easily, and it's fine for what it is. But it's not this." He set the next plank on his knee and pointed to a section where the grain shifted direction slightly. "See that? That's a branch scar that healed over. The tree took a hit, lost a limb, and grew right around it. Sealed itself up and kept going. That's what makes old-growth stronger than plantation timber. It's been through something."

Ethan nodded. "My dad would have spent an hour with this plank."

"He would have," Bill said. "Phil and I looked at a lot of wood together over the years. He'd come by the mill, and we'd stand in the yard talking about grain and species until Maggie or Olivia called to ask if we'd fallen in a hole somewhere." Bill pulled another nail and dropped it in the can. "He was the same way at the lake. We'd be out fishing on a Saturday at the crack of dawn, and Phil would notice a stand of timber on the far bank and spend twenty minutes talking about the species composition from the boat. I'd tell him I was trying to catch a fish, and he'd say the fish would wait." The corner of Bill's mouth lifted. "He was right. They always waited."

Ethan smiled. "He talked about those fishing trips a lot. He said you were the only person he knew who could sit in a boat for four hours without saying a word and call it a good time."

"That is a good time," Bill said.

They went back to work side by side, and Sarah watched. Her father and Ethan worked the way men work when trust had been built. There was no performance in it. No trying. Just two men pulling nails from a stage floor, talking about wood and fish, and understanding each other in the language of hands and honest labor.

She picked up her pry bar and got back to it.

The afternoon moved at the pace of the work. Boards came up. Sawdust and decades of accumulated grit sifted through the gaps in the subfloor. Tim called out conditions as each new section was exposed, his voice carrying across the stage in the shorthand Sarah's crew had used for years. "Clean here." "Soft spot, two feet from the east wing." "Nail pattern's different in this row. Somebody did a repair, maybe forty years ago." Sarah moved between sections, inspecting the subfloor and the joists as they appeared, making real-time decisions about what stayed and what needed reinforcement. The work was physical and exacting, the kind of labor that put grit under your nails and left your shoulders aching by late afternoon, and Sarah was in the middle of it, not standing back giving orders. She was on her knees beside her crew, pulling boards, checking conditions, and getting as dirty as anyone else on the stage.

Ethan worked beside her for stretches, then moved away to photograph and document, then returned. Their conversations were brief and functional, the shorthand of two professionals who had found a working rhythm over weeks of shared labor. He'd call her over to look at something. She'd give her assessment. He'd make a note or take a photograph. They moved around each other on the stage like partners in a dance they'd rehearsed without realizing it, anticipating where the other needed to be, stepping aside or stepping in without a word exchanged.

"Sarah!" Tim hollered from the far side of the stage. He was standing over an open section where three planks had been removed, looking down with an expression she'd seen enough times to know it meant something unexpected.

She crossed the stage and looked down. A section of the subfloor boards had been cut and refitted, a rectangular opening about two feet by three feet that had been carefully sealed and blended into the surrounding floor. The cuts were clean and deliberate, not the ragged edges of a repair.

"That's not structural," Tim said.

"No, it's not." Sarah crouched and ran her fingers along the seam. The boards had been nailed back into place with finishing nails. If the stage planks hadn't come up, nobody would have ever known it was there.

"Ethan," she called.

He was already moving toward them. He knelt beside her, and she pointed to the cut lines in the subfloor. Ethan studied the edges. He pulled a utility knife from his pocket and carefully scored along the seam where the filler had sealed the joints, working the blade slowly. Tim handed him a thin, flat bar, and Ethan worked it into the gap until the panel shifted. He looked at Sarah.

"Together?"

She nodded. They each took a side and lifted the panel free. It came up with a soft, dry exhale of trapped air, and beneath it, nestled in the cavity between the subfloor and the joist bay, was a metal box.

It was rectangular, about the size of a large shoebox; the surface dulled to a matte gray with age. The lid was fitted but not locked. What was left of a piece of cloth, once white, now yellowed to the color of old paper, had been wrapped around it and tied with twine that had gone brittle and dark.

Nobody moved for a moment.

"Daddy... come here," Sarah said.

Her father came across the stage and looked into the opening.

"That's been there a long time," Bill said.

Sarah looked at Ethan.

"This would have been placed here when the stage was built," Ethan said. "Before the flooring was laid."

"Your grandparents," Sarah said.

He nodded once. "And my great-grandparents. They were both involved in the construction." He reached into the cavity and lifted the box out carefully. The cloth wrapping crumbled slightly where his fingers pressed against it, tiny fibers drifting down like dust. He set the box on the subfloor between them and untied what was left of the twine.

Brian and Luke had stopped working. Tim stood with his arms crossed, watching. Bill was beside Sarah, his hand resting on the back of his neck.

Ethan lifted the lid.

Inside, arranged with care, were the contents of a time capsule that had been sleeping beneath the Granville stage for over seventy years. A folded newspaper clipping from the Serenity Crossing Gazette, the paper browned and fragile, with a headline about the theater's groundbreaking. A handful of photographs, small and square with scalloped edges, the images faded but still legible: men in work clothes standing on the unfinished stage frame, a woman in a print dress holding a lunch pail, a group photo of the construction crew squinting into the sun in front of the half-built facade. Handwritten notes, the paper thin as tissue. Two coins, one a penny and one a quarter, both dated the year of construction. A small glass bottle, corked, with a rolled piece of paper inside. And beneath everything, a handwritten letter on lined paper, the ink faded to a pale brown, the handwriting careful and deliberate.

Ethan picked up the letter and unfolded it slowly.

Sarah watched his eyes move across the page. She watched his jaw work once. She watched him press his lips together and look up at the ceiling of the auditorium for a long moment before he looked back down.

"It's from my grandfather," he said. "Addressed to whoever finds this." He paused. "He wrote about why they built the theater. About what they wanted it to be for the town. He said a building isn't finished when the last nail goes in. A building is finished when the first person walks through the door and feels like they belong there."

"There's a list," Ethan continued. "Names of everyone who worked on the original construction. Every carpenter, every mason, every electrician. The date each section was completed." He turned the page over. "And a note at the bottom from my grandmother. She wrote, 'To the ones who come after us. Take care of this place. It was built with love, and love is the only thing that keeps a building standing.'"

Sarah looked at her father. Bill's hand had moved from his neck to his chest, resting flat over his heart, and he was looking at the letter in Ethan's hands with an expression she had seen only a few times in her life. The expression her father wore when something moved him deeply enough to show on his face.

"That needs to be preserved," Bill said. "Every piece of it."

"It will be," Sarah said, and then she turned to Ethan. "Did you notice your mama had snuck in?"

She pointed toward the auditorium seating. Sarah had noticed them about an hour ago: the two women sitting side by side in the old velvet seats, watching the stage work. Olivia had been taking photographs with her phone. Maggie had been leaning forward with her hands folded in her lap, her eyes following the progress.

Now Maggie was standing, one hand on the seat back in front of her, the other hand over her mouth. She'd heard Ethan read the letter. The acoustics of the old auditorium carried sound from the stage to the seats the way the building was designed to, and every word had traveled.

"Ethan," Maggie said. "Bring it here."

Ethan gathered the contents and the box and carried them to the edge of the stage. Sarah's crew had built a temporary set of wooden steps at stage right for access during the demolition phase. Maggie met him at the bottom, and Olivia was right beside her, one hand on Maggie's back.

Ethan set the box on the armrest of the nearest theater seat, and Maggie looked inside. She picked up the photographs first, holding them close, tilting them toward the light from the high side windows.

"That's your grandpa," she said, pointing to a man in the crew photo. "Right there. Second from the left. And that woman with the lunch pail, that's your great-grandmother. I was told she brought lunch to the construction crew every day until the building was finished. Every single day." She touched the edge of the photograph with her fingertip. "I have a photo just like this at the house. Your daddy kept a copy in his desk."

She set the photographs down and picked up the newspaper clipping, reading the headline, her lips moving slightly over the words. She examined the coins, turning them in her palm. She uncorked the glass bottle and tipped the rolled paper into her hand, unrolling it to reveal a small pencil sketch of the theater's facade, drawn by someone with a steady hand and a clear vision of what the finished building would look like.

"That's his drawing," Maggie said. "Your grandpa drew this before the building was finished... I'm sure of it. He used to sketch everything. Philip was the same way. And now you." She looked at Ethan, and her eyes were bright with tears.

"He left all of this here on purpose," Ethan said.

"Of course he did. He was building something he wanted to last. And he wanted the people who came after him to know why." Maggie picked up the letter and read it, her eyes moving across her father-in-law's handwriting. When she finished, she folded it along its original creases with the tenderness of a woman handling a living thing and placed it back in the box.

Olivia put her arm around Maggie's shoulders. "That is a treasure," Olivia said. "An absolute treasure."

"It is," Maggie said. She wiped her cheek with the back of her hand, took a deep breath, looked up at the open stage where half the floor was missing, and smiled.

"Well," she said. "I suppose you'd better get back to work. That stage isn't going to rebuild itself."

Ethan laughed. It was a short, surprised sound, and it broke the tension in the room the way laughter does when it arrives at exactly the right moment.

Sarah stepped forward. "Maggie, we'll photograph every item in that box and catalog it properly for the grant file. The original letter and the photographs should be archivally preserved. I know a conservator in Knoxville who works with documents like these. I can make that call for you if you'd like."

Maggie looked at Sarah for a long moment. "I would like that very much. Thank you, Sarah."

"Yes, ma'am."

Maggie reached out and squeezed Sarah's hand once, briefly, and then released it and turned back to Olivia. The two women gathered the items and the metal box and walked up the aisle together. They settled back into their seats, and Maggie opened her purse and pulled out a tissue and pressed it to her eyes.

Sarah climbed the temporary stairs back up to the stage. The crew was already returning to their positions, picking up tools, and finding their places. The work resumed. Boards came up. The stage gave up its secrets one plank at a time.

Bill was standing near the spot where the time capsule had been, looking into the empty cavity in the subfloor. Sarah walked over and stood beside him.

"That letter," Bill said.

"I know."

He looked at her. "A building is finished when the first person walks through the door and feels like they belong there." He shook his head slowly. "That's the truest thing I've heard in a long time."

Chapter 21

Art was standing on the top step of a ten-foot ladder with a cordless drill, loosening the mounting plate of a wall sconce, while Liam held the ladder base steady. Ethan stood at the marble concession counter with a roll of acid-free tissue paper, a stack of numbered labels, and a catalog sheet he'd printed at the office that morning, watching them.

The sconce came away from the wall in one piece. Art passed it down to Liam, who cradled it in both hands and brought it to Ethan at the counter. The fixture was heavier than it looked, solid brass beneath the tarnish, the tulip-shaped frosted glass shade still intact, no chips, no cracks. Ethan turned it over and examined the backplate. He could see the stamp of the manufacturer pressed into the metal, faint but legible. Chattanooga.

From the other side of the lobby, through the open double doors leading into the auditorium, he could hear the sounds of Sarah's crew. The rhythmic crack of pry bars. Tim's voice calling a condition report.

Sarah's voice cut through it all, clear and steady, directing the next section of work.

He set the sconce on a bed of tissue paper and wrote the label. Sconce #1, lobby east wall, right of the auditorium entrance. Brass, tulip shade, frosted glass. Manufacturer stamp: Chattanooga Lighting Co. Condition: excellent. He photographed it from three angles with his camera, then wrapped it carefully.

The lobby doors opened behind him, and Maggie came through carrying a canvas tote bag over one arm and a cardboard box of packing supplies under the other. She wore a cotton blouse with the sleeves already rolled to her elbows and a pair of flat-soled shoes that said she had come prepared to stand on terrazzo all day.

"I brought more tissue paper," she said, setting the box on the counter beside Ethan's station. "And these." She pulled out a roll of small adhesive labels, a fine-point marker, and a stack of gallon-sized zip-lock bags. "For the small hardware. Each bag gets labeled with the fixture number and the location it came from. That way, when it's time to put everything back, we're not guessing which screws belong where."

Ethan looked at her.

"Your daddy taught me this. He'd take something apart and put every hinge, every screw, or every pull in a bag with a number on it. I used to tease him about it. He told me that any man who lost a screw and blamed the screw instead of himself didn't deserve to own a screwdriver."

"That sounds like Dad."

She set the marker beside the bags and looked around the lobby, taking in the space. Her eyes moved across the ceiling, the chandelier still hanging from its center medallion, the sconce on the wall where the second fixture had not yet been removed, the ticket booth standing in its glass-walled octagon to the right. She took it all in, and then she nodded once, the nod of a woman who had made her peace with being here and was ready to work.

"Where do you need me?" she said.

"Right here. Art and Liam are handling anything that's hard-wired. The sconces, the chandelier when we get to it, and a few small fixtures in the hallway near the restrooms. As each piece comes down, it comes to us. We photograph it, label it, wrap it, and box it. Between the electrical pieces coming down, you and I are going to work through the rest of the lobby. Ticket booth hardware, concession details, the menu boards, and the brass trim around the entrance doors."

Maggie pulled a pair of cotton work gloves from her tote and put them on. "All right. Let's start."

They fell into a rhythm. Art brought down the second sconce and passed it to Liam, who brought it to the counter. Ethan handled the photography and the catalog sheets. Maggie handled the packing and the small hardware bags, labeling each one in her neat, precise handwriting.

While Art and Liam moved to the hallway fixtures, Ethan and Maggie crossed the lobby to the ticket booth. The narrow swinging door at the back hung on brass hinges that had gone stiff with age. A small latch on the inside of the counter, the kind a ticket seller would flip to secure the booth at the end of the night, was green with patina but still functional.

Ethan started with the latch. He worked a flat-head screwdriver into the mounting screws, turning slowly, and the screws resisted and then gave. The latch came away from the wood with a faint pop, and he held it in his palm.

"Your grandma had a system," Maggie said. She was standing beside the booth with her hand resting on the glass panel, looking at the narrow shelf inside where a stack of yellowed ticket stubs still sat fused to one another by decades of humidity. "Every Friday and Saturday night, she'd count the cash drawer twice before she left. Not because she didn't trust herself the first time. Because she said a theater that couldn't account for every nickel didn't deserve the town's trust. She kept a ledger. Handwritten. Every ticket sold, every night, for years. Even after they started using a register, she kept the ledger going."

Ethan placed the latch in a Ziploc bag and labeled it. "Do we still have that ledger?"

"I believe so. It should be in the filing cabinet in his office at home." She pulled her hand from the glass and looked at him. "Remind me, and I'll look for it this evening."

They removed the hinges from the swinging door next, working in tandem, Ethan on the screws and Maggie holding the door steady so it wouldn't swing and crack the glass. The hinges were brass, matching the latch, and they came off clean with only minor resistance. Ethan bagged and labeled each one.

They worked through the ticket booth methodically. The metal cash drawer built into the counter. The small brass plate around the speaking hole in the glass, the one that allowed the ticket seller to talk to customers without opening the window. A decorative brass frame around the booth's interior light fixture. Each piece came away from the booth with the reluctance of hardware that had been in place long enough to consider itself permanent.

"Mr. Cole, we're ready to work on the chandelier. Is that okay?" Art asked.

"Go ahead," Ethan said.

Maggie watched Art climb the ladder. "I keep thinking about something."

"What's that?" Ethan asked.

"Yesterday, when you showed me the time capsule photographs. Your grandfather in that crew photo. The expression on his face." She turned from the chandelier and looked at Ethan. "He looked like a man who was building something he believed in. Not just constructing it. Believing in it. There's a difference."

"There is."

"Your father had that same look. When he'd come home from this building when we were first married, even at the end of a long day, there was something in his face that I could read from across the kitchen. Satisfied. That's the word. Not happy, exactly. Satisfied. Like the work had given him something back."

She picked up a sheet of tissue paper and folded it absently, creasing the edges with her fingernails. "Your daddy was funny about this lobby. Did I ever tell you about the night he tried to fix the terrazzo?"

"No."

"This was before you were born. A few years after we were married. A section of the floor near the entrance had developed a crack; nothing structural, just cosmetic, but it bothered your grandfather terribly. He wanted to hire a tile specialist from Knoxville. Phil told him that he could handle it. Said he'd researched the repair process, and it was straightforward." She shook her head. "He went to the hardware store and bought what he thought was the right filler compound, and he came here on a Saturday morning and spent four hours on his hands and knees working on that crack. When he finished, he called me to come look, very proud of himself. I walked in, and the repair was a completely different color than the rest of the floor. Not close. Not in the same family. It looked like someone had drawn a white line across the terrazzo with chalk."

Ethan laughed.

"Your grandfather came in behind me, looked at it, and didn't say a word. Just stood there with his arms crossed. Phil looked at the floor and looked at his father, and said, 'I'll call the specialist in the morning.' Your grandfather said, 'That would be wise, son.' And then the two of them went to Minnie's for lunch and never spoke of it again."

"That's a dad story," Ethan said.

"That is a Phil story through and through. He was brilliant with a pencil and a blueprint. Brilliant. But the man did not have hands for repair work. He tried. He always tried. But your father was a designer, not a fixer. He could draw you a building that would stand for a hundred years, and he could not hang a curtain rod straight to save his life."

They moved to the concession area. The hand-lettered menu boards were mounted on brackets above the back wall. Popcorn 75¢. Coke 50¢. The lettering was clean and confident, painted by someone with a steady hand, and Ethan photographed them in place before he and Maggie lifted them carefully from their brackets.

Behind the counter, the old popcorn machine sat with its chrome trim clouded but complete. It was too large to remove today, and it wasn't on the electrical scope, so it would stay in place for now. But the chrome trim pieces along the front panel were decorative and removable, and Ethan carefully detached them, working each one free with a flathead and setting them on the counter for Maggie to wrap.

"Your grandmother made the best popcorn," Maggie said, buffing a smudge from one of the chrome strips with the edge of her glove. "She used real butter. Melted it in a saucepan on a hot plate behind the counter and poured it over every batch. People would walk in the door, and the smell would hit them, and they'd buy popcorn before they even bought a ticket. She always said popcorn was half the reason people came to the movies, and she was probably right."

They worked through the concession area piece by piece. The chrome trim. The brass rail that ran along the front edge of the counter, a decorative piece that had prevented customers from leaning too far over the marble.

"Ethan," she said as she set down the marker she had been using. "I'm not trying to pry, and I'm not going to push myself into your business. But talk to me, son." She folded her hands on the counter. "I see the way you look at Sarah. And I can tell she's important to you."

Ethan set the camera down and leaned against the counter.

"She's not like anyone I've ever known," he said. "And I don't mean that the way people say it when they're trying to sound... well, I'm not sure. I mean it literally."

Maggie waited.

"With Kelly, I was always thinking three moves ahead. Planning. Strategizing. Trying to make the relationship work the way I'd make a project work, with milestones and timelines and the right amount of effort applied at the right time. And it didn't work. It couldn't work because she was a person, not a floor plan, and I treated her like something I could manage instead of someone I needed to show up for."

He picked up one of the brass screws from the counter and turned it between his fingers. "With Sarah, I'm present in a way I've never been with anyone. She changed something in me that doesn't want to move back. I don't have a better way to say it. It's like breathing. It's just there. It's natural. I just know."

"You know what, son?"

He looked at his mother. "That she's it. She's the one, Mama."

Maggie studied his face. "When did you know?"

"I knew the first time we walked through this theater, before the contract was even signed. It was a little feeling, just subtle, but it was there. It grew gradually. She walked into a room, and something shifted in me. It kept shifting and getting bigger, a little more every day, every conversation, every time she laughed or pushed back. It just happened."

"That's how it works," Maggie said. "When it's real."

She pulled off her cotton gloves and set them on the counter, and her hands were bare and still. The wedding ring she still wore caught a thread of light from the front window.

"I knew with your father right away. Not hoped. Not wondered. I knew." She shook her head slightly and smiled. "I remember telling my mother that I'd just met the man I was going to marry, and she laughed and said I was being dramatic, and I said, 'Mama, I am not being dramatic.'"

"Son...people will tell you that kind of certainty is naïve," Maggie continued. "That real love takes time and caution and all the sensible things. And I don't disagree with any of that. But I also know what I know. When God places someone in your path, and you feel that pull, that recognition, that thing in your chest that says pay attention, this one matters, that is not an accident. That's not infatuation. That is God in motion. Putting two people in the same room at the same time for a reason that's bigger than either one of them." She looked at him steadily. "I felt it with your father. I never once doubted it. Not once."

"Sarah is a good woman," Maggie said. "I've known her for years. I watched her grow from a cute little thing into a beautiful woman full of spunk and character. I've watched the way she treats you and the way she treats me, and I see what's in her. She has a good heart, Ethan. She cares about this place, and she cares about you, and she doesn't perform either one of those things. They're real."

"They are," Ethan said.

"Then don't overthink it. Don't plan it to death. Don't turn it into a project." She reached across the counter and put her hand over his. "Just be there. Be present. The way your daddy was."

Ethan turned his hand over beneath hers and held it. "Thank you, Mama."

"Don't thank me. I'm your mother. This is what I'm for." She squeezed his hand once and released it, picked up her gloves, and pulled them back on. "Now. We've got a chandelier to pack. Let's go."

Chapter 22

Sarah had the iPad propped against the old brass plan weight on the marble concession counter and was halfway through the week's progress log when she realized she'd been staring at the same line for two minutes without reading it. She blinked, scrolled back to the top of the entry, and started again. Stage subfloor demolition; sections A through D complete. Joist inspection ongoing; structural engineer's report due Monday. Electrical rough-in, lobby circuits sixty percent complete, auditorium circuits scheduled for next week.

Sarah typed the last of her scheduling notes and saved the file. She closed the progress log and opened the grant folder, checking the photo documentation against the milestone checklist. Everything was current. Everything was on track.

The lobby doors opened behind her.

She knew it was Ethan before she turned around. "You're early."

"I brought a bribe."

She turned. He was standing just inside the lobby doors, holding two paper cups from The Daily Grind, steam curling from the lids.

He crossed the lobby and set one of the cups on the marble counter beside her iPad.

Sarah picked it up. The cup was hot in her hands, and she could smell it before she took the first sip. "You have no idea how much I needed this."

He leaned against the counter beside her and took a sip from his own cup. "How's the documentation looking?"

"Current. I wanted to get the progress log and the grant file squared away before the crew gets here. Easier to think when this building isn't full of noise."

"What about the electrical?"

"Art says lobby circuits are about sixty percent. They'll finish the east wall runs today and start on the auditorium side Monday. No surprises in the wiring so far, which in a building this old is a small miracle."

"The stage?"

"Still in progress. My dad's been helping all week. The joist replacement on the downstage sections is done, but there's a run along the back wall that Tim flagged. The structural engineer is coming Monday to evaluate before we proceed." She pulled up a photo on the iPad and turned it toward him. "This section here. See how the joist has deflected? That's not rot; it's load distribution. The original framing wasn't designed for the weight they ended up putting on it when they added the fly system in the fifties."

Ethan studied the photograph. "What's Tim's read?"

"He thinks sister joists will handle it, but he wants the engineer's sign-off before we commit. Which is the right call."

"Agreed."

Sarah set the iPad down and picked up her coffee again.

"How long have you been here this morning?" he said.

"I got here a little after seven."

"On a Friday."

"Doesn't matter what day it is... I like starting early sometimes. Nobody bothers me. I can think."

"Nobody except me."

"You brought coffee. You're exempt."

"Good to know," he said. "This week felt like a turning point. The time capsule. The fixture cataloging. The electrical is on pace. We're actually getting somewhere."

"We are."

"Your dad's been out here every day this week."

"He has. I think the physical work feeds something in him that sitting behind a desk at the mill just doesn't do."

"He's good... he's really a remarkable man. Tim told me yesterday that your father spotted a split in one of the replacement joists before anyone else caught it."

"That's Daddy. He can read a board the way some people read a book."

Ethan set his coffee down and turned toward her. His hand came up, and she felt his fingertips brush the side of her face, light and unhurried, tucking a strand of hair behind her ear that had come loose from her ponytail.

"Ethan Cole," she said. "What are you up to?"

"Nothing. Just fixing your hair."

"My hair was fine."

"It was in your face."

"It's been in my face all morning, and I managed."

"I know you managed. I just wanted to be the one to fix it."

She looked at him.

"Have dinner with me," he said.

"We've had dinner."

"Not a to-go bag on a job site dinner." He held her gaze. "A real dinner. Tomorrow night. Just us."

"Okay," she said. "But not Minnie's."

"I wasn't going to suggest Minnie's."

"And not anywhere in Serenity Crossing. Somewhere outside of town. Somewhere nice. Somewhere I can wear a dress and heels."

"You want to dress up."

"I want to dress up. I spend five days a week in work boots and jeans, and I am very good at that, and I enjoy it, but tomorrow night I want to put on something pretty and sit across a table from you in a restaurant where nobody knows my framing crew by name."

"Any other requirements?"

"Surprise me."

He looked at her. "Surprise you."

"Completely. I don't want to know where we're going. I don't want to know the name, the menu, or the neighborhood. You pick it. You plan it. All of it."

"You're giving me full control of the restaurant selection."

"I am giving you full control. And before you say anything, yes, I'm aware of what that means coming from me. I know exactly how significant it is that Sarah Hartwell is handing over the planning of anything to another human being. Take the win, Ethan. Don't make a speech about it."

"I wasn't going to make a speech."

"You were composing one. I could see it. And you're going to need my address."

"I was wondering when we'd get to that."

She pulled her phone from the back pocket of her jeans, typed out her address, and texted it to him. His phone buzzed in his pocket.

"I'll be ready by five o'clock," she said.

"Five o'clock."

Outside, a truck pulled up in front of the theater, then another. The crews were arriving.

Ethan straightened up from the counter. "What can I do today?"

"My dad should be here any minute. The stage work continues. You can help him and Tim with the joist replacement if you want."

"I can do that."

"Then go get changed and get to work."

"Yes, Ma'am."

He looked at her for a beat. Then he leaned down and pressed a kiss to the top of her head. He straightened, picked up his coffee, and turned and walked toward the auditorium doors without saying a word.

Chapter 23

Sarah's home was a Craftsman cottage, with a low-pitched gable roof, wide overhanging eaves, and exposed rafter tails, set on roughly two acres where the last residential streets of Serenity Crossing gave way to wooded foothills. Natural wood siding stained a warm brown, board-and-batten on the lower sections and horizontal lap siding on the upper. The combination gave the facade a depth and texture that made the house look as if it had grown out of the land rather than been placed on it. A stacked fieldstone foundation was visible at the base, the kind of detail that a person who built for a living would choose because it was right, not because it was fashionable.

Ethan sat in his truck and studied it the way he studied every building, reading the proportions and the material choices and the sightlines, and what he read was this: a woman who understood craft at the bone level had designed and built a home that said everything about her without saying a word too much. The roofline was clean. The eaves overhang was generous. The windows were placed with intention. Every choice was purposeful, every material was of quality, and there was not a single element that existed for show.

He got out of the truck and admired the front porch that ran the full width of the house. Square timber columns. A simple railing. Tongue-and-groove porch boards, sanded smooth and sealed.

He walked up the stone path that connected the driveway to the porch steps. A detached two-car garage sat to the side, built of the same materials and style. Native plantings lined the edges of the property: black-eyed Susans and coneflowers, and mountain laurel, practical and low-maintenance but far from neglected. Mature oaks and hickories shaded the south side. The lawn was kept but had a natural quality at the edges where it met the treeline, as if the house and the land had come to a quiet agreement about where one ended and the other began.

He climbed the porch steps. His shoes were polished. His sport coat was navy, his collared shirt was white, and his tie was a deep blue. The front door opened seconds after he knocked, and the world inside his head went quiet.

She stood in the doorway in a red satin dress. The dress fit her in a way that made the surrounding air seem insufficient. A full skirt that landed just above her ankles, elegant and simple and precisely right, the kind of dress a woman chooses when she wants to feel beautiful and succeeds without trying. Red satin strappy heels. Her hair was down, falling past her shoulders in soft waves, thick and dark and loose in a way he had only seen a handful of times outside a job site. A touch of makeup, light and natural, mascara, and a little color on her lips.

"You're beautiful," he said.

Sarah tilted her head. "You clean up pretty well yourself."

He held out his hand. She took it. Her fingers were warm in his, and he lifted her arm and turned her in a slow spin right there on the porch. The skirt of her dress flared and caught the air, and settled again.

"Where are we going?" she said.

"Nice try."

"I had to ask."

"You didn't. You wanted to. There's a difference."

She laughed. He offered his arm, and she took it, and they walked down the porch steps together. He opened the passenger door of his truck, and she climbed in, gathering the skirt of the dress with one hand.

He walked around to the driver's side, got in, and started the engine.

***

The route left the tighter mountain roads within fifteen minutes and opened into foothill country. Pastureland stretched on both sides, soft ridgelines rolling into long views that seemed to widen the sky. Fence lines ran along the road, and cattle stood in the far fields like dark shapes painted against the green. The light was warm and heavy with the particular quality of early September in the Tennessee foothills, the color of the afternoon leaning toward gold without having arrived there yet.

Sarah sat in the passenger seat with her window cracked an inch. The air that came through smelled like cut hay and warm grass.

"You're not going to tell me," she said.

"I am not."

"Not even a hint."

"Not even half a hint."

"A general direction."

"We're heading east. That's all you get."

The road wound through a corridor of old hardwoods, light shifting through the canopy in moving patterns across the windshield, and then opened again into long pasture views. They talked the way they had been talking for weeks, easy and unhurried, the particular comfort of two people who had stopped performing for each other. She told him about Lizzie calling her that afternoon to ask if she was going to a ball because Aunt Rebecca had told her that tonight Auntie Sarah was going to be a princess. He told her about his mother laying out three different tie options on his bed before settling on the one.

"Your mother picked your tie," Sarah said.

"She did."

"She dressed you for our date."

"She offered a single accessory recommendation."

"She dressed you for our date."

"Fine. She dressed me for our date. And she enjoyed every second of it."

The road curved south, and the land opened further, the ridgelines settling into softer shapes, and then the lake appeared between the trees. Flashes of water through the trunks, bright and flat and catching the late light, and the glimpses grew longer and wider as the road followed the shoreline.

Sarah sat up straighter. She was looking at the water, then at the road ahead, then at a sign that appeared on the right side of the road, discreet and well-lettered on dark wood.

BELLEHAVEN LANDING.

She turned to him. "Ethan."

He kept his eyes on the road.

"Ethan Cole. The Bellehaven?"

"I don't know what you're talking about."

"The Bellehaven. The riverboat. The paddlewheel dinner cruise on Douglas Lake. I've read about this place. I've heard about it from different women at church." Sarah's voice had lifted in a way he had never heard from her, a bright, unguarded excitement. "This is where you're taking me."

"This is where I'm taking you."

She pressed her hand to her mouth and looked out the windshield as the paved lane descended through manicured grounds. The lake widened ahead of them, and she didn't say anything for a long stretch because she was taking it all in. A stone-and-wood welcome pavilion. Manicured lawns rolling down to the water's edge. A wide dock lined with planters of late-season white blooms and greenery, the petals glowing in the afternoon light. And at the end of the dock, moored with a quiet sense of ceremony, was the Bellehaven.

It was not a small dinner boat.

It was a full, old-world paddlewheel riverboat, three decks, a crisp white exterior, dark wood trim, and brass railings that caught the light in thin gold lines. Tall windows wrapped the main dining salon, and the paddlewheel sat at the stern like a polished emblem. Small flags stirred in the breeze. The scale of it, sitting there on the calm water with the mountains behind it, was the kind of thing that made a person stop and simply look.

Ethan pulled into the parking area, turned off the engine, and looked at Sarah.

She was staring at the boat. Her hand was still near her mouth, and when she turned to him, the expression on her face was worth every phone call, every reservation detail, and every moment he had spent making sure tonight would be exactly right.

"Ethan," she said. "This is perfect."

He got out and walked around to her side and opened her door. She stepped down from the truck, gathering the skirt of her dress, and stood beside him and looked at the boat and the lake and the mountains, and then she looked at him.

The smile on her face was the one he had been working toward since yesterday morning in a stripped-down theater lobby. He offered his arm. She took it. They walked across the lawn toward the dock.

The lake was calm, and the mountains sat in the distance like a painted backdrop. Staff in formal attire stood at the gangway beneath a white canopy, greeting guests. A woman in a dark dress welcomed them and gestured them forward. Ethan placed his hand on the small of Sarah's back as they stepped onto the gangway.

The gangway led onto the main deck, and the interior changed the atmosphere from marina and open air to evening formal. Gleaming dark wood floors stretched ahead of them. Soft lighting from sconces and chandeliers replaced the outdoor brightness with a warm, layered glow. A grand staircase curved upward with a carved banister. Framed black-and-white photographs lined the corridor, depicting early lake life and historic boats, and vintage mountain resorts, and the total effect was one of legacy held carefully, a space that knew its own history and wore it with quiet confidence.

Sarah was looking at everything in awe. The polished brass. The pressed linens. The fresh florals were arranged low and elegantly in the small parlor lounge they passed, where tufted settees sat beneath tall windows looking out to the water.

"This is stunning," she said.

"Wait until you see the dining room. The pictures I saw online were amazing."

A host led them down the corridor. Double doors opened, and the main dining salon spread before them, a long, refined panoramic space with windows on both sides. White linen tables spaced for privacy. A ceiling trimmed in subtle crown detail that nodded to classic riverboat style. Crystal water glasses were set at the top right of each place setting, catching the light. Folded linens, crisp and precise. Small candles in hurricane glass, unlit, waiting for dusk. Silverware gleamed.

They sat at a table that was near the windows on the starboard side. The host pulled Sarah's chair, and she sat, and the skirt of the red dress settled around her. Ethan sat across from her.

"This is incredible," she said. "You did good, Ethan. This is better than anything I could have imagined."

A server appeared and filled their water glasses and offered a brief explanation of the evening's menu, describing the seasonal courses with quiet warmth before disappearing. Ethan watched Sarah pick up her water glass and take a sip, and look out the window at the lake, and the light from the water reflected onto her face.

The boat eased away from the dock. The paddlewheel's rhythm became a low, steady pulse beneath them, felt more than heard, a vibration in the floorboards that was soothing rather than mechanical. Light moved across the table linen as the boat turned into open water. The lake widened.

Sarah looked across the table at him. "No work talk tonight."

"No work talk."

"No theater talk."

"None."

"Just us."

"Just you and me."

The first course arrived with a brief, soft explanation from the server: a delicate starter built around fresh herbs and late-summer produce, the presentation clean and precise on a white plate. They ate slowly. The food was exceptional, with flavors that were bright and layered—the kind of cooking that understood restraint.

"Okay," Sarah said. "What's your favorite movie? Your all-time favorite. One answer."

"The Shawshank Redemption."

"That was fast. Why that movie?"

"Because it's a movie about a man who refuses to let the worst thing that happened to him become the truest thing about him. He builds something, even in a place designed to break people. The ending, when he's standing on that beach in the rain, that's what hope looks like to me. Not the pretty kind. The kind that costs you everything and still holds."

Sarah set her fork down. "That is a really good answer."

"Your turn."

"You've Got Mail."

He raised an eyebrow.

"Don't look at me like that, Ethan Cole. You've Got Mail is a perfect movie. The bookshop. The emails. The autumn in New York. Tom Hanks and Meg Ryan circling each other the entire film, and the audience knows before they do. That is exactly how a love story should work."

"You sure do like love stories."

"I build things for a living. I read blueprints, pour concrete, and argue with county inspectors about setback requirements. When I sit down at the end of the day, yes, I want a love story. I want the bookshop and the emails and two people who figure it out. That's not a guilty pleasure. That's a preference."

"I didn't say it was a guilty pleasure."

"You raised your eyebrow."

"I raise my eyebrow at lots of things. It's a reflex."

"It's an editorial comment."

"It was a surprise. I would have guessed action movies."

"You would have guessed wrong." She picked up her fork and took another bite. "Funniest high school memory. Go."

Ethan leaned back in his chair. "Our junior year. The homecoming float. Do you remember this?"

"Oh, no."

"Oh yes. The senior class built a float with a papier mâché Wildcat that was supposed to breathe actual smoke from a fog machine hidden inside."

"I remember."

"The fog machine shorted out, and the Wildcat caught fire on Main Street during the parade. Full flames. The marching band scattered. Principal Hodges tried to put it out with a cup of lemonade. A cup. Of lemonade."

Sarah was laughing now, her hand flat on the table, her shoulders shaking. "He threw lemonade on a fire. I don't remember that part."

"With absolute confidence. Like lemonade was a known firefighting agent. And then Coach Rivera ran over with a fire extinguisher and got the foam all over Mrs. Patterson's new convertible, and she chased him up the sidewalk in her parade sash."

"Mrs. Patterson... the mayor's wife?"

"The one and only. In heels. Running. With a sash that said 'Serenity Crossing Spirit.' I was standing on the curb with Mark Bell, and we laughed until we couldn't breathe."

Sarah wiped the corner of her eye. "That was the same year Rebecca entered the talent show and forgot the words to her song and just stood onstage and waved until they made her get off."

"I didn't know that."

"She has never let any of us bring it up. Never."

The courses changed. The server cleared the starter plates with quiet efficiency and refreshed the table, crumbs swept, glasses refilled, and linens kept clean. The entrée arrived, a beautifully composed plate built around regional trout with seasonal vegetables; the presentation was refined without being fussy. At the front of the dining salon, a small performance nook held a piano and a violin, and the music drifted through the room, slow and romantic.

"Favorite cake," Sarah said.

"Chocolate. Dark chocolate. With chocolate ganache."

"No."

"What do you mean, no?"

"I mean no. That's wrong. The correct answer is coconut cake with cream cheese icing."

"That is your answer. My answer is chocolate."

"Your answer is wrong."

"There is no wrong answer to a favorite cake."

"There is when someone says chocolate ganache with a straight face when coconut cake exists in the world."

Ethan laughed. "You feel strongly about this."

"I feel correctly about it. My mother makes the best coconut cake in the state of Tennessee, and I will take that claim to my grave."

"I've had your mother's cooking. I believe you."

The banter moved between them the way it always had, the back-and-forth volleys that had been their language since the first week of the Granville project. The competitive edge had softened into something playful, the push and pull not of two people testing each other but of two people who enjoyed each other so thoroughly that every exchange felt like a gift.

"Perfect Sunday afternoon," Sarah said. "What does yours look like?"

Ethan thought about it. "Church in the morning. Come home. Make lunch, something simple. Sit on the porch with a sketchpad and let the afternoon be whatever it wants to be. No schedule. No project list. Just the mountains and peace and quiet."

"You sit still?"

"I'm learning to."

"Interesting."

"A lot of things are interesting."

She held his gaze across the table, and the look lasted a beat longer than casual, and she didn't look away first.

"Mine is almost the same," she said. "Church. Then Mama and Daddy's for dinner. The whole family around the table, the noise and the chaos, Lizzie telling stories, and my brothers arguing about football." She turned her water glass slowly on the linen. "Then home. The back porch and a good book. I love the noise of my family, and I love the quiet of my house afterward. I need both."

"I understand that."

"I know you do."

The candles were being lit. A server moved from table to table, and the small flames caught and held behind the hurricane glass, and the white linen turned to soft gold.

"Tell me something you've always wanted to try...like a bucket list item," Ethan said.

"Skydiving."

He stared at her.

"I'm serious. I've wanted to try it for years now. The free fall. The openness. Nothing between you and the ground except trust."

"Sarah Hartwell wants to jump out of an airplane."

"Sarah Hartwell builds structures for a living. She understands load-bearing capacity and wind resistance, and the physics of gravity better than most people. And she would like to experience gravity from the other direction, just once."

"You are full of surprises."

"Good. What about you?"

"I would like to learn to flyfish. Real fly-fishing, not just casting. The kind where you tie your own flies and read the water and stand in a river at dawn and wait."

"Your dad fished; tell me more about him."

"He fished every chance he got. Mostly at dawn. Never fly-fishing, though. He always said he wanted to try it. We were going to go together." Ethan paused. He looked at the candle on the table, the small flame steady behind the glass. "But...we never got to."

Sarah reached across the table and put her hand over his, and her fingers were warm and steady.

After a moment, he turned his hand over beneath hers and held it. They sat like that while the music drifted through the salon, piano and violin weaving something slow and sweet. The lake darkened outside the windows and the candles brightened inside, and the world on the water grew smaller and warmer.

Their dessert arrived, a composed plate built around ripe fruit, vanilla-flavored cream, and warm spice. They separated their hands to eat, and the conversation picked back up, circling through the kinds of things that two people share when they are genuinely curious about the person across the table.

He learned that she sang in the church choir in middle school and couldn't carry a tune. She learned that he had broken his finger in middle school and tried to hide it from his parents because he didn't want to be benched during basketball season. For two full days he hid it before his mom discovered it and dragged him to the hospital. She told him about the time Rebecca dared her to jump off the rope swing at Hawthorne Lake, and she landed so hard in a belly flop that the sound echoed off the far bank. He told her about the time he tried to cook Thanksgiving dinner for himself in Nashville and set off every smoke alarm in the building, and the fire department showed up, and three of them stayed for pie.

She laughed at that one until she had to press her napkin to her face. Ethan watched her laugh and the candlelight on her skin and the way her hair fell forward when she leaned in, and he felt the precise fullness of the moment, the woman across the table from him in a red satin dress who had been so far behind her walls when he'd first walked back into her life that he'd wondered if he'd ever get through.

Sarah pushed her dessert plate aside and looked at him across the table, with the candlelight in her eyes.

"Dance with me," she said and stood before he could answer. She held out her hand, and Ethan took it and rose from his chair. She turned and led him through the dining salon toward the wide staircase.

The staircase curved upward, and the music from the dining salon faded behind them as they climbed.

The Lantern Deck spread before them, an open-air space partially covered by a white canopy. A polished wooden dance floor was centered in front of a small deck stage framed in wood and brass railing. The stage was low and intimate, softly lit now as the sky deepened. An acoustic ensemble sat in place: a man with a guitar, fingers picking gently at the strings; another with an upright bass providing a steady, easy pulse; and a woman with a fiddle drawing long, honeyed lines that carried across the water. The sound was unmistakably Smoky Mountain, warm and unhurried, the kind of music that belonged to this place and this evening.

The railings along the deck were lined with lantern-style fixtures. String lights woven into the canopy beams above the dance floor glowed against the deepening sky, a soft constellation of warm light.

Several couples stood at the railing or sat at small tables near the edge of the deck. A few were already on the dance floor, swaying in the easy way of people who had found the rhythm and let it carry them.

Sarah turned to face him at the edge of the dance floor. The lantern light caught the red satin of her dress and held it. Her hair moved in the breeze off the lake.

"Well?" she said.

His right hand found the small of her back, her left hand settling on his shoulder, and the fit was immediate. Natural.

The ensemble played. The guitar carried the melody with gentle fingerpicking that sounded like warmth itself. The bass held the pulse. The fiddle wove above it all, long notes that felt like mountain air. They moved across the polished wood floor, and Ethan led her through a slow turn, and she followed without a bit of hesitation. Her body moved the way her mind worked: quick and capable and completely attuned to the person beside her.

One song became two. Two became three. The space between them closed gradually. She moved with him through turns and changes and the occasional flourish he offered, and every time he led her into something new, she was already there, matching him, answering him, her balance and timing as sure as his.

He was an excellent dancer. His mother had made certain of that. Maggie Cole had insisted on dance lessons when Ethan was fifteen, over his loud and sustained objections, and the muscle memory of those mortifying Saturday afternoons at Mrs. Hargrove's studio had never left him. Sarah, who had never danced with him before, moved as if she had been doing it for years. She trusted his lead.

A vocalist joined the ensemble for a song. A woman with a voice that stayed close and warm, more intimate storytelling than performance, the lyrics landing softly in the open air. Ethan drew Sarah closer, her hand sliding from his shoulder to the back of his neck, and they moved together in the small, private way of two people who had forgotten the rest of the world existed.

The string lights above them glowed brighter as the sky darkened. The lanterns along the railing flickered and held. The lake was black glass now, and the boat moved through it like a vessel of light.

The ensemble returned to instrumentals. Slow-dance timing. Lingering notes. The fiddle carried a melody that was old and sweet and patient, the kind of song that had been played on porches and in dance halls in these mountains for a hundred years. Ethan led Sarah through a series of turns that were smooth and unhurried, moving her across the floor with the easy confidence of a man who knew exactly where he was taking her and was in no rush to arrive. She matched every step. Her eyes stayed on his. Other couples were present on the deck, sitting, standing, a few still dancing, but they existed at the edge of his awareness the way furniture exists in a room you've stopped noticing.

The song built. The fiddle climbed. The guitar picked up, and the bass deepened, and the melody swelled into something full and warm, and Ethan's hand tightened on her back as he guided her into a dip. Slow. Smooth. Unhurried. She arched back in his arms with the trust of a woman who knew she would not be dropped, and his arm held her steady, her weight balanced perfectly against his.

He brought her up slowly. The music resolved. And the deck erupted in applause.

Ethan and Sarah surfaced from their private world they had built on that dance floor and found that the other couples had moved back. They were standing at the edges of the floor, some at the railing, some near the tables, and they were clapping. An older woman near the stage had both hands pressed to her chest. A man at the railing raised his water glass in a quiet salute.

Sarah looked at Ethan. He looked at her. And they both laughed, the real kind, the kind that breaks through surprise and lands somewhere between joy and disbelief. They had been so completely inside their dancing that the existence of an audience had genuinely not occurred to either of them.

"I think we had spectators," she said.

"I think we created fans."

The applause faded. The ensemble picked up another song, something slow and gentle, and the deck settled back into its easy rhythm. A few couples returned to the floor. The lantern light swayed.

They moved back into the center of the dance floor. Her head came to rest against his shoulder, and he felt her breath warm through the fabric of his shirt. He rested his cheek against her hair, and the music played, and the sky was full of stars that had appeared one at a time while they weren't looking.

She lifted her head from his shoulder. He looked down at her. The space between them was measured in inches, and the inches were closing with the slow, steady certainty of something that had been building for weeks and was finished waiting.

Her eyes were on his. Her hand was warm against the back of his neck. The lantern light was on her face, on the red satin, on the dark waves of her hair, and the music was soft and the water was still and the world had narrowed to the space between two people on a dance floor on a lake in the Smoky Mountains.

He kissed her gently as his hand came up and cradled the side of her face.

Sarah's hand tightened on the back of his neck as she kissed him back. Warm and sure.

When the kiss ended, neither of them moved away. They stood on the dance floor under the string lights with their foreheads touching and their breath mingling in the warm September air.

"Ethan."

"I know."

They danced slowly and closely and quietly until the boat eased toward the dock, and the paddlewheel slowed.

Chapter 24

Ethan pulled up outside The Fluff & Curl just after one o'clock and left the engine running. He watched the salon through the front windshield. The front door was propped open with a cast-iron doorstop shaped like a rooster, and he could hear music drifting out, something folksy, and the layered hum of women's voices.

Sarah stepped out, dressed for a full day of hiking. Lightweight pants, a fitted green athletic top, and trail boots. Her hair was braided, a single thick braid that started high and fell over one shoulder. Sunglasses perched up on top of her head.

Rebecca appeared and walked to his window. He rolled it down.

"Bring her back in one piece. I just spent three hours pampering her."

"Yes, ma'am."

Rebecca held his eyes for one more beat, the look carrying everything a younger sister could pack into a single glance. Then she smiled, patted the side of his truck twice, and turned back toward the salon.

Sarah opened the passenger door and climbed in. She pulled the door shut and looked at him. "Let me guess... she threatened you."

"She expressed a preference for your safe return. It was very diplomatic."

"That was not diplomatic. That was Rebecca being Rebecca."

"Well... I understand my assignment."

Sarah shook her head and buckled her seatbelt. "All right. Where are we going?"

"East."

"You said that last time."

"Worked last time."

She gave him a look that was half protest and half amusement, and he pulled away from the curb and pointed the truck toward the foothills.

***

The trailhead was forty minutes outside town, past the last of the paved county roads, where a gravel lot held space for maybe six vehicles beneath a stand of old tulip poplars. Sarah stood at the edge of the lot and looked at the trail marker and the ridge rising above the tree line.

"I know this trail," she said. "I haven't been out here in years. Rebecca and Anna came with me once, and both of them wanted to turn back before we hit the first switchback. Anna's shoes were wrong, and Rebecca decided the elevation was a personal attack on her hair. We were back in town by noon."

Ethan pulled the packs from the truck bed and handed Sarah hers. He shouldered his own and clipped the chest strap. "Today you're going all the way."

"You don't know that. You don't know what's up there."

"I have an idea. I hiked the first two miles Wednesday evening to scout it."

She looked at him. "You scouted the trail."

"I scouted the trail."

"You are unbelievable."

"I'm thorough."

She tightened her pack straps and stepped onto the trail, and Ethan fell in beside her, and within fifty yards the parking lot disappeared behind them and the mountains took over.

The trail started gradually through hardwood forest, the canopy thick enough to break the September afternoon into moving pieces of light on the ground. Oaks and maples and the occasional birch, their trunks straight and close.

Their pace found itself defied within the first quarter mile. Matched stride. Matched rhythm. The same unconscious calibration that happened every time they ran together in the mornings now translated to a climb that would ask more of them as the elevation gained.

"The switchbacks start in about half a mile," Ethan said. "It gets steep."

"Good."

"I'm serious. The elevation gain is real."

Sarah looked at him sideways without breaking stride. "Ethan. I carry lumber for a living. I think I can handle a hill."

"I'm just saying, if you need a break at any point, there's no shame in it."

"If I need a break, I'll let you know. And if you need a break, I'll pretend not to notice and bring it up later at the worst possible moment."

He laughed, and the sound carried into the trees and scattered a pair of blue jays from a low branch.

The switchbacks arrived as promised, and the trail tilted hard. The grade changed the character of the hike entirely, turning what had been a walk into real work. The path cut back and forth across the face of the ridge in long zigzags, each turn gaining ten or fifteen feet of elevation, and the air changed with every hundred feet they climbed. Cooler. Thinner. The late-summer heat that still hung in the valley didn't reach this high, and the breeze that moved through the trees carried something sharper, the particular bite of altitude that the mountains held onto even in September.

Sarah pushed the pace. She pushed it the way she pushed everything, lengthening her stride on the switchbacks and attacking the turns with the kind of footwork that came from years of running on uneven ground.

"You're sandbagging," she said over her shoulder at the third switchback.

"I am not."

"You're two steps behind me, and you're not even breathing hard. You're letting me lead."

"You're navigating well. I'm being strategic."

"You're being chivalrous, and I didn't ask for it."

He lengthened his stride and pulled even with her, and they climbed the next switchback side by side, their boots finding the same rhythm on the packed dirt.

The forest began to change as they gained elevation. The hardwoods thinned, and the understory opened, and the light came through in wider columns. Rhododendrons crowded the trail in places, their dark, waxy leaves creating tunnels that blocked the view and then released it suddenly into clearings where the valley opened below them in long green folds. Every clearing was bigger than the last. Every view reached further.

Sarah stopped at one of these clearings and took a long drink from her hydration pack.

"You picked a really good trail," she said.

"I picked a trail worthy of you."

She looked at the view for another beat, and then she turned and started climbing again.

The trail hit a scramble section where the path gave way to exposed rock, a series of natural stone steps worn smooth by water and time. The angle was steep enough that hands were useful, and Ethan went first, finding the holds and testing each ledge before moving up. He reached the top of the section and turned and extended his hand down to her.

Her grip was strong and sure, and exactly what he expected from a woman who worked with her hands every day. He pulled, and she pushed, and she came up over the ledge in one clean motion. When she stood beside him on the narrow shelf, she didn't let go right away. Her fingers stayed in his.

"Thanks," she said.

"Anytime."

They continued the climb. The trail delivered everything Ethan had hoped it would: challenge after challenge, the kind of terrain that demanded the full attention of two athletic people and rewarded that attention with increasingly staggering views. They read the trail differently, Sarah watching the ground three steps ahead with the eye of a builder who understood terrain and load, Ethan scanned the route from a wider angle, tracking the switchbacks above them and estimating the remaining elevation gain by the tree line. They traded observations about the route the way they traded observations on the Granville site, each one's expertise complementing the other's.

The sound reached them before the trail revealed its source. Water. Not the distant murmur of a creek below the ridge, but something closer, fuller, with a steady percussion that grew louder with every step. The trail curved left around a massive boulder and dropped into a hollow, and the forest opened, and the waterfall appeared.

It fell from a rock ledge thirty feet above into a pool at the base of the hollow. The water came down in a single clean sheet that broke into white spray where it met the rocks. The pool below was dark and clear, fed by the falls and draining slowly into a creek that wound away downhill. Ferns and moss covered every surface near the water.

Sarah stood at the edge of the pool and looked up at the falls with an expression Ethan had seen on her face exactly twice before: once when the Bellehaven appeared around the curve in the road and once on the Lantern Deck when the notes of the fiddle carried across the water. It was the look of a woman who had been given something she didn't know she was missing.

"I've lived here my whole life, and I've never been here."

Ethan dropped his pack on a flat rock near the pool's edge and unzipped the cooler portion. "Then it's a good day."

They ate lunch sitting on the rock shelf. He had packed thick sandwiches, apples, trail mix, and two bottles of sweet tea.

They finished eating, and Ethan packed the trash back into the pack as Sarah sat forward on the rock and looked at the pool. It was maybe fifteen feet across at its widest point, ringed with smooth stones, and the water was so clear that the bottom was visible.

She unlaced her boots. Pulled off her socks. Rolled the cuffs of her hiking pants above her calves and stepped into the water.

The sound she made was involuntary. A sharp intake of breath, followed by a laugh that echoed off the rock walls of the hollow. "Cold."

"Mountain water."

"That is icy cold, Ethan."

"Mountain water in September."

She waded further. The water climbed to mid-calf, and she stood in the pool with the falls crashing ten feet away. She looked back at him with a challenge in her eyes that he recognized.

He unlaced his boots.

The water was cold enough to make his jaw tight. He stepped in carefully, finding his footing on the slick stones.

"Come closer," she said, raising her voice over the falls.

He waded closer. The water was above his ankles, numbingly cold, and the stones beneath his feet shifted and settled. She was three feet away, then two, and the spray from the falls caught the light and hung between them in the air.

"Isn't this amazing?" She asked.

"It is."

"I have something important to tell you."

"What?"

"You have water on your nose."

She splashed him. A full, deliberate, two-handed scoop of mountain water that caught him square on his chest. The cold seized his lungs, and the shock erased every thought in his head except one, which was that Sarah Hartwell had started something she was not equipped to finish.

He splashed her back. Not gently. She gasped and retreated two steps, slipped on a stone, and caught herself. Then came back at him with another volley that soaked the rest of his shirt. They were both laughing and splashing like children, the sound of their laughter mixing with the falls. She was fast and accurate and ruthless, and he was bigger and had a longer reach, and neither advantage mattered because the pool was small enough that there was no safe distance, and every retreat led to a counterattack.

She lunged for a big scoop, and her foot slipped on the stones. He caught her arm. She caught his shoulder. They collided in the middle of the pool, off-balance and laughing, and his arm went around her waist to keep her upright. She grabbed the front of his soaked shirt with both hands, and they stood there, breathing hard, ankle-deep in mountain water, the falls roaring beside them.

He kissed her. Quick and joyful and tasting of sweet tea and mountain water. Two people standing barefoot in a freezing pool with their clothes soaked and their guards completely down.

"Your lips are cold," she said.

"Your hands are freezing."

"This was your idea."

"You got in first."

She let go of his shirt, grinned, and pushed him, a gentle shove that sent him back one step on the slippery stones, and she turned and waded toward the edge of the pool. He followed her, and they climbed out onto the warm rock shelf and sat in a patch of sun.

They sat close, side by side on the flat rock, their bare feet drying in the warmth. The spray from the falls reached them in occasional gusts, fine and cool, and the hollow held the heat of the afternoon within its sheltered walls.

"Ready for the rest?" he asked.

"There's more?"

"The top," he said as he pointed.

She looked at the ridge above them, visible through the trees, the trail continuing upward past the hollow.

"Lead the way, Cole."

They laced their boots over damp socks, shouldered their packs, and left the waterfall behind. The trail climbed harder past the hollow, steeper pitches, and tighter switchbacks, the forest thinning steadily as the elevation pushed above the hardwood line. The scramble sections came more frequently, hands-and-feet climbing over rock ledges where the trail threaded through gaps in the stone. They worked through them as a unit, reading the rock, testing holds, and reaching back for each other with hands that gripped and pulled and steadied without hesitation.

A section of exposed trail ran along a narrow ridge with views on both sides, and Sarah paused and looked out, and said nothing.

The world was enormous. Ridgelines stacked in layers of green and blue, each one fainter than the last, dissolving into haze at the horizon. To the west, the valley they'd climbed out of was a green basin holding the thin silver thread of a creek. To the east, more mountains, more ridges, and more sky than a person could account for.

"Keep going," Ethan said. "I have a feeling it's gonna get better."

"It does not get better than this."

"It might."

She looked at him with open skepticism and started climbing.

It got better.

The trail broke through the last of the tree cover and delivered them onto a broad rock outcropping at the summit. The ridge fell away on three sides, and the view opened in a full panorama that made every step of the climb make sense. The Great Smoky Mountains spread before them in every direction, ridge after ridge after ridge, the nearest dark green and detailed, the middle layers fading to blue, the farthest barely distinguishable from the sky itself. The scale of it defeated description. It was not a view. It was a continent tilted on its side.

Ethan checked his watch. Right on time.

They sat on a rock. The stone was warm beneath them, holding the day's heat, and the air up here moved with a steady breeze that cooled the sweat on their skin and carried the particular clean emptiness of high elevation.

A deer appeared on the ridgeline below them, picking its way along a game trail through the low scrub. Then a second, smaller one followed. They moved with a careful, deliberate grace that wild animals carry in their territory, unhurried and perfectly aware of their surroundings. Ethan and Sarah watched in silence as the pair crossed the ridge and vanished into the treeline on the far side.

"There," Sarah said.

Ethan followed her gaze and saw an eagle circling on a thermal above the valley, wings spread wide and motionless, riding the current in long, unhurried arcs.

They watched it until it drifted beyond the far ridge and disappeared.

Eventually, the light began to change. The sun was lower now, and the color of the mountains was shifting. The sky above was still bright and blue, but the western horizon was beginning to gather color, the first streaks of amber and coral appearing above the range.

Sarah reached for his hand, and they sat on the warm rock at the top of the mountain and watched the light do its work. The transformation was slow and steady. The gold deepened. The purple spread. The amber on the horizon intensified into something rich and layered, and the ridgelines became a kind of staircase descending into color, each one a different shade, each shade more impossible than the last.

"I have a question," Sarah said. She was looking at the mountains, not at him.

"Okay."

"The Bellehaven. This trail. You plan things."

"I do."

"You planned the timing today. You planned for us to arrive at the top right now, right when the light would be doing this."

"I did."

She was quiet for a moment. The breeze moved through the scrub below them, and the light continued its slow transformation, the western sky building color the way a painter builds a canvas, layer over layer.

"The Bellehaven was the most beautiful evening I've ever had," she said. "The boat and the dancing and the dinner... all of it. It was perfect. Like something out of a story. You gave me my new favorite romance novel in real life."

"But?"

"Not but. And." She turned her head and looked at him. "And this is where I want to be. Right here with you. On a rock. In hiking boots. With wet socks and sore shoulders."

She looked back at the mountains. "This view is extraordinary. And the fact that you planned a whole day so that we'd end up here, right now, watching this..."

She didn't finish the sentence. She didn't need to. She leaned into him, and they sat on the summit while the sky gave everything it had.

Chapter 25

The plaster section on the west wall had let go at 2:47 in the afternoon.

Sarah knew the time because she'd been standing twelve feet away reviewing the electrical rough-in schedule with Tim when the crack traveled from the ceiling line to the chair rail in a single clean split. A four-foot section of a seventy-year-old wall fell onto the auditorium floor in a cloud of white dust that coated everything within fifteen feet. Nobody was hurt. Nobody was even close. But the sound of it, that particular crack followed by the heavy, crumbling thud of old lath and horsehair plaster hitting hardwood, went through Sarah's chest like a door slamming.

Tim had walked to the debris pile and crouched, and looked at the exposed wall behind it for a full minute without speaking. When he stood, he brushed the plaster dust off his knees and looked at her.

"Water damage behind the lath," he said. "Old. Probably from a roof leak years ago. Ran down the inside of the wall and weakened the key. The plaster lost its grip."

"How much more of this wall is compromised?"

Tim looked at the remaining plaster stretching another twenty feet toward the stage. "Won't know until I sound it. Could be just this section. Could run the whole length."

"Sound it. Today. Before the crew leaves."

He'd sounded it. It ran the whole length.

That was the last straw on a week that had been stacking up against them since Monday. The tile supplier in Knoxville had shipped the wrong grade of mortar for the lobby restoration work, and the replacement wouldn't arrive until next Wednesday, which pushed the concession area timeline back by five days. A permit revision she'd submitted a week ago came back with questions from the county inspector, which meant another round of paperwork, another visit to the county office, and another afternoon she didn't have. The structural engineer's report on the backstage corridor had flagged two additional joists that needed sistering, work that wasn't in the original scope and would have to be documented separately for the grant compliance file. And this morning the compressor on the crew's primary nail gun had failed at 9:15, which meant Tim had to send Brian into Gatlinburg for the backup unit. Which meant Brian wasn't on site for the first two hours of the day, which meant the framing work in the auditorium fell behind.

None of it was catastrophic. All of it was cumulative. Five days of problems landing on top of each other with the steady, relentless rhythm of water finding every crack in a foundation. Sarah had sent her crew home at four. It had been a long week, and they all needed a break. Sarah was standing alone in the Granville lobby with her iPad on the marble concession counter, and her jaw was set so tight her teeth ached.

She spread the revised schedule across the counter beside the iPad and started reworking the timeline. The plaster failure changed everything on the west wall. If the damage ran the full length, which Tim's sounding suggested it did, the auditorium renovation sequence would have to be restructured. The rest of the plaster would have to come down, the lath stripped, and the framing assessed before any finish work could proceed. That could take weeks, depending on what they found after opening the entire wall. Not days. Weeks.

She wrote the new task sequence on the back of the schedule printout, her handwriting tight and fast. Demolition. Assessment. Framing repairs, if needed. The electrical. New lath. New plaster. Cure time. She ran the numbers in her head and didn't like what they told her.

Ethan came up beside her and looked at the schedule spread across the counter. He didn't say anything. He set his bag on the floor, leaned one hip against the counter, and waited.

"The west wall in the auditorium let go," Sarah said. She kept her eyes on the schedule. "A section of plaster came down this afternoon. Tim sounded the rest of it. The damage runs the full length, all the way to the stage."

"I saw the debris on my way through," Ethan said.

"That's not even the worst part. The worst part is that it changes the entire auditorium sequence. We're looking at weeks, Ethan. Weeks on a wall I had scheduled for finish work by the end of the month."

She pushed back from the counter and walked three steps toward the center of the lobby and turned around, and walked back. Her hands moved as she talked, punctuating the words.

"And that's just today. That's just the cherry on top of a week that started with the wrong mortar from Knoxville, a permit revision that should have been approved the first time, two additional joists in the backstage corridor that nobody anticipated, and a compressor failure that cost me two hours of framing work." The color was climbing in her cheeks, and her voice was getting faster and sharper. "I have been putting out fires all week. Every single day this week I have walked into this building, and something else has gone wrong. I have handled every single problem because that is what I do, but today, right now, I am telling you that I'm tired. I feel beaten to a pulp."

Ethan stood at the counter and listened. His arms were at his sides. His eyes were on her.

"I am tired of being the person who fixes everything. I am tired of being the one who reworks the schedule and calls the supplier and drives to the county office and documents the changes and keeps the crew on track, and makes it all look like it's under control when it is not under control. It is not under control, Ethan. This week has not been under control since Monday, and I have been holding it together with both hands for five days, and I am done holding it together."

"The tile supplier doesn't care that my timeline is tight. The county inspector doesn't care that I've already built thirty buildings that passed every code review the first time. The plaster doesn't care that I had a beautiful schedule that was on track until 2:47 this afternoon. None of it cares. And I know that. I know that's construction. I know that's the job. I have been doing this job for years. I know that things go wrong, and you adapt, and you solve them, and you move on. I know all of that." She stopped moving. She was standing in the middle of the terrazzo floor, and her shoulders were high and tight, and her jaw was clenched. "But right now, today, this Friday, I am mad. I am frustrated, and I am mad, and I needed to say that out loud to someone, and you're the only one still in this building."

Sarah stood in the quiet that followed her own voice. Her shoulders were still tight. The week was still sitting on her like a physical load that had compressed into a knot between her shoulder blades.

She tipped her head back and looked at the pressed-tin ceiling, and opened her mouth and let out a scream. Not a shriek. Not a cry. A full, deliberate, from-the-gut sound that came up through her chest and out into the Granville's lobby.

When she was done, she dropped her chin and let out a long, slow exhale that emptied her lungs and loosened something in her chest.

She looked up, and Ethan was there. She opened her mouth to speak, and he placed one finger against her lips.

"Shhhh."

He lowered his finger from her lips.

He pulled his phone from his back pocket, and she watched him scroll for a moment, his thumb moving across the screen. He found what he was looking for and tapped it, and music came through the phone's speaker, a song she didn't recognize, something slow and acoustic, a guitar and a voice. He walked to the marble counter and set the phone down.

He walked back to her. He stood in front of her on the terrazzo floor and extended his hand.

Sarah looked at his hand and took it.

He drew her in slowly, his other hand settling against her lower back. Her free hand found his shoulder, and the tension that had been living in her body for five days began to slowly come apart.

Ethan had not said a single word since shhhh. He was saying everything with his hand on her back, his shoulder under her palm, and the slow, steady way he moved them across the floor.

She rested her head on his shoulder. The fabric of his shirt smelled like sawdust and coffee and the clean soap he used, and she closed her eyes and let him lead. She stopped thinking about the schedule and the plaster and the mortar and the permit and the joists and the compressor and every other thing that had stacked itself on her shoulders this week.

When the music ended, Ethan pressed his lips to her forehead. The kiss was warm and unhurried, and Sarah felt the last of the week's tension leave her.

She lifted her head from his shoulder and looked at him. "Thank you."

"You're welcome."

"I needed that."

"I know."

She stepped back.

"My mom's making chicken casserole tonight," he said. "Nothing fancy. Just food, probably a movie afterward. Come over."

"Yes."

He looked at her, a slight lift at the corner of his mouth. "That was fast."

"I've been running on adrenaline and a granola bar since noon. You had me at casserole." She picked up her iPad from the counter and slid it into her bag. "But we're stopping for ice cream on the way."

"We don't have to. Mom keeps ice cream in the freezer."

"This is not a negotiation, Ethan. This is a statement of fact. We are stopping. For ice cream. On the way." She slung her bag over her shoulder and looked at him. "I have had the worst week of this entire project. I screamed like a lunatic in front of you. You danced with me in the middle of a construction site. The only thing that makes this evening complete is a stop at Millie's, and I am getting two scoops, and you are not going to say a word about it."

He picked up his phone from the counter and slid it into his pocket. "I was going to get two scoops myself."

"Good. Then we understand each other."

Chapter 26

Maggie was at the counter slicing sourdough bread when Ethan and Sarah entered the kitchen.

"Hey, Mama. I brought company for dinner."

She turned with the serrated knife still in her hand, and when she saw Sarah standing beside him, the knife went down on the counter, her hands went up, and her face broke into a smile.

"Sarah. Oh, my goodness." Maggie wiped her hands on her apron, came around the counter with her arms already open, and pulled Sarah into a hug. "Well, this is the best surprise."

"Thank you for having me, Maggie."

"Having you? Honey, you just made my whole evening." She held Sarah at arm's length and looked at her. "Sit down. Let me get you some sweet tea."

Maggie was already pulling a glass from the cabinet. She filled it from the pitcher in the refrigerator and set it on the counter in front of Sarah. "Dinner won't be long. That casserole's been in there for a while, and it's almost ready."

"It smells wonderful."

"It's nothing fancy. Chicken and stuffing." She said as she went back to cutting the bread. "How about I whip up a good salad to go with it?"

"I can help with that," Sarah said.

Maggie pointed the knife toward the refrigerator. "There's romaine in the crisper, and tomatoes and a cucumber. Ethan, grab the red onion from the pantry and wash everything, will you?"

"Yes, ma'am."

Ethan washed the vegetables at the sink and handed them to Sarah, who stood at the cutting board Maggie had pointed her toward, chopping romaine into ribbons.

"Where's your salad bowl, Maggie?"

"Second shelf, left of the stove. The big wooden one."

Sarah reached up and pulled it down and set it on the counter, and kept chopping.

"You look tired, sweetheart," Maggie said.

Sarah scraped the romaine into the bowl and started on the tomatoes. "It's been a tough week. But it's Friday, and the workweek is over, and I'm standing in your kitchen about to eat a homemade casserole. So I'm calling it a win."

Maggie arranged the bread slices on a plate and covered them with a cloth napkin. She pulled three place settings from the cabinet and carried them to the round table in the breakfast nook.

"Ethan, check that casserole for me."

He opened the oven door and looked. The top was browned and bubbling at the edges. "Done."

"Perfect timing." Maggie pulled a trivet from the drawer beside the stove and set it on the table. Ethan carried the casserole dish with two oven mitts and set it down, and Sarah brought the salad bowl and the bread plate, and the three of them took their seats.

Maggie reached for their hands. Ethan took his mother's hand on his left and Sarah's on his right.

Maggie bowed her head. "Lord, thank You for this food and for the hands that prepared it. Thank You for my son beside me and for Sarah at our table tonight. You have blessed this home with good people and warm company, and I am grateful for every bit of it. Bless this food for the nourishment of our bodies and bless these people for the nourishment of each other. In Your name we pray. Amen."

"Amen," Ethan and Sarah said.

Maggie served the casserole with the generous hand of a woman who believed food was love made visible. Sarah took a bite and closed her eyes for a moment.

"Maggie, this is incredible."

"Oh, it's just a casserole. Nothing special."

"It's special," Sarah said.

"Well," Maggie smoothed her napkin in her lap, and her cheeks colored slightly. "I'm glad you think so."

The conversation moved easily. Maggie told a story about Ethan's first day of kindergarten, how she'd walked him to the door and he'd turned around and told her she could go now; he had it from here.

"He did not," Sarah said.

"He did. Five years old. Backpack half his size. He looked at me as if I were embarrassing him in front of people he hadn't even met yet."

"I was establishing independence," Ethan said.

"You were breaking my heart, is what you were doing," Maggie said. "I sat in the truck and cried for twenty minutes."

"Has this house been in your family a long time?" Sarah asked, buttering a piece of sourdough.

"We built it," Maggie said. "Well, Phil designed it, and we hired a crew, and then Phil drove that crew half crazy because he kept changing things during construction. He'd show up in the morning with a sketch on a napkin and say he'd had a better idea for the mudroom, and the foreman would just look at him."

"Daddy says architects who change things mid-build are the worst kind of clients."

"Your daddy is right. And Phil was the worst of the worst. But the house turned out exactly the way it should have, so I forgave him." She broke off a piece of bread. "We moved in the summer of '93. Ethan was born the following spring. Your daddy helped us, actually. Bill brought a truckload of lumber from the mill for the porch framing. Wouldn't let Phil pay full price. Said a man building his first house deserved a neighbor's discount."

"That sounds like Daddy."

"Those two," Maggie said, shaking her head. "Phil and Bill. They were a pair."

Sarah smiled. "Mama still says he was the only man in Serenity Crossing who could out-talk Daddy about wood grain."

"That is the truth."

The conversation kept moving, warm and unhurried. Ethan ate his casserole and listened to his mom tell Sarah stories she might not have offered otherwise.

When the casserole was gone, the salad bowl was nearly empty, and the bread plate held nothing but crumbs, Maggie set her napkin on the table and straightened.

"Oh. I almost forgot." She looked at Ethan. "That ledger. Your grandmother's ledger. I found it."

Ethan set his fork down. "You did?"

"It wasn't in the filing cabinet. I finally found it in a box of your daddy's things in the closet of his office. There are photo albums in there too. Old ones. From the theater's earlier years. Photographs I haven't looked at in a long time."

"Can we see it?" Sarah asked.

Maggie looked at her and smiled. "I was hoping you'd want to."

They cleared the table. Sarah carried the dishes to the sink and started washing them before Maggie could protest. Ethan dried. Then Maggie led them down the hallway toward Philip's study.

Ethan opened the door and stepped aside to let Sarah enter first.

The room was small. A drafting table sat under the window, and bookshelves lined two walls, heavy with volumes. Framed photographs of completed projects. Rolled blueprints standing upright in the corner like sentries. The desk was neat and organized, with a cup of pencils and various drafting supplies.

Sarah moved to the photographs on the wall and recognized several of the buildings. The Serenity Crossing library renovation. The community center addition. A farmhouse out on Route 12 that Phillip had designed in the early years.

Maggie went to the closet and pulled out a cardboard storage box, nothing fancy, the kind you buy at an office supply store.

They settled on the floor. Sarah and Ethan sat side by side, their backs against the front of the desk. Maggie pulled the desk chair closer so she could see and lowered herself into it.

Ethan lifted the lid, and the ledger was on top. A hardbound book, the kind with a marbled cover and lined pages inside.

He opened it and saw his grandmother's handwriting. Precise, consistent, and slanted slightly to the right, every letter formed with the careful penmanship of a woman who had been taught that handwriting was a reflection of character. Dates in one column. Amounts in another. Notes in the margins, small and neat.

Friday showing, full house. Saturday matinee, 142 tickets. Rain, lower attendance.

Christmas play, standing room only, extra chairs from the church. Every ticket sold, every night, for years.

He handed it to Sarah.

She took the ledger and turned the pages slowly. Her fingers moved along the columns, and she paused at a margin note that read:

Mrs. Piedmont brought her entire Sunday school class. 47 children. Charged half price for the little ones.

Sarah smiled.

"She accounted for everything," Sarah said.

"Down to the last nickel," Maggie said. "I thoroughly enjoyed reading through that ledger; so many of her little notes are precious."

Sarah turned another page and another. The entries spanned years; the handwriting never changed, the precision never slipping.

Ethan reached into the box and pulled out the photo albums. Two of them, the old kind with black paper pages and photographs held in place by adhesive corners. He opened the first one and held it between them so Sarah could see.

Black-and-white photographs. The Granville lobby. The ticket booth occupied by a woman Ethan recognized as his grandmother. A young woman in a dark dress, her hair pinned up, her posture straight, a roll of tickets in one hand.

"Those were from opening night," Maggie said as she leaned forward in the chair. "Your grandfather had the photographs taken by a man from Knoxville."

The next page held several images of the auditorium. Every seat was occupied in each of the photographs. People in their good clothes, programs in their laps, faces turned toward the stage.

"It used to be back in those days everyone turned out on Friday night. The theater was basically the community hub," Maggie said.

Sarah leaned closer to the album, and she studied the faces in the photographs. Pictures of several people who were dressed in what appeared to be their Sunday best.

He turned the page. A community event of some kind. Tables set up in the lobby, food laid out, children sitting cross-legged on the terrazzo floor. A banner across the far wall that Ethan couldn't quite read in the photograph.

"That was the Harvest Festival," Maggie said. "Back then it was always held in October. The lobby of the Granville was the gathering place for various children's activities. Your grandmother ran that festival for years. She organized the food, the games for the children, and the decorations. Your grandfather just did whatever she told him to do, which was exactly how that marriage worked."

Sarah laughed.

More pages. A man on a ladder changing the marquee letters. A group of teenagers on the sidewalk outside the theater, the girls in skirts and the boys in rolled-up jeans, leaned against the building as if they owned it. A photograph of the concession counter with a woman Ethan didn't recognize standing behind it, the popcorn machine running, and a line of customers reaching back toward the doors.

"That's Dorothy Fields," Maggie said, pointing. "She worked the concession stand occasionally. Her caramel popcorn was famous."

Ethan turned to the last pages of the first album. A Christmas photograph. The lobby was decorated with garlands, candles in the windows, and a small tree near the ticket booth. The chandelier overhead. Families standing in clusters, children holding candy canes. The Granville at its finest.

"Your grandfather said a theater is a living room for a whole town," Maggie said. She was looking at the Christmas photograph.

Sarah was still. She was looking at the photograph with the expression she wore when something landed deep, the quiet attention that Ethan had come to recognize as the truest version of how Sarah Hartwell received the world.

He reached over and took her hand. Her fingers closed around his, warm and certain, and she kept looking at the photograph while Maggie leaned forward in the desk chair and pointed to a face in the crowd.

"Now, that man right there," Maggie said, tapping the page gently, "that's Harold Liemans. He owned the mercantile on Main Street for forty years. Your grandmother couldn't stand him because he overcharged her for light bulbs, and she told him so every single time she went into that store. He never changed the price, and she never stopped going and buying her bulbs there either."

Sarah's thumb moved slowly across the back of Ethan's hand.

Maggie turned another page of the album and stopped.

"Oh," she said. Her hand hovered over a photograph Ethan hadn't seen before. Two men standing in front of the Granville, their sleeves rolled up, a set of blueprints spread across the hood of a truck between them. One of the men was his grandfather. The other was younger, barely out of his twenties, with a pencil behind his ear and a look on his face that Ethan knew in his own mirror.

"Your daddy," Maggie said. "That was the day your grandfather handed over an extra set of keys he had made. That's the day the Granville started transitioning from one generation to the next." She looked at Ethan. "And now it's passing again. Isn't life grand?"

Chapter 27

The county inspector's office had been his last call of the day, and it had gone better than any of the others.

Ethan sat in his office chair with his legal pad on the desk in front of him, the yellow pages covered in his handwriting from margin to margin. Three pages. Every item crossed through with a single clean line, the way he'd crossed off punch list items since his first year of practice. Completed. Resolved. Handled.

He leaned back and read through the list one more time.

The plaster specialist in Nashville, a man named Gerald Fisk who had done restoration work on two of Ethan's projects during his years with the firm, had answered on the second ring Saturday morning. Ethan explained the scope. West wall of the auditorium. Horsehair plaster over original lath, water damage behind the key, the full length compromised. Fisk had asked the right questions, the questions a man asks when he knows plaster the way Ethan knew architectural things, and by the end of the call they had a preliminary plan. Fisk would come on Thursday with two of his crew. They'd assess the wall in person, work alongside the existing team, and begin the restoration sequence that same day. Three additional sets of hands. Skilled hands. The kind of hands that could cut weeks off a timeline.

The grant board liaison had been Monday morning, first thing. Ethan had spent Sunday evening organizing the documentation for the backstage joist modification, pulling the structural engineer's report, cross-referencing the revised cost projections against the original grant submission, and drafting a scope modification summary that was thorough enough to answer every question the liaison might have before she asked it. He'd emailed it at 7:15 this morning with a follow-up call at 8:30. The liaison confirmed receipt, reviewed the summary, and told him that the documentation was exactly what they needed. She'd process the modification this week.

The county inspector's office had been the final piece. The permit revision that had come back with questions last week involved architectural specifications that Ethan could clarify faster than anyone because they were his specifications. He'd prepared supplemental documentation over the weekend, detailed drawings and load calculations that addressed each question point by point, and hand-delivered them to the county office this afternoon. The inspector on duty had reviewed the package, compared it against the original submission, and told Ethan he expected the revision to clear without requiring another site visit.

Three problems. Three solutions. One weekend and a Monday spent doing what he did best.

He looked at the clock on his office wall. 3:17. Sarah had texted him around noon asking where he was, and he'd told her he was finishing up some work at the office and would be there later. He hadn't lied. He just hadn't told her what the work was, because he wanted to walk in with the answers, not the questions.

Ethan closed his legal pad, tucked it under his arm, and drove to the Granville.

He parked on Beech Street and walked through the lobby, the smell of old plaster dust and fresh-cut wood meeting him at the auditorium doors.

The stage was alive with work. Half of it, anyway. The left side had been opened up, the old subfloor removed and replaced with new material, and across that new surface, heart pine planks were being laid in careful, measured rows. The wood was beautiful even from the back of the house; its grain caught the work lights with a warmth that the fluorescent fixtures couldn't flatten. The right side of the stage remained untouched, blocked off where the joist issue waited on the county permit.

Tim was on his knees near the front edge, fitting a plank into position with the steady patience of a man who understood that rushing wood was a waste of everyone's time. Brian and Luke worked behind him, setting the previous rows with a nail gun whose rhythmic punch echoed through the auditorium like a metronome. Melvin and Dan were further back, measuring and cutting at a makeshift station near the wing. Bill was beside Tim, his sleeves rolled to his elbows, a pencil behind his ear and sawdust on his forearms.

Sarah was crouched near the center of the work area with a level in one hand and her other palm flat against a newly laid plank, checking the seam where it met its neighbor. Her ponytail hung over one shoulder. Her tool belt sat low on her hips.

Ethan started down the aisle. His boots were quiet on the old carpet, but Sarah's head came up before he was halfway there. She tracked him as he walked, and he saw her register the legal pad under his arm.

She stood, brushed sawdust from her knees, and came toward the temporary steps at the stage's edge. She came down them and met him at the base, standing close enough that he could see the fine layer of dust across her cheekbones.

"Well, look who decided to show up," she said.

"I had a productive day."

"So did we. Half a stage floor." She nodded toward the stage behind her. "You missed some good work."

"I can see that." He looked past her at the rows of planks gleaming under the lights. "That wood is stunning."

She tilted her head. "You look like a man who's about to show me his homework."

"Something like that."

She crossed her arms and waited as Ethan flipped through some of the pages of his legal pad.

"I've been working on a few things since Saturday," he said. "Some of the issues from last week. I wanted to walk you through what I've put together."

Sarah's eyebrows lifted slightly, but she didn't speak. Behind her on the stage, the nail gun punched, and the work continued.

"First. The west wall. I know a plaster restoration specialist in Nashville. Gerald Fisk. I've worked with him on two previous projects, and his crew is one of the best in the state for period-accurate plaster repair. I called him Saturday morning, walked him through the scope of the damage, and he's available. He's bringing two of his men, and they'll be here Thursday to begin the restoration work alongside your crew." Ethan glanced up from his notes. Sarah's arms were still crossed. Her jaw had shifted slightly, a small lateral movement. He kept going. "Three more skilled hands on that wall, which should cut the timeline significantly. Fisk already has a preliminary approach based on what I described. He'll confirm everything on-site Thursday."

He turned to the next page. "The grant board. The scope modification for the backstage joists. I put the documentation package together over the weekend. The structural engineer's report, the revised cost projections, everything formatted to the grant board's submission standards. I sent it to the liaison this morning and followed up with a call. She confirmed receipt and said the documentation was clean. She's processing the modification this week."

Sarah had begun to move. Not away from him. Sideways. Short, tight lines; three steps to her left, pivot, three steps back. Her arms stayed crossed, her hands gripping her elbows.

Ethan noticed the pacing. He attributed it to impatience, the way she moved when she was processing information fast and waiting for the next piece. He turned to the third page.

"And the county permit. The revision that came back with questions. The issues were architectural, all related to specifications I drew, so I prepared supplemental documentation addressing each question with updated drawings and load calculations. I drove it to the county office this afternoon. The inspector reviewed the package and said he expects it to clear without another site visit."

He looked up from the legal pad.

Sarah had stopped pacing. She was standing four feet in front of him, square to him, her arms still locked across her chest. Her jaw was working.

Ethan closed the legal pad and held it at his side. He waited for the relief. For the exhale. For the look he'd been carrying in his mind of Sarah hearing that the three biggest problems on her plate had been addressed, that someone had taken the weight she'd been carrying

alone and shared it because that's what you did when you loved someone.

"I know last week was brutal," he said. "I wanted to help."

Sarah looked at him. And the thing that moved across her face was
not relief.

"You called a plaster specialist," she said. "You hired him and two
of his crewmembers to come to my job site. You submitted documentation to the grant board for my company's project. You drove to the
county inspector's office and handed over revised specifications for a
permit that has my contractor's license number on it." She paused. "Is
that accurate?"

"I was trying to help, Sarah."

"That's not what I asked. Is that accurate?"

"Yes."

"And at any point during this weekend or this morning, during the
hours you spent making calls and organizing paperwork and scheduling a specialist to arrive at my job site on Thursday, did you pick up
the phone and call me?"

The question landed in the quiet between them, and Ethan heard
it the way he heard a crack in a load-bearing wall. Clean. Structural.

"I wanted to have the answers before I brought it to you," he said.

"That's not what I asked either."

"No. I didn't call you first."

Sarah took one step closer to him. "You spent three days making
decisions about my project. My company's project. Decisions that
involve my crew, my grant compliance, my permits. You contacted
people on my behalf without my knowledge. You scheduled work at
my job site without consulting me." Her voice hadn't risen. It had
tightened, each word drawn like a wire pulled to its limit. "And you

walked in here with your legal pad and your checkmarks, and you expected me to be grateful."

"I expected you to see that someone was trying to share the workload."

"No. What I see is a man who looked at me struggling and decided I needed to be handled. Managed. That my problems were his to solve. That he could go around me, over my head, behind my back, because he knew better."

Up on the stage, the nail gun had gone quiet. Ethan's peripheral vision registered stillness where there had been motion. Tim had set down his tools. Brian and Luke were motionless. Melvin and Dan had stopped cutting. Bill was standing near the front edge of the stage, his hands at his sides, watching.

"Sarah, that is not what this was."

"Then what was it? Because from where I'm standing, it looks like a man who spent three days rearranging my professional life without asking me if I wanted it rearranged. You didn't consult me. You didn't include me. You made choices about my work, my relationships with inspectors and grant boards and subcontractors, and you presented them to me like a finished product. Like all I had to do was say thank you."

Her voice was shaking now from the effort of keeping it level while something enormous pushed against it from underneath.

"I have spent years building relationships with county offices and grant boards, and every supplier and subcontractor I work with. Years, Ethan. Those relationships have my name on them. My reputation. My word. And you stepped into the middle of them without asking whether I wanted you there."

Bill moved. Ethan saw it from the corner of his eye: the quiet, unhurried motion of a man who had read a room the way other men read blueprints. Bill set his tools down on the stage floor. He stood and looked at the crew.

"Boys," he said. His voice was calm, carrying the weight of a man who had run a lumber mill and raised six children. "Let's take a coffee break and head over to Minnie's. A cup of coffee and a slice of pie. My treat."

Tim didn't hesitate. He nodded once, and the crew moved. They set their tools down in the careful, quiet way men set things down when they understand they are not the ones needed in the room. Brian and Luke climbed down from the stage. Melvin and Dan followed. Tim came last, and he didn't look at Sarah or Ethan as he passed. He just walked up the aisle with the steady gait of a man who trusted his boss to handle what needed handling.

Bill didn't follow immediately. He stepped down from the stage and stood beside his daughter. Sarah was standing with her arms locked across her chest, her jaw set.

Bill looked at her. "Don't punish a good man for what a bad one did."

Seven words. Then he turned, walked up the center aisle, and followed his crew out of the auditorium. The double doors closed behind him with a sound that settled into the empty theater like the last note of a hymn.

Sarah stood still. Her arms hadn't moved. Her jaw hadn't unclenched. But something behind her eyes flickered, a fracture so fast that Ethan almost missed it.

Ethan set the legal pad on the edge of the stage, and then he looked at Sarah. "I know what's happening right now," he said. "I can see it. And I need you to hear me, Sarah, because I am only going to say this once."

She didn't move.

"I am not the man who told you to be less. I have never once looked at you and seen a woman who needed to be smaller, or quieter, or more manageable. Not once. I see the whole of who you are, and I've never flinched from it."

Sarah's chin lifted a fraction. Her jaw was still tight, her hands still gripping her elbows, but her eyes were on his and she hadn't looked away.

"I made a mistake. I should have called you first. I should have brought you the problems and worked through them beside you instead of handing you solutions like they were mine to give. I see that now. I own it. Fine. But I know you know I did this from the goodness of my heart. I know you know I was only trying to take some of the stress off you."

He paused.

"But don't you dare put me in that box. Don't look at me and see a man who was trying to diminish you, because that is not who I am and you know it. I wasn't managing you. I was loving you. But I did it wrong. The reason behind every call on that legal pad was because I watched you carry the stress of this project alone for five days last week, and it broke something in me to see it. I didn't want to fix you. I wanted to fix the things that were hurting you, the things that were stressing you out. There's a difference, and I think you know what it is."

Sarah stared at him. A hundred things crossed her face in the space of a breath. Anger and grief and recognition and something that looked like fear, the specific fear of a woman who has just been seen clearly by the one person she cannot hide from.

"I will stand here as long as you need me to," Ethan said. "But I will not stand here and be someone I'm not. Not for you. Not for anyone."

Sarah's arms dropped to her sides. She looked at him for another long moment, and whatever war was being waged behind those eyes was not one she was going to let him witness. She reached for her tool belt, unbuckled it, and set it on the stage beside his legal pad.

Then she turned and walked up the center aisle. She didn't look back. She pushed through the auditorium doors, and the sound of them closing echoed through the empty theater and faded into nothing.

Ethan stood beside the stage. His legal pad sat on the edge beside her tool belt.

He hadn't yelled. He hadn't chased her. He had said the truest words he'd ever spoken to another person, and she had left them on the floor of the Granville and walked away.

He lowered himself to the floor and tipped his head back and looked up at the ceiling, at the ornate plasterwork and the curved beams and the high windows where the late afternoon light was fading.

"Lord," he said to the empty room. "I could use a little help down here."

Chapter 28

Sarah drove home with the windows down and the radio cranked all the way up.

The two-lane road between the Granville and the edge of town was a straight shot she could drive blindfolded, and she made it on autopilot, her hands at ten and two, her jaw clamped shut. She pulled into her driveway, cut the engine, and went inside her house.

She kicked off her boots in the mudroom, went to her bedroom, and changed out of her work clothes. She pulled on worn cotton sleeping pants and an old sweatshirt that had been washed so many times the lettering across the front had faded to a ghost of itself.

She stood in front of the bathroom mirror and pulled the elastic from her ponytail, letting her hair fall. She washed her face, dried it, and looked at the woman looking back at her.

"Well," she said to her reflection. "This day ended up about as bad as it could. Nice job, Hartwell."

The coffee maker was a one-touch operation she could perform in the dark, and she did it now without thinking, measuring the grounds, filling the reservoir, pressing the button. After a few moments, the invigorating scent of coffee filled her kitchen, and she poured a full mug and carried it through the back door onto the smaller porch that faced the foothills.

The Adirondack chair caught her weight. She tucked her bare feet up underneath her and wrapped both hands around the mug. The air had the bite of a September evening, cool enough to notice against her skin, warm enough that the sweatshirt was sufficient. Crickets in the treeline. A whippoorwill somewhere in the distance, its three-note call repeating at intervals that were almost, but not quite, regular.

Sarah drank her coffee and replayed the auditorium.

She started with herself. She owed herself that much. She went through what she had said to Ethan, line by line, the way she would review a punch list after a walkthrough, checking every item against the facts.

He had called a plaster specialist and scheduled him to arrive at her job site without telling her. Fact. He had submitted documentation to the grant board on behalf of her company without her knowledge or consent. Fact. He had driven revised architectural specifications to the county inspector's office for a permit that carried her contractor's license number. Fact. Three professional decisions, three actions that involved her business relationships, her reputation, her name, and he had made all three of them without picking up the phone to consult with her.

She wasn't wrong. The argument she had made in the auditorium was accurate. Every point she had raised was legitimate, every boundary she had named in the past was real, and if she had been standing in front of any other man on any other job site saying those words, she would have been right and she would have been done.

But she hadn't been standing in front of any other man. She had been standing in front of Ethan. And the facts, as accurate as they were, weren't the entire structure.

She drank her coffee. The whippoorwill called again.

Don't punish a good man for what a bad one did.

Her father's voice landed in the quiet, and Sarah closed her eyes against it.

Seven words. Her father, who had not once in her thirty years told her how to handle her personal life. Her father, who trusted his children to make their own decisions and live with the consequences. Bill Hartwell had looked at his daughter, looked at the man standing in front of her, and had broken a lifetime pattern to say those seven words.

And then he had taken charge of her crew. Walked them out of the building. That was the part that kept circling back. Her father didn't overstep in her business. Not ever. He respected her authority on a job site the same way he respected it in every other part of her life. But today he had looked at the situation, made a judgment, and moved the crew out of that auditorium because he saw something that required it.

"He's wrong," she said out loud, to the foothills and the crickets and the dark. "He doesn't know what it felt like, standing there, hearing Ethan list off everything he'd done behind my back."

The foothills didn't answer. The crickets kept their rhythm.

"He went around me. He made decisions about my company. My relationships. My permits. He treated my project as if it were his to manage."

She heard the words come out of her mouth, and they were true. They were accurate. And they were beginning to sound like a wall she was building while she talked.

"Daddy doesn't know how badly Daniel hurt me."

But that was a lie, and she knew it before the sentence finished. Bill Hartwell knew exactly what Daniel had done to his daughter. He had been on the homestead porch the night she drove over after the breakup and sat beside her mother and didn't say a word. He sat there and listened. He had watched her rebuild herself for four years. He had never said a word about Daniel, never offered an opinion on the man or the relationship, because that wasn't his way. And today, for the first time in her entire life, he had spoken into her personal business, and the thing he chose to say was: *Don't punish a good man for what a bad one did.*

Sarah opened her eyes and stared at the treeline.

"Geez... why does he have to be right? Dead on correct. Good job, Daddy."

Her father had never been wrong about the character of a man. Not once. Not about Jim's business partners, not about Dave's coaching staff, not about Mike's late wife's family, not about the men he employed at the mill. Bill Hartwell sized up a man the way he sized up a piece of timber: by the grain, by the weight, by whether it would hold when the load came. And Bill had looked at Ethan Cole and seen a man worth defending with the only seven words he had to spare.

She drank her coffee.

Then she let herself hear Ethan.

I wasn't managing you. I was loving you.

She had been standing four feet from him when he said it, her arms locked across her chest, her jaw set, every defense she owned engaged and operational. And he had not backed down. He hadn't apologized for who he was. He had not told her that she was overreacting. He hadn't made it about her being too much.

Daniel would have. That was the thought that arrived with the blunt force of something she had been carrying without realizing she was still holding on to it with a fierce grip. Daniel would have said she was overreacting. Daniel would have turned it around, made her anger the problem, made her the one who needed to calm down, be reasonable, stop being so intense about everything. Daniel would have retreated or attacked, and either way, the message would have been the same: You are too much, and this is why.

Ethan hadn't done that. Ethan had stood in the aisle of the Granville Theater and said: I made a mistake. I should have called you. I own it. And then, in the same breath, without flinching, without raising his voice, he had said: But don't you dare put me in that box.

He had held her accountable and held her with respect at the same time. He had told her she was right about the mistake and wrong about the motive. He had refused to become the man she was treating him as, and he had done it not by defending himself but by standing his ground and telling her the truth.

That was not what Daniel did. That had never been what Daniel did. And sitting on her porch with her coffee going cold, Sarah knew it.

She uncurled her feet from under her and set them flat on the porch boards. The wood was cool and smooth against her soles, solid beneath her, the same boards she had measured and cut and laid herself because she didn't trust anyone else with the work.

Didn't trust anyone else with the work.

She sat with that for a long time.

Her coffee went cold. She didn't get up to make more. The whippoorwill had gone silent, and the only sounds were the crickets and the wind in the trees and the slow creak of the chair when she shifted her weight.

She thought about the lake. The afternoon on Hawthorne Lake when she had told Ethan about Daniel, every word of it, the full weight of two years laid out in the open air between their kayak paddles. She had told him she waited for the other shoe to drop. She had told him she expected every man who got close to eventually decide she was too much. And Ethan had listened without flinching and then told her about Kelly, about choosing control over vulnerability, about having the best example of love in his own father and spending a decade proving he hadn't learned a thing.

Two people on a lakeshore who had hurt and been hurt in opposite directions, and both of them sitting there at thirty, trying to figure out how to be different.

And then today. When Ethan had made a genuine mistake born from genuine love, she had treated him like Daniel. She had looked at a man who was trying to share her workload and ease her stress, who had spent hours solving her problems because watching her carry them alone was breaking his heart, and she had heard Daniel's voice instead of Ethan's.

"Lord," the word came out rough, unpolished, nothing like the prayers she offered at church or around her mother's table. She wasn't sitting up straight. She wasn't folding her hands. She was slouched in an Adirondack chair on her back porch with bare feet on cold boards, and the prayer that came was as stripped down as she was.

"I don't know how to do this. I don't know how to let someone in without bracing for the hit. I've been managing everything, Lord. You know that. Every project, every relationship, every piece of my life, I've managed it the way I manage a job site. Controlled. Planned. Every variable accounted for. And I've been managing You the same way. Trusting You with the blueprint and then running every detail myself, like You need a project manager."

She stared at the dark outline of the foothills against the sky.

"I was wrong today. Not about the facts. The facts were right. But I was wrong about the man, and I knew it while I was saying it, and I said it anyway because it was easier to be right than to be honest." Her throat tightened. "I let what Daniel did to me become the thing I build everything in my life on. Every wall I've put up since him, every time I've walked away instead of answering from my heart, every time someone got close enough to help and I heard it as doubt. That's Daniel's foundation. And I've been building on it for four years like it was solid, and it's not. It's cracked, Lord. The whole thing is cracked, and I've been building on it anyway because tearing it out felt like admitting I let him win. I really messed up. I messed up big this time, Lord."

She pressed her palms against her knees.

"I need help. Help me change. I'm asking You to show me the truth about myself, and I'm asking You to help me do something about it. Because I see the pattern... I see the patterns I keep choosing to follow. I can see it all so clearly; it makes me sick. Every time Ethan stepped toward me with something good, I flinched. Every time he showed me he wasn't Daniel, I tested him again. And today he passed the test, and I punished him for it. I am so mad at myself right now, Lord. I did this to myself because I'm so bullheaded."

The night was full around her. Stars above the treeline, scattered and bright where the sky was clear between the clouds. No sound but the world breathing in the dark.

"This is going to take some work within me, Lord. I'm not gonna be an overnight fix and I know it. I honestly know that. But I am asking You to work in me, because I can't do this alone and I'm tired of pretending I can."

She sat for a long time after that. The prayer wasn't finished so much as it had run its course, the way a hard rain runs its course and leaves the ground soft and quiet underneath. She didn't feel fixed. She didn't feel resolved. She felt scraped clean, like a wall stripped back to the lath, ready for new plaster but not yet repaired.

But she could see it now. The pattern. The way Daniel's words had become load-bearing in her life, supporting every wall she'd built since, and the way she had laid each course with such care and precision that she'd mistaken the fortress for a home.

Ethan had never once made the pivot she kept waiting for. Not when she challenged him in the first week on the Granville. Not when she told him about the house she'd built for a family she didn't have. Not when she threw a hissy fit and screamed in the auditorium last week, not when she was sharp with him, not when she was difficult, not when she was fully, entirely herself. He had seen every piece of Sarah Hartwell, and he had moved closer, not away.

And today, when he'd gotten it wrong, when he'd overstepped with the best of intentions, he hadn't made excuses. He'd stood there and said the truest thing anyone had ever said to her: I wasn't managing you. I was loving you. But I did it wrong. And then he'd drawn a line. Not to push her away. To show her who he was and refuse to be mistaken for someone else.

That took a kind of strength she recognized. It was the same strength her father had. The quiet, unshakable kind that didn't need to raise its voice because it knew where it stood.

She wasn't going to resolve everything tonight. That wasn't how she worked, and she knew herself well enough to know that the distance between seeing a thing clearly and living differently because of it was measured in days, not hours. But something had shifted on this porch, in the space between the prayer and the silence that followed it. A decision. Not a plan. Not a schedule. A decision made at the bedrock level, below the foundation, where the ground either held or it didn't.

She wasn't going to let a man who didn't deserve her define how she treated the man who did.

Sarah stood up, walked to the porch railing, and tipped the last of the cold coffee over the edge.

She looked up. The sky above the foothills was enormous, clear in patches between slow-moving clouds, the stars close and sharp in the September air.

"All right," she said. "I'm going to need You for what comes next."

Chapter 29

Sarah pulled up to the Granville a little after nine the next morning and parked behind Tim's truck at the curb. The crew's vehicles lined Beech Street in the same order they appeared every morning: Tim first, then Brian and Luke in Brian's Silverado, then Melvin and Dan in the work van.

She didn't get out of the truck. She pulled her phone from the cup holder and typed a message to Tim:

Come outside for a sec.

She set the phone on the dash and waited. Through the Granville's front windows she could see the faint glow of work lights and the occasional shadow of movement, but the sounds of the job site were muffled behind brick and glass.

Tim came out the front door less than a minute later. He saw her sitting in the cab and walked over to the driver's side. Sarah rolled down the window.

"You're in charge today," she said. "Work on whatever's moving forward on the stage. The areas you've got clearance on."

Tim looked at her. He didn't ask why. He didn't ask where she was going. He stood with his arms at his sides and his salt-and-pepper beard catching the morning light, and he read his boss the way he'd been reading her for years.

Sarah reached into her purse on the passenger seat and pulled out the company credit card. She held it out the window. "Take the crew to lunch. Two-hour break, paid. Let everyone know."

Tim took the card and slid it into his shirt pocket. "You good, Boss?"

"I'm working on it."

He nodded once and turned and walked back toward the Granville, and Sarah watched him pull the door open and disappear inside before she put the truck in gear and pulled away from the curb.

She drove south on Beech Street, past the storefronts and the converted Victorians that lined the blocks between downtown and the residential streets beyond. Cole Architecture sat on the near edge of the transition, the two-story Victorian with its warm slate exterior and white trim and the modest sign in the front yard that read "Cole & Associates Architecture" in the clean lettering Phillip Cole had chosen decades ago. Maggie's car was parked out front. Ethan's truck was not.

Sarah kept driving.

The Cole family home sat on a quiet street on the east side of Serenity Crossing, a neighborhood of mature trees and generous lots where the houses had been built by people who intended to stay. Phillip Cole had designed this house and then driven his building crew half crazy during construction, changing details mid-build with napkin sketches and better ideas, and the result was a home that looked exactly the way it should. Sarah had sat at the table inside that house five days ago eating Maggie's casserole and listening to stories about the man who built it, and she had felt something that evening that she hadn't let herself name until last night on her porch.

Ethan's truck was in the driveway.

Sarah parked behind it and cut the engine. She sat with her hands on the steering wheel and looked at the front porch. The same porch her daddy had delivered lumber at a neighbor's discount in 1993. The same porch she'd walked across Friday evening to eat dinner with Maggie, the evening that had felt like a glimpse of something she wanted badly enough to terrify her.

"All right, Lord," she said quietly. "I've been talking to You all night and most of this morning. You know what I came here to do. I'm asking You to give me the words and the guts to say them. And if my voice shakes, that's fine. I'd rather be honest and shaking than polished and hiding."

She took the keys from the ignition, got out of the truck, and walked up to the porch.

She knocked.

Footsteps inside, and then the door opened, and Ethan was standing in front of her. He was in jeans and a gray T-shirt, no shoes, and he looked like a man who hadn't slept much and had spent the hours doing something harder than sleeping. His eyes moved over her face, and what she saw in them wasn't anger. Not coldness. It was the quiet love of a man who had said the truest words he knew how to say and then watched the woman he loved walk away from them.

He opened the door wider.

"Can we sit outside?" Sarah said. "On the porch."

Ethan stepped out and pulled the door closed behind him. Two chairs sat near the railing, angled toward each other with a small table between them. They sat down. The street was quiet. A cardinal was working through a sequence in the oak tree at the edge of the yard, and somewhere down the block a lawn mower hummed.

Sarah leaned forward with her elbows on her knees and her hands clasped. She looked at the porch boards between her feet, and then she looked at Ethan.

"I need to say some things, and I need you to let me get through them."

"I'm listening."

"You should have called me first." She said it cleanly, without anger, without the heat that had been in her voice in the auditorium. A fact stated on level ground. "Every one of those calls you made, every piece of documentation you submitted, every meeting you took. You should have picked up the phone and talked to me before any of it happened. Not because the work wasn't good. It was good. I know it was good, Ethan. You're thorough and smart, and you care about that project, and I have zero doubt that everything you did was done right. But those are my professional relationships. My permits. My grant compliance. My name on the line. And a partnership, business or personal, means two people making decisions side by side. Not one person carrying the load while the other one solves it in the background. I don't want to be rescued. I want to be consulted... involved. I need that. That's not negotiable."

Ethan nodded. His jaw was set, and his eyes were steady on hers.

"What you did was kind," she said. "I want you to hear that, because I didn't say it yesterday, and you deserved to hear it. The impulse behind every call on that legal pad was love. I know that. You watched me drowning last week, and you did what you know how to do. You fixed things. You solved problems. You took action. And the fact that you spent an entire weekend and most of Monday working on my problems because you couldn't stand to see me carrying them alone."

She paused. "That is one of the most generous things anyone has ever done for me. I should have said that in the auditorium instead of the things I did say."

She sat back in the chair and looked out at the street. The cardinal had finished its song and gone quiet.

"Now here's the part that's harder for me."

She turned back to him.

"My daddy said seven words to me yesterday before he walked out of that auditorium with my crew. And I sat with those seven words all night on my back porch until my coffee went cold and the stars came out and I ran out of arguments against them." She pressed her palms flat against the arms of the chair. "He was right. I was punishing you for something you didn't do. I was standing four feet away from you, hearing every word you said, and I was measuring those words against a man who has no business being in the same room as you, and I knew it while I was doing it, Ethan. I knew it, and I did it anyway, because the pattern was easier than the truth."

Her throat tightened, but she kept going.

"I have spent four years building steel walls out of what Daniel did to me. Four years treating his words like load-bearing walls in my life, building everything on top of them —my business, my independence, my relationships, every part of how I move through the world. And I built them so well and so carefully that I convinced myself that within those walls was a home. But it's not. It's a fortress. And last night I finally saw it for what it is. A cracked foundation with bad mortar. The whole structure built on something that was never solid to begin with."

She looked at him and held his gaze.

"That pattern is not going to break overnight. I wish I could sit here and tell you I'm fixed, but I'm not. I've lived inside my fortress for four years, and it's a stubborn building, and so am I. There's gonna be days when something happens and my first instinct is to flinch. To pull back. To measure you against a template you never built and don't deserve to be held to. And when that happens, I need you to call me on it. I need you to be strong enough to stand in front of me and say, 'Sarah, that's not me. That's the old pattern. Come back.' And I might need a minute. I might need to walk away and sit on my porch and wrestle with myself before I can come back and admit you're right. But I will come back. Every time. Because I know who you are, Ethan. I've known it for weeks. You're the man my daddy stood up for, and Bill Hartwell has never been wrong about the character of a man. Not once."

She straightened in the chair.

"So here are my terms. And these are not an ultimatum. These are the foundation. The terms I want to use to build something with you, and I am choosing that word on purpose because it's the only language I've ever trusted completely." She looked him straight in the eye. "Never make a professional decision about our project without me in the room. Not behind my back. Not as a surprise. Not with good intentions. If it involves my company, my crew, my permits, or my name, we talk about it first. We decide it side by side. That is the deal."

"That's fair," Ethan said. "And you're right. That was my mistake. Control disguised as help. I won't make it again."

"Good," Sarah leaned forward. "Now. Those were my professional terms. I have personal ones."

The corner of Ethan's mouth moved. Just barely.

"Don't ever stop doing the little things," she said. "The things that have nothing to do with plaster specialists and grant boards and everything to do with the fact that you pay attention to me in a way nobody else ever has. I want the flowers that show up for no reason. I want coffee in a to-go cup on a job site because you thought I might need it. I want hikes on trails you scouted because you knew I'd love the view at the top. I want dinners where you surprise me and I don't get to see the menu ahead of time. I want fried chicken on a Friday when I've had the worst week of my life."

She was smiling now. The genuine kind. The kind that started in her chest and climbed.

"And Ethan Cole, don't you ever, ever stop rewriting our romance novel. Because I have read hundreds of them, and not a single one of those heroes has danced with me on a construction site on a Friday afternoon or argued with me about vanilla ice cream in a grocery store or told me I was beautiful on my own front porch before I could even say hello. That's you. That's our story. And I don't want the edited version. I want every chapter."

Ethan was looking at her the way he'd looked at her on the paddle-wheel boat and the way he'd looked at her in the Granville lobby last Friday. The steady, unhurried attention of a man who had chosen her and had not wavered from that choice for a single second.

"Are you done?" he said.

"For now."

"Then it's my turn."

She lifted her chin.

"You were right about the phone call. You were right about the boundary. I accept your terms, every one of them, and I will honor them because they're not demands, Sarah. They're blueprints. You just handed me the plans for what this looks like when it's built right, and I know how to read plans." He held her gaze. "I'm not going anywhere. I told you that in the auditorium, and I meant it, and nothing that happened between then and now has changed a single thing about where I stand."

"Now. My terms."

Sarah raised an eyebrow.

"Don't ever change who you are. Not for me. Not for anyone. Don't soften the edges, don't quiet down, don't make yourself smaller so I'm more comfortable. I fell in love with a woman who builds houses with her bare hands and runs mountain trails at five in the morning, and eats six different kinds of ice cream without apology. That woman. Every day. That's what I want."

"I have never apologized for my ice cream."

"I know. Don't start." He leaned forward. "Keep dragging me to places I'd never go on my own. Keep surprising me. Keep beating me up mountain trails and pretending you're not winded at the top when I know you are."

"I am never winded."

"You were winded at the overlook, and you covered it by pretending to admire the view."

"I was admiring the view."

"You were gasping for air and looking at trees."

She laughed. The sound came out bright and loose and surprised, the way laughter sounds when it breaks through something that's been held too tight for too long.

"And keep reading your romance novels," Ethan said. "I wanna know about the ones that make you cry... the ones that make you laugh... and the ones that make you stop and think.. Keep comparing me to fictional heroes and tell me where I fall short."

"You have never fallen short."

Ethan looked at her.

"Dance with me," Sarah said.

"There's no music."

"We don't need music." She stood up from the chair and held out her hand. "I need you."

Ethan took her hand and stood up. His other hand found the small of her back, and her free hand settled on his shoulder, and the fit was the same as it had always been. Immediate. Natural. The kind of fit that doesn't require adjustment or negotiation, just two people who know where they belong in relation to each other.

They moved across the porch boards in a slow, easy rhythm that belonged to no song and needed none. The September air was warm against her skin. The cardinal had started up again in the oak tree, working through its sequence as if it had been hired for the occasion. Down the street the lawn mower had gone quiet, and the neighborhood held the particular stillness of a Tuesday morning when the rest of the world was at work and two people on a porch had decided that the rest of the world could wait.

In the Granville lobby, he had led. He had pulled his phone from his pocket and found the music and extended his hand and taken her weight when she was too tired to carry it. That dance had been a rescue. Comfort after a breakdown.

This one was hers.

She had driven here. She had knocked on his door. She had said the words. She had held out her hand. And now she was dancing with this man on his front porch on a Tuesday morning because she had spent the hardest night of her life chipping away at every wall she had seamlessly built and had walked out the other side still standing.

Ethan pulled back just enough to look at her. "What are your plans for the rest of the day?"

"I took the day off. Tim's running the site."

He stopped moving. He looked at her the way a man looks at a woman who has just announced she's moving to the moon.

"Sarah Hartwell took a day off."

"I did."

"From her own job site."

"Yep. I handed Tim the company credit card too, and told him to buy the crew lunch. Two hours paid."

"Who are you and what have you done with my girlfriend?"

She grinned. Reached into the back pocket of her jeans and pulled out two tickets. She held them up between her index and middle fingers, the way a poker player holds a winning hand.

Ethan took them. Read them. His eyes came back to hers, and the look on his face was worth every dollar she'd spent.

"Skydiving," he said.

"Tandem jump. Pigeon Forge. We need to be there in two hours."

The laugh that came out of him came from somewhere deep and real, the kind of laugh that shakes through a man's whole body and changes the surrounding air. He tipped his head back, and the sound carried across the porch and into the quiet street, and Sarah stood there and watched him laugh and enjoyed every moment.

"Are there any conditions?" he asked.

Sarah took his hand. Laced her fingers through his. Held on.

"Just that we jump at the same time," she said. "And you hold my hand while we free-fall."

Ethan looked down at their joined hands and then back at her face, and whatever he saw there made him tighten his grip.

"Get your shoes," Sarah said. "We're burning daylight."

Epilogue

The gravel pullout held six vehicles by the time Sarah climbed out of her truck and pulled on the fleece she'd tied around her waist. Ethan's truck was already there, parked at the far end near a white Ford with a rod rack bolted to the roof and a bumper sticker that read I Fish Therefore I Lie. Her daddy's truck sat beside Ethan's, and Jim's was next to that, and the rest of the Hartwell vehicles lined up along the river road like a caravan that had found its destination and settled in.

October had done its work on the Smokies. The mountains burned in every direction, the maples in full flame, red and amber and a deep, saturated orange that looked like something poured from a jar. The oaks held their color lower, bronze and rust and the warm brown of old leather, and the poplars had gone to gold. The ridgelines stacked against the sky in layers of color so vivid that the whole landscape felt lit from inside, and above it all the sky was the particular blue that October gives to Tennessee, high and clean and sharp enough to cut.

Little River ran beside the road, clear and low, the water moving over smooth stones with unhurried patience.

Ethan appeared from behind the white Ford with a pair of waders draped over his arm. He was grinning.

"Everybody's down at the bank," he said. "Cal's already got your daddy in waders."

"My daddy is in waders."

"Your daddy is in waders and looks like he was born in them. Your mama took one look at the river and asked for a camp chair and a thermos."

Sarah laughed as she opened her tailgate and sat down to pull on the waders Ethan handed her.

They walked down the slope to the riverbank, and Sarah saw her family.

Bill was standing at the water's edge in chest waders that looked like they'd been tailored for him, listening to a wiry man in a faded canvas vest explain something about the angle of a fly rod. The wiry man was Cal, the man Ethan had hired to teach them all how to fly-fish. His beard was close-trimmed and silver. His hands moved with economy when he demonstrated a casting stroke, the rod loading and releasing in a clean arc that put the fly line exactly where he intended.

Bill watched the demonstration once, picked up his rod, and replicated the motion with a precision that made Cal pause and look at him.

"You sure you haven't done this before?" Cal asked.

"First time," Bill said.

Cal nodded slowly, the way a man nods when he's recalculating his expectations for the day.

Olivia was already stationed on a flat rock above the bank, a canvas camp chair unfolded beneath her and a thermos of coffee at her feet. She had a blanket across her lap and a contentment on her face that said she had found her spot and had no plans to leave it. Maggie sat beside her in a second chair. Maggie was in waders. Her hair was pulled back under a ball cap; the brim softened from years of wear, and she was watching the river.

Jim was downstream with Grace, already in the water up to his knees, his casting motion aggressive and overpowered because Jim did everything with the full force of his personality, and fly-fishing was apparently no exception. Grace stood beside him, watching.

Dave was on the bank, studying his fly rod with the methodical attention he gave to tax returns. He had the reel apart and was examining the drag mechanism, and Sarah knew without asking that he would be the last person in the water and the most technically proficient once he got there.

Mike stood in the shallows with Lizzie, helping her hold a rod that was nearly as tall as she was. Lizzie's waders were child-sized and purple, and she was gripping the cork handle with both hands and looking at the water with the same intensity she brought to touchdown runs in the Hartwell front yard.

Rebecca was already in the water. She had cast once, hooked a branch on the far bank, and was now attempting to free her line with a series of sharp tugs that were making the situation progressively worse.

"I need help," Rebecca announced to no one in particular.

"You need to stop pulling," Jim called from downstream.

"I'm not pulling. I'm negotiating."

Anna was on the bank with her phone out, photographing everything. She had that particular stillness she carried when she was seeing something worth capturing, her eye moving from the mountains to the river to her family scattered across the water and the rocks.

Sarah waded in.

The water hit her boots first, then rose around her shins, then her knees, cold and clear and alive with the kind of current that made you aware of your own weight. The riverbed beneath her feet was smooth stone, slick in places, solid in others, and she picked her way out to a spot where the current split around a boulder and created a seam of slower water along its downstream edge. Ethan followed her in and stood beside her, and Cal waded over to them with two rods already rigged.

"The trout are holding in the deeper runs today," Cal said. He handed Sarah a rod with a small fly tied to the tippet, something delicate and dark that looked like a beetle with ambitions. "Water's low and clear, so we're going light. Ten o'clock to two o'clock on your cast. Let the line load before you come forward. Don't muscle it."

Sarah took the rod and stripped out line the way Cal showed her, feeding it through the guides with her left hand while her right hand held the grip. She made her first cast. The line rolled out in a loop that wasn't pretty but landed where she'd aimed; the fly settling onto the surface with a soft kiss and drifting downstream along the seam.

"Good," Cal said. "Natural. Strip in slow."

She did, and the fly moved through the current, and nothing happened, which was fine because the sound of the river and the feel of the water against her legs and the mountains standing watch around her were already more than enough for a Saturday morning.

Ethan's first cast was shorter and more controlled. He watched the line load and released it with the measured timing of a man who understood mechanics and wasn't interested in rushing the process. The fly landed upstream of Sarah's position, and they fished side by side while Cal moved between them, adjusting technique and offering quiet corrections.

The morning unfolded the way mornings unfold on moving water, slowly and without any particular interest in keeping to a schedule. Sarah found a rhythm with the rod. The casting motion lived in her shoulders and her wrists, and after twenty minutes she was placing the fly within a foot of where she wanted it, reading the water the way she read a building, looking for the structure beneath the surface.

Ethan was slower to find the rhythm, but once he had it, his casting was cleaner than hers, more precise. He had an architect's eye for the geometry of the line in the air, and he adjusted angles the way he adjusted design elements, with small corrections that accumulated into something elegant.

Bill, meanwhile, had moved downstream to a run Cal had pointed out, and he was fishing it with the quiet concentration of a man who had found something he'd been looking for without knowing he'd been looking for it. His line moved in that clean arc, back and forward, and the fly landed softly and drifted true, and Cal watched from the bank with his arms folded and admiration on his face.

"Your daddy... he's something else," Ethan said.

"I know."

"It's his first time."

"He's Bill Hartwell. He does everything like that. He's just good."

A shriek from upstream. Rebecca had hooked something, and based on the bend in her rod and the volume of her reaction, it was either a fish or another branch.

It was a fish. A rainbow trout that Cal estimated at ten inches, and Rebecca held it up with both hands while Anna photographed it from three angles. Rebecca's face was pure, uncomplicated joy. Jim slow-clapped from his position downstream. Grace laughed. Dave looked up from his drag mechanism and offered a single nod of acknowledgment, which from Dave was the equivalent of a standing ovation.

Lizzie caught the next one. Or rather, the fish caught Lizzie, because her rod bent and she screamed and Mike grabbed the rod before it went into the river, and the two of them brought in a small brown trout that Lizzie declared was the biggest fish she had ever seen. Cal knelt beside her and showed her how to hold it in the current, the trout's body cradled in her small hands, its gills working, and Lizzie looked at the fish with something close to reverence before she released it and it disappeared into the deeper water.

"I want to keep it," Lizzie said.

"We let them go," Mike said.

"But it was mine."

"It was yours for a minute. That's how today's fishing works. It's catch and release, Lizzie."

Lizzie considered this. "Can I catch another one?"

"You can catch as many as you want."

She picked up the rod again with the single-mindedness of a six-year-old who had discovered a new obsession.

The hours moved. Sarah lost count of casts. She caught two trout and released them both, feeling the pulse of each fish against her palm before she opened her hands in the current and watched it swim away. Ethan caught one, a rainbow that hit his fly in a pool behind a boulder, and the surprise on his face when the rod bent and the line went tight was something Sarah filed away to remember.

They ate lunch on the bank. Cal produced a cooler from the back of his truck, and the food was simple and good. Sandwiches. Apples. Thermoses of coffee and hot cider. The family gathered on the rocks, camp chairs and blankets, and the conversation moved the way it always moved when the Hartwells were in one place, in overlapping currents and cross-conversations and the occasional eruption of laughter that sent birds scattering from the trees.

Rebecca sat beside Anna and gave a detailed account of her catch, which grew more dramatic with each retelling. Jim ate his sandwich in four bites and went back to the water. Dave opened a discussion about the physics of fly casting that Mike tolerated for approximately ninety seconds before changing the subject to Lizzie's trout. Bill sat on a rock with his Styrofoam plate on his knee and looked out at the river, and Sarah caught him watching Ethan, and the expression on her father's face was one she knew well. It was the expression her daddy wore when he'd made up his mind about a man and was at peace with his conclusion.

Olivia and Maggie shared a blanket. Maggie was telling Olivia something that made Olivia reach over and squeeze her hand, and the two women sat like that for a long moment, hand in hand, two mothers on a riverbank watching their families fill up the same space.

After lunch, the group drifted back toward the water.

The afternoon light had shifted. The color on the mountains had deepened, the reds richer, the golds warmer, and the river carried the reflection of it all on its surface, broken and reassembled by the current into something abstract and beautiful. A leaf drifted past Sarah's waders, a single maple leaf the color of fire, turning slowly in the current before it disappeared downstream.

Ethan was quiet beside her. He'd reeled in his line and was holding his rod loosely at his side, and he was looking downstream at the mountains where the river curved out of sight.

"My dad would have loved this," he said.

Sarah stopped casting. She held her rod still and looked at him.

"Not the fishing, specifically. All of it. The family. Your family. My mom is on the bank with your mom. Lizzie screaming when she caught that trout." He paused. "He would have been standing right about here. Probably with Mama on one side and your Daddy on the other. And probably giving Cal unsolicited advice about the best spots on the river because he would have read three books about it the week before."

Sarah smiled.

"He wanted to learn how to do this. He wanted to stand in a river with someone he loved and cast a fly and wait." Ethan looked at the water moving past his legs. "I'm glad we're here."

"I'm glad we're here too."

"Reel in your line."

She looked at him. Something in his voice had changed. "Okay... should I be worried?" She asked as she reeled in her line.

Behind them, on the bank, Rebecca had gone still. Sarah registered it the way she registered details on a job site, automatically, peripherally. Rebecca was never still. Jim had moved to a position downstream where he could see them clearly. Bill had reeled in and was standing in the shallows with his arms at his sides. The guide had stepped away from the group and was standing near the trucks with his hands in his pockets. Olivia had reached for Maggie's hand on the blanket.

Sarah saw all of it and catalogued none of it, because Ethan had set down his rod on a boulder behind him and was reaching into the chest pocket of his fishing vest.

He took out a small box. Everything around her seemed to stop.

"This ring belonged to my grandmother," Ethan said. "My grandfather proposed with it on the balcony of the Granville Theater after a Saturday matinee. Sixty years ago. The stone has been in my family for three generations. My mama kept it in her dresser after my grandma passed it to her, and she gave it to me three weeks ago. I took it to my drafting table, and I designed a new setting for it." He opened the box. "Because the woman who is helping restore the building where my grandparents' love story began deserves a ring that carries that history forward."

Sarah looked at the ring. A single stone, beautiful and clear, catching the afternoon light, set in a band that was unlike anything she'd ever seen. The setting was precise and intentional, clean lines that held the center stone with an architect's eye for balance, and surrounding it were eleven smaller stones, each one distinct, each one placed with the kind of care that only comes from a man who draws every line on purpose.

"Eleven stones," Ethan said. "One for each person standing on this bank and in this river who loves you and one for the man that's in heaven that I know would have loved you. Your mama and daddy. My mama and dad. Jim. Grace. Dave. Mike. Lizzie. Anna. Rebecca."

Sarah's vision began to blur.

"I want to build a life with you, Sarah. Not a building. A life. A partnership where neither of us carries anything alone, ever again. Sunday mornings and shared meals, and a porch to sit on when we're old. I want all of you. Every dimension. The steel-toed boots and the painted nails, and all the red satin dresses. The builder and the woman. I have never once wanted less."

He went down on one knee in the river. The water moved around him, and his waders creased at the bend, and he held the ring box open in front of her.

Sarah started laughing and crying all at once.

It came up from somewhere deep and ancient and entirely her own, a laugh that broke across her face and rang out over the water, bright and full and startled. Because this man, this impossibly thoughtful, quietly romantic, maddening, wonderful man, had just proposed to her in a river during a fly-fishing lesson he'd organized to honor his father, with a ring his grandfather had used sixty years ago in the theater they were restoring, and every single person she loved was standing on the bank or in the shallows watching, and not one of them had told her, and the absolute perfection of it, the way it fit them, the way nothing about this moment was borrowed from a script or a formula but was entirely, specifically, irreplaceably theirs, hit her all at once and the only response her body knew was joy.

She wasn't laughing at him. She was laughing at the beautiful absurdity of standing in a river in waders on a Saturday afternoon in October and being asked the most important question of her life by a man who was kneeling in the current and looking up at her like she was the only woman in the world.

"Yes. Double yes. You better believe I'll marry you," she said.

Rebecca screamed. It was the kind of scream that sent birds from trees and echoed off the ridgeline and probably startled trout for a quarter mile in both directions. Olivia was crying, her hand pressed to her mouth, tears running freely. Maggie was crying too. Bill was standing downstream with his arms folded and his chin dipped, and his eyes bright, and when Sarah caught his eye across the water, he nodded once. Jim started a slow clap that Dave picked up, and then Mike joined, and the sound of it carried across the water.

Lizzie's voice cut through all of it. "Does this mean Uncle Ethan is gonna live at Aunt Sarah's house now? Because her house is really cool."

Ethan was still on one knee. The water moved around him. His eyes hadn't left Sarah's face.

He took the ring from the box and reached for her hand. The metal was cool against her skin.

Sarah pulled him up from the water and into her arms and held on. Her face pressed against his neck, and her arms locked around his shoulders. She held on with the grip of a woman who knows what it means to hold something that matters. He lifted her. Her boots left the riverbed, and the water streamed from her waders, and he spun her around.

Rebecca reached them first, and she grabbed Sarah's left hand and held it up, and examined the ring with the forensic attention of a woman who had opinions about jewelry and intended to express every one of them. "Ethan Cole," she said. "You designed this?"

"I did."

"At your drafting table."

"Yes."

"With your little architect's pencils."

"They're not little."

"This is the most beautiful ring I have ever seen in my life."

Jim pulled Ethan into a hug that involved a firm grip and a hard clap on the back and words spoken close to his ear that Sarah didn't hear but that made Ethan's jaw tighten in the way it tightened when he was keeping himself steady.

Grace hugged Sarah and said, "Welcome to the engaged club," and her smile was warm and real.

Dave shook Ethan's hand with the gravity of a man ratifying a contract and said, "Good job."

Mike hugged Sarah and said nothing, because Mike said the important things through his actions.

Lizzie tugged on Sarah's waders and asked to see the ring, and Sarah held out her hand. Lizzie studied the stones with enormous concentration.

"There are a lot of sparkles," Lizzie said.

"There are."

"And one of those is mine?"

"One of them is yours."

Lizzie beamed. "Cool."

Anna had been photographing the entire thing from the bank, and Sarah knew without asking that somewhere in those photos was the moment she'd frame and hang on her wall.

Bill came last. He waded through the shallows and stood in front of Ethan, and the two men looked at each other as Bill extended his hand.

Then Bill turned to Sarah and put his hand on her shoulder and squeezed once.

"You picked a good one, baby girl," he said.

Maggie was the last to reach them. She came slowly, picking her way across the rocks, and when she got to Sarah, she took Sarah's face in both her hands. Her palms were warm. Her eyes were wet. She held Sarah's face and looked at her for a long moment, and then she said something quietly, meant only for the two of them.

Sarah nodded. Maggie kissed her forehead and then turned to her son and held him the way only a mother holds her child, with the full measure of a love that had carried him since before he took his first breath.

The family moved back to the bank. Cal had produced a second cooler from somewhere, and there was more food and sweet tea to go around.

Sarah and Ethan stood in the river together as Sarah looked at the ring on her finger. The old stone caught the light and held it, and the eleven smaller stones around it glinted like points on a compass.

She looked at Ethan.

"You know what I love about foundations?" she asked. "You can't see them when the building's done. But every single thing that stands, stands because the foundation held."

Sarah took his hand. Laced her fingers through his and held on.

"Our foundation's gonna hold something beautiful," she said.

Leave A Review

If you enjoyed this book, please consider leaving an honest review on Amazon

Visit Our Website:

www.tarabaisden.com

Visit Our Amazon Author Page HERE

Find Us On Social Media:

Facebook

Facebook Author Page

Instagram

Also by Tara Baisden

<u>**Serenity Crossing: The Hartwell's Series**</u>

#1 Hometown Sweethearts

#2 Hearts Restored

#3 The Art of Starting Over – coming April 3, 2026

#4 Love in God's Timing – coming May 1, 2026

#5 Wildflower Heart – coming June 5, 2026

#6 Brave Enough to Love – coming July 3, 2026

<u>**Laurel Ridge Series**</u>

#1. Season of Hope

#2. Finding Grace

#3. His Perfect Plan

#4. Love Redeemed

#5 Snowbound Blessings

#6 Sheltered Hearts

#7 Restoring Faith

#8 Love Rekindled

#9 Where She Belongs

#10 Shelter in His Arms

#11 Where Love Stands

#12 The Pieces We Mend

#13 Where Love Grows

#14 Where Hearts Heal

#15 Harvest of the Heart

#16 Heart of the Season

#17 Season of Forgiveness

#18 Threads of Grace

<u>Riverbend Valley Series</u>

#1 A Cowboy's Second Chance

#2 Wanderlust & Wild Horses

#3 Heartstrings on the Horizon

#4 Runaway in Riverbend Valley

#5 Mended Hearts

#6 Healing Hearts

#7 Home to Lost Creek

<u>Mistletoe Falls Series</u>

#1 Whisk Me Under the Mistletoe

#2 Once Upon a Christmas

#3 The Mistletoe Express

#4 Candy Canes & Sweet Dreams

#5 Wrapped Up in Christmas

#6 Jingle All the Way Home

About The Author

Tara Baisden is a Contemporary Christian Inspirational Romance author who proudly calls the beautiful state of West Virginia her home. Nestled on a sprawling mountainous property, she is surrounded by the peace and serenity of nature. Her days are happily spent in the quiet of country life, writing heartwarming stories of love, faith, and second chances. Tara also enjoys quilting, working in her garden, tending to her beloved pets, and soaking in the beauty of her surroundings.

With deep roots in West Virginia, family is everything to Tara. One of her favorite pastimes is gathering on the front porch with loved ones, sharing stories, laughter, and enjoying the simple, meaningful moments that life offers. When she's not crafting her novels, Tara can often be found exploring the rich history of her home state, visiting local historical sites, and, of course, stopping by every bookstore she passes! Her passion for reading and discovery always fuels her next adventure.

Tara is the author of the Laurel Ridges series of novels, as well as the Riverbend Valley series of novels, of which have been beloved by fans of inspirational romance. Her novels reflect her love for faith, family, and the timeless beauty of the world we live in.

Known for her sweet and clean romances, she creates characters that feel like family and settings that make readers want to visit again and again.

You can find out more about Tara and her latest releases at www.tarabaisden.com or follow her on social media for updates and behind-the-scenes glimpses of her writing process. Stay connected—you won't want to miss the heartfelt stories of love and family she has in store!

About Serenity Crossing

Nestled in a valley of the Great Smoky Mountains, Serenity Crossing, Tennessee, is the kind of small town that makes everyday life feel a little softer around the edges. Around 8,200 neighbors call it home—enough to keep things lively, but small enough that a wave from a porch swing still counts as a proper greeting. Downtown curves around a historic square with a beloved gazebo at its heart, framed by timeworn brick storefronts and wide sidewalks where it's easy to linger. The coffee is always brewing at The Daily Grind. Minnie's Diner always seems to have a seat, and shop owners tend to learn a newcomer's name by the second visit.

Life here is stitched together by simple pleasures and steady rhythms: morning mist settling in the valley and lifting by midmorning, church bells chiming at eight, and quiet kindness that shows up in casseroles, carpools, and prayers offered without fanfare. News travels fast—often faster than anyone means it to—but so does help when it's needed. Serenity Crossing has a way of rallying that feels less like a decision and more like instinct.

Nature isn't "nearby" in Serenity Crossing—it's part of the daily scenery. Hawthorne Lake sparkles just beyond town with walking paths, fishing piers, and secluded coves made for unhurried conversations. The Rolling and Flint Rivers curl along the valley's edges beneath old stone bridges, while the ridgeline offers overlooks locals swear are best at sunrise. And tucked away on a moderate two-mile hike, Serenity Falls has earned a reputation as the town's favorite spot for big questions and brave promises.

Serenity Crossing knows how to celebrate, too. Thursday evenings typically bring music to the gazebo, and Saturday mornings (April through October) fill the square with a farmers market and familiar faces. Come the last weekend of September, the Harvest Festival turns the town into pure cozy delight—pie contests, craft booths, live music, and an apple butter competition taken very seriously, right down to the crowning of the Apple Queen. Winter brings its own magic with the Christmas Stroll, hot cider and cookies, carolers in the square, a tree lighting, and Santa arriving by antique fire truck.

In Serenity Crossing, faith runs deep, community runs strong, and love has room to grow—slowly, sincerely, and surrounded by the kind of belonging that makes visitors want to stay awhile.

9 781966 093503